COLLIN JOHNSON

Psychedelic Turnpikes

"…we were back at home, and I had returned to that reassuring but profoundly unsatisfactory state known as 'being in one's right mind."

— Aldous Huxley, The Doors of Perception

Contents

1

…Thus Departs

GRIEF IS a cold, heartless bitch who is said to come in stages. The first of which, of course, is doubting whether or not she came at all.

When Tarron Faust received the call informing him of his best friend's suicide, it was raining. It really put a damper on his mood when he woke up that morning and was the first clichéd indication that Grief herself had arrived in full. It was the harsh sort of November rain, local to Wyoming, that cuts cold and chills you to the bone. Rain like this was nothing but a bloody inconvenience—just a tad too warm for snow but cold enough to ruin the day. Akin to getting a call that a person you had unresolved trauma with just killed himself. In the abridged words of Winnie the Pooh, *oh-fucking-bother.*

He hung up the phone without a word. The caller, Sean Hart, a long-disregarded childhood friend, Tarron figured wouldn't take much offense. He didn't want to waste another second and risk being late to meet Lady Grief for a drink. He left Sean to wonder on his own about phone etiquette.

When someone you love passes away, the unfortunate

predicament you may find yourself in is having people who want to help you through it. But more often than not, that just includes them offering to bring you food and ask how you're doing.

Not good, man. Not good, Tarron thought.

It exhausted Tarron when his father passed away, and he was already exhausted thinking of the maelstrom of people he hadn't talked to in years going out of their way to give him hollow words of consolation. Sean, being the first one to call him, was the best example. He hadn't even thought of Sean for several years now, yet he, of all possible candidates, was the one to break the news. Sean, the goddamned third wheel of a friend that Jack and he quickly shed after high school. Look who's left now!

Tarron sat in his kitchen, pouring over pictures of himself and Jack with tears welling up in both eyes. A bottle of Jägermeister was uncapped for his consideration. It would've been a waste to dirty a glass tonight.

It had been near twilight when Sean called, but when the bottle was emptied, his clock read 2:30 AM. Tarron dropped the bottle bluntly into the trash and stumbled into his bedroom. Face-down into bed. Jeans and T-shirt still on.

Sometime later, he blinked his eyes awake, and it was still bloody raining. His watch read 2 pm, which meant he had to be at the bar for his shift in an hour. Just enough time to sit in the shower for thirty minutes and practice his chipper customer service voice.

He made it exactly one and a half hours through his shift before he decided he was tired of serving drinks to other people and being sober. He left early, asking the other bartender to cover for him. Called it a family emergency—which was not altogether false but not entirely the truth. His nose may have only slightly grown if anyone asked, but the fuck-off look he tried to maintain on his face worked as intended.

And he used to be such a nice guy.

The rain eventually turned into snow the next week as the temperature dropped and the news of Jack's death spread. Glenrock, Wyoming was a tiny town among tiny towns in a state with barely half a million people living in it; news here moved like wildfire. With fire came smoke and people to call him and blow the aforementioned smoke up his ass.

A couple of calls came from former high school friends and one from the football coach. The man loved to brag that the Jack and Tarron were "the best out of Glenrock High sports in a generation," with state champion trophies brought home in football as well as a myriad of track events. Jack went on to pick up a full ride for Arizona State's track team in the decathlon. And Tarron, in his best hopes to follow his best friend, was awarded just enough scholarship money to manage out-of-state tuition for the Tempe-based university. Friends who knew them well enough would joke that wherever Jack went, Tarron followed—be it sports, girls, or school.

Girls used to call me the funny one and Jack the cute one, Tarron thought.

His brother. Not by blood but by enough of a shared life experience to matter.

Family.

Tarron had also knocked up an ex-girlfriend of Jack and later blamed him for her walking out, something that had put a *slight* rift in that love triangle. Sometimes you get the girl and lose your friends. Sometimes you choose friendship over companionship. Sometimes it seems that you lose both. And that's what had brought him back to Glenrock. In his case, the girl left him and took their daughter. He seethed, knowing that he never apologized to his now deceased best friend for the blame he placed on him for that.

Tarron disconnected his phone after the sixth call of condolence came. He decided to retreat to the liquor store to replace his sorrows with spirits. Walking the aisles like an aimless wraith, he filled the entire handcart. He didn't respond when the store clerk made a corny joke about the amount he was buying and asked where the party was. Plenty of intrusive thoughts of something snide to say raced through his head as he handed over the bills to pay for the 18 rack of Coors banquet, a replacement bottle of Jägermeister, and a bottle of Brennivín.

Yes, I am going to drink all this myself. No, everything is not alright. No, I don't want to talk about it.

"And your change is $2.37. Would you like a bag?" The clerk asked earnestly.

"Keep it, man," Tarron mumbled as he bagged the alcohol himself and trudged out the door.

Tarron opened one of the cans of Coors and floored his truck to make the exceedingly short (but too long and cold to walk) drive home. The wet snow made for rough roads, but Tarron knew local PD wouldn't give other locals trouble. Maybe he could bawl his eyes out if he got pulled over and try to get off with a pity warning.

Tarron knew for a fact that Jack Finnegan wanted to be unceremoniously cremated and his ashes spread in the mountains, but here was Tarron's own mother texting him about a post she just saw on Facebook. The post was for a very private funeral Jack's father was hosting. Family only.

This was curious, considering James was the only relative Jack would've had left in Wyoming after his mother divorced his father and took his baby brother along with her.

Tarron knew he should be the one to call Mr. Finnegan and ask simply, "what the fuck" and if he and his mother were invited, but his stomach churned at the thought of having to make that call. When he arrived home and sat down at his tiny dining room table, he opened his second Coors. It was still early in the day, and he figured he could call Mr. Finnegan before he ran through the 18-rack at the earliest.

Hours later found him going through more pictures, each doing wonders for his mental health. He figured he'd skip right over anger and bargaining and go straight to depression. Miss Grief was one he didn't want to keep expectant. Tarron remembered how his mother went through her own journey to acceptance after his father died. Tarron couldn't fathom how his mother had faced this sort of pain soberly.

This current flavor of loss he tasted was new but not altogether unfamiliar. When Celeste walked out on him, she took their daughter Alina to the next town over to move in with a guy she had previously assured Tarron was not a problem for him to worry about. That was the last time he remembered this sort of hurt, in a lesser magnitude at least. He still got weekends with Alina, at least.

A week had passed since the news, but it felt as though absolutely no time had transpired. He was seated in his kitchen once more, alcohol and bad intentions within reach. The Jägermeister was gone. Scratching his beard out of habit, he reached for the bottle of Brennivín he had brought home and read the label.

Produced and bottled in Iceland. Almost makes me miss those dumb Nordic bastards, he thought before uncorking the bottle and tipping it gingerly into his mouth. The black licorice taste of the drink danced around on his tongue, filling Tarron with a mix of nostalgia and nausea.

Traditionally, Brennivín was labeled with a skull and called "Black Death" because of the prohibition laws in Iceland; those who made the drink wanted it to sound as terrible as possible. At least that is what Jack and Tarron's Icelandic roommates had told them when they brought out the smuggled bottles in their dorm room. They were a pair of brothers, free from their parents in America, to go to school. They had specifically chosen Arizona State University for the party scene rather than academic pedigree. The four of them were all transplants and bonded over the fact.

That was another call he wasn't looking forward to making.

Magnús and Jóhann had begged Jack and Tarron to visit them in Reykjavik once they had all graduated one unspecified day in the future. But they both left to finish school in Europe the following semester, and Tarron dropped out two semesters after that. Following the years after Jack got his degree, they had barely spoken a word to each other.

Jack had just finished his master's degree last fall and broke the silence. Reaching out to him about finally making the trip. It was the first time in over a year that they had spoken to each other. The trip was something that seemed almost impossible given Tarron's financial situation—which was a fancy way of saying "broke."

But Jack had insisted they set a date to finally go.

It was always something that came up. Tarron wasn't able to get work off, this was his weekend to see his daughter, or his mom was in town. Some of the best-laid plans are laid to rest instead.

A third call Tarron bemoaned having to make, albeit less emotionally damning, was to his boss to politely tell the man he needed to take another day off. Tarron quickly settled that this would be the most painless one, so he pulled out his cell, rehearsing what he'd say as the line rang. He felt the Black Death take over as soon as his boss answered.

"Yeah, what is it, Tarron?"

"Not gon' come in. Findsomeone to cover," he slurred before pulling the phone away from his face to retch in the sink.

***

He didn't think she was going to call. And she didn't. Even after he reconnected the landline the following morning with a bit of hope, still, Tarron couldn't help but feel annoyed by it. Celeste had dated Jack for less than a year, but she and Tarron stayed together well over five times that. Though, the last four months he remembered as a waking hell of passive-aggressive arguments, half-assed attempts at date nights, taking care of their toddler, and loveless sex. Purgatory was probably more accurate, waking or not.

His head was pounding. He mentally apologized to his liver and simultaneously thanked it for its service. All curtains were drawn, setting the room in darkness so he could concentrate, firstly, on not dying. This was accented by the continued quest to dig up old pictures of him and Jack from any source he could think of.

He thought about writing a speech, but as soon as he held a pen to a notebook, the blank page shouted at him impatiently. An anxious voice in his head suggested that maybe he wouldn't even be invited to the funeral. Jack's father had never liked him, and it's not as if they were related, truly.

Or would he go with Celeste? And bring Alina to the burial of a man she didn't even know, but ironically, was the reason for her coming into the world. But still, Celeste had not called.

Silence. Digital and physical. The snowfall dampened any sounds of passersby, and the absolute stillness irked Tarron. He was left alone to think. A luxury he usually coveted but not today.

He flipped through more pictures. From some tucked away in yearbooks and one's taken on the cheap disposable cameras of his childhood. He backtracked and started searching through his laptop for any digital remnants he might've missed. After all, sources were exhausted, he stayed looking at three pictures. Some of the happiest memories he could recall. Captured in full color.

Jack and he after their senior year state track meet.

Jack and he during a Jackson Hole ski trip.

Jack holding his legs to do a keg-stand at a college house party (the picture being the only surviving evidence of them ever attending).

There was one missing. A picture of them after high school graduation. There was scratching in the back of his brain, begging him to find the picture. After he double-checked all possible places, the itch had subsided to an ache.

Bargaining, was that you? Madame Grief, you work in mysterious ways.

The physical pain besides the mental was something people fail to mention when you lose someone you loved. There was an idea Tarron remembered from college that someone's life only continues after their physical life ends by way of people's memories. Not as much as their "life" but the idea and memory of the person. This was a dictating maxim behind

Día de Muertos in the Mexican Catholic culture, the professor explained. It was up to the family to uphold this, and Tarron couldn't picture Jack's father lighting a candle in his son's vigil every year, let alone at his funeral.

But Jack had mentioned reaching out to his mom the last time we talked. Hadn't he? It seems so long ago.

It first had been nearly a year ago over the phone. Tarron remembered that Jack was planning on visiting his mother in Tahoe since he'd finished up his degree and was talking about some big revelation he had. About how shitty his family was and how that shouldn't affect his life any longer. He was going to stop in Glenrock to meet with his dad first and wanted to see if Tarron was available to get a beer. He had said he hated how complicated their friendship had become. That there wasn't enough time to hold on to bad blood.

But that was right after Celeste had walked out. Things were not well, Tarron thought sardonically.

He could still remember the look on his friend's face. The consternation when he told him to leave him the fuck alone.

Jack didn't give up on his friend that day or the next. He stayed until he made sure Tarron could walk on his own and had a plan to keep moving.

Working as a bartender at Ozzie's seemed like a good start.

Tarron's phone buzzed with a text. Speak of the devil. His boss informed him very passive-aggressively that the Sunday day-shift bartender caught the flu and Tarron needed to work a double to make up for it. He swore and picked up the bottle of Brennivín from below the table. Upon seeing it was empty, he swore again.

2

Just Begins

THE LAST melancholy notes of Led Zeppelin's *Stairway to Heaven* had just rung out as a beer glass shattered to the floor. What followed was a cacophony of male aggression, many racial slurs, and the dull crashing of a barstool over the instigator of the yelling's head. Tarron instinctively reached below the counter of the bar to withdraw a decades-old Remington model 870 shotgun.

The black gentleman had raised another barstool high to serve justice to the unfortunate man lying on the floor, which, in turn, started fumbling around for his own firearm. The metallic clack of a shell racking into the chamber of the 12 gauge froze them both in place.

"I'm gonna stop you two right there. One barstool was fair, but two is a problem. And I'd really appreciate it if no one got shot during my shift," Tarron said calmly.

The man lying on the floor retreated his hand from the holstered pistol and quickly scampered off akin to a hurt rabbit, pausing to boldly shout the N-word once more before out the door.

The other man looked at Tarron apologetically and put down the barstool.

"I'm sorry about that, man. But I just got off my shift at the mill, and that fuck started being aggressive towards me, and I called him a honky as a joke and—"

"Hey, don't worry about it," Tarron cut him off "assholes like that… they're not worth it. Just pay for your drink and the stool, then cool off. It's only six pm, for chrissakes."

The mill worker opened his mouth to protest, then stopped and clenched his jaw before pulling out his wallet—tossing a small wad of bills on the counter. Finishing his whiskey, he walked out to Glenrock's snow-duster streets. Tarron sighed and replaced the shotgun under the counter. It was loaded with beanbag rounds anyway, which hurt like hell but not entirely enough to prevent a potential vagrant from retaliation. So he was told.

Ozzie's had no real theme to it, but one may call similar bars that go for a "rustic" look a bit derivative. Every piece of furniture or decoration here had real meaning. From the boar's head above the bar, the small collection of German cuckoo clocks on the far wall, or the fact that nearly every table, chair, or barstool was handmade with local timber. The lighting was moody and dark, the jukebox typically stuck on Neon Moon radio, and drinks were always served with a small bowl of pistachios.

This also being the only actual bar in Glenrock, Tarron had become accustomed to the locals that would frequent slow Sunday nights such as these. Mostly workers from the Sawmill or a half-dozen 30-somethings that made their weekly attempts to find someone that shared the desire for a quick fuck without the guilt in a nearby motel. Sometimes foreign passersby would roll through, most often on their way to Casper city or anywhere but this tiny personal hell that Tarron had grown tired of.

Tarron and Jack had actually worked here before. As barbacks in the summers of high school. Mr. Osmond Hartford, the owner, didn't care too much about underage kids serving drinks as much as he did about the job they did. And he always paid under the table, in cash. Ideal for a couple of dumb high school kids with more fleeting ambitions to carry out idiotic acts of teenage fuckery rather than college applications. Mr. Hartford loved them dearly and taught them everything he knew.

When the time came for them to leave for ASU, he was kind enough to give each a $500 bonus with a wink for "textbooks" and even offered to hang a Sun Devil banner next to the Casper Thunderbird one above the bar in their honor.

Unfortunately, Mr. Hartford passed away a couple of years later, and the bar went up for sale. Tarron knew he could never afford such a venture, but he looked at least to uphold one of the lasting conditions in Mr. Hartford's verbal will. Being that his beloved bar "bears the same resemblance to the day, I leave it" and never becomes "a liberal, blue, punk-ass disco bar that serves micro-brews that taste like shitty IPAs." Referring to the typical college town bars in places like Boulder, Colorado—where he grew up.

A kid younger than Tarron purchased the place with his parent's money—bringing along with him big ideas from his University of Wyoming MBA. His big ideas revolved around re-branding, but Tarron would go to the stake before he undermined his former boss's dying wish.

Tarron walked around the bar to grab a broom and a dustpan

to clean the mess the mill worker and racist drunkard had left for him. As he bent over and started sweeping, a pair of hands outstretched to him from a nearby table.

"Hi! I saw the whole thing. Terrible huh? You seem bushed; I can clean that for ya." the voice said. The hands belonged to a spray-tanned, towering, lanky man wearing a ski cap. He had been sitting towards the back for a couple of hours and seemed contently nose-deep in a book until a minute ago. The spray tan was good, though, almost unnoticeable except that he stood out execrably.

"What's that? Uh, no thanks, man," Tarron mumbled, barely glancing up.

"Oh, it's no problem. I was just about to a good stopping point when those two started at it. Glad I could catch a glimpse of the violence." The man said. He looked at Tarron again in the eyes, back down at the dusk pan and back at Tarron, and nodded his head forward.

A ghost stood before him, in the flesh. Tarron's heart skipped.

The over-eager lively tone of the voice was what caught him off-guard at first. But he was sure it was the same cheekbones and toothy grin. Same pair of blue-white eyes. He looked at the man for a second more before asking, in disbelief:

"Do I know you? Did you go to high school around these parts? I swear you look just like—" he felt his heartbeat speed up as he spoke.

"I grew up here, yeah, but my mom and I moved to Cali when she and my dad split up."

Realization washed over Tarron akin to a waterboarding victim.

"Wait? Shit, are you Jack's brother? I barely recognized you,

Darian. I'm sorry. I know you didn't know him much, but Jack was…." Tarron paused, his throat catching "he was like my brother." He sputtered before rubbing his eyes with the blade of his hand.

He tried to convince himself everything was okay and to breathe and relax. He didn't believe himself, but the breathing helped.

"Yeah," Darian's face darkened, "Someone told me he used to work here, and I never really drink, so I figured 'what the heck,' ya know?"

Tarron finished collecting the remains of the whiskey glass without responding again and walked back behind the bar to dump it in the trashcan. When he turned back around, Darian had set up shop one seat down from the now broken barstool. Tarron gathered the remains of the once beautifully handcrafted stool and dumped it unceremoniously in the trash atop the shattered glass.

Tarron initially locked eyes with Darian and was about to ask if he could get him anything, but the man turned his gaze to his book and did not look back up. There was still busy work to be done and still more beer to serve. Curiosity got the better of him, though, and Tarron started to rack his brain, remembering how long ago Jack and Darian's parents had split up.

Jack had to be 8 or 9, which means Darian was probably three at the time. Every time I'd come over when we were kids, Jack would make a point to play outside away from him. The kid always seemed glued to his momma's side.

"He talked about you a lot!" Darian said suddenly.

Tarron turned sharply, startled by the outburst, "What's that?"

"Jack had reached out to Ma and me to reconnect for the first time about a year ago. We'd talk for hours on the phone, and he always seemed really jazzed whenever he'd talk about his best bud Tarron."

"That's flattering. He and I uh—actually never mind, it's not important. Can I get you anything, man?"

"Milk. Please! Chilled 16-ounce glass. I tried a beer already and hated it"

"Was it an IPA?"

"A what?"

"Did it taste like water soaked in moldy bread?"

"That's… yeah, that describes exactly what it tasted like."

"Maybe try a cider next time."

"Next time! For now, though, milk, please."

Tarron decided he would not let another night shift or this interaction with Darian be ruined by his pre-disposition for self-hatred (or chance of making tips). He also wanted to take his daughter fishing this weekend. Might as well get a head start on practicing a happy face. He was unsure how long it would be before her mother inevitably took away visitation rights since she had moved in with Ian, the divorce lawyer.

"My milk, sir!" Darian reminded him. Tarron realized he was dozing off while holding the gallon jug in one hand with the glass in the other.

Tarron passed the glass with a napkin underneath to Darian, along with a bowl of pistachios, Ozzie's bar staple. A patron had once remarked how regular bars had pretzels or peanuts, but the green-shelled snack gave the place a sense of class.

It took the new owner one month to complain to Tarron about how the price gouge of ordering pistachios every week was damaging profits. Tarron could only shrug and told him that Oz was allergic to almonds and the pistachios were probably half the reason people drink here.

Tarron started routinely cleaning glasses when Darian opened his mouth in between sips of milk to chat.

"I think when you plant a tree, you give a little bit of your soul to the earth," Darian said.

"How do you figure that?" Tarron asked.

"The earth is dying, man. But not in the way things should die, no, not at all. I firmly believe the cyclical nature of life and death is a beautiful and natural thing. Catholics have a phrase I actually really like."

"And what's that?" Tarron put the glasses he was previously cleaning down.

"That we are from dust and to dust we will return. Jack and I talked about this a lot. He always asked what I was doing to better myself. But the Earth, man! How the hell do we better it? It would've been, like, millions of years before it turns into dust if humans ain't here. We're the fire. Guys like you and me can't do shit about it."

"Hey now, I recycle," Tarron protested.

"And honestly, bless you for doing that," Darian said, excitedly rambling on, "but giving a glass a new purpose when you recycle is taking only a drop of water away from the tsunami that's gonna fuckin' wreck us."

"But a tree is more than a drop, I'm assuming?"

"A tree is life. Something that we can give almost selflessly. We breathe out the CO2, and a tree takes that and turns it into the air that sustains us. And not just trees! They said on Nat Geo that sea plankton does this too! But I haven't figured out how to plant plankton yet."

"So, you're trying to save the world, is that it?"

Darian just smiled warmly. This time Tarron wasn't un-nerved by it.

"I want to live in it. Before I pass on. Like the lady in that Led Zeppelin song," Darian said calmly.

"I always thought that line in Stairway to Heaven meant she was too rich to buy herself into the real world. And then she died. You know, like 'halfway to heaven' but have to repent, type-thing. I dunno. I'm just talking out of my ass at this point."

"Nah, man, that's an interesting take. You're funny, though. I'll give you that. Jack said you had a sense of humor. He did, too; I can really see how y'all rubbed off on each other."

A silence hung over the two of them. Tarron felt his heart swell again and fought back the sudden urge to run into the storeroom and smash bottles over his head. He felt like shouting, belting his lungs, destroying every glass and barstool in the place. Taking fire and setting alight every piece of brick and cinder. He counted to ten slowly like a good boy before breathing in deeply.

"He had talked about going to Iceland, ya know?" Darian said again, breaking the noiselessness that lay between them "he said you, and he had some friends there. Said he wanted to bring me 'cause I wanted to see the northern lights."

"Iceland was something we always talked about but never did, ya know? Something always came up." Tarron replied.

"That's kinda tragic, man. You gotta chase those dreams. Or find a way to walk towards your path. Jack was the reason I started school. He helped me apply for the nursing program."

"You moved here all the way from Tahoe?"

"Kinda? I was on the road for a while. I wanted to see Wyoming again before I died and just kinda hung around.

Met up with Jack once, traveled around some more, and came back…." Darian started to trail off.

"Oh… So, you're a real-life vagabond, huh?"

Darian didn't respond. He had already dived back into his hardback. Tarron looked at the title: *American Gods* by Neil Gaiman. Tarron shrugged and returned to work.

Darian stayed for another hour before silently leaving. Tarron had almost missed him while tending to other barflies but caught his glancing grin before he went out the front door. The fly's eventually shuffled out respectively as the night wore on.

When cashing out for the night, Tarron realized two things. The millworker had paid him around $200 for the stool and glass (and the trouble of breaking it), and Darian had left him a note. Neatly spaced handwriting etched carefully onto a napkin.

Find some time :)

The note was folded around a small plastic baggie with a dozen or so small, black and white seeds encased.

***

The walk to his beaten-up Toyota Hilux after closing Ozzie's usually held a melancholy weight in Tarron's heart. He could blame it on seasonal depression, although he had no way of knowing if he really was clinically depressed or just sad and melodramatic. He didn't want to see a doctor or any sort of therapist that would just prescribe him medication. Would rather beg for his ex's forgiveness than take pills.

But tonight, genuinely felt different; the short-lived bar fight that had started out his shift had the potential to sour the next 6 hours that he would spend behind the counter, but after talking with Darian, the friendly giant, he found himself actually striving to work rather than run on auto-pilot. By the end of his shift, he surprised himself when he checked his watch and saw it was time to close.

Although the jukebox had played out sad, yee-haw tunes for most of the night, Tarron still had the lines of *Stairway to Heaven* on repeat in his head. He had a strange habit of waking up from dreamless sleep with a song stuck in his head. More often than not, the song was one he hadn't remembered listening to. This Led Zeppelin song reminded him of that.

He was really looking forward to taking Alina, his daughter, fishing next weekend. His own father, Martin Faust, had a coveted fishing spot less than an hour outside Glenrock. Tarron had fond memories of that place, tucked into the hills. When the wind was quiet, and birds stopped chirping, he remembered he could hear his heartbeat.

He hadn't asked Alina's mother yet. The last time he proposed it, she wouldn't hear it. She was a self-proclaimed changed woman after she had left him. Taking up a new workout routine and a vegan, keto-friendly, non-GMO diet or whatever it was now. She told him repeatedly that it was a lifestyle choice. Tarron had voiced criticisms to her directly but admitted to himself in private that she looked dammed fine since they had split.

It had been some time since he had made the drive down to Casper to visit. He felt guilty, but he figured it wasn't *all* his fault. He and Celeste never married, and she liked to remind him of this whenever he asked to see their daughter.

He sat stationary in his truck, pondering all this and feeling weightless in time. Snowfall had begun to leave little white impressions on his windshield. He dug into his pockets and retrieved the bag of seeds and note Darian had left him.

The entire interaction left a lasting impression on his mind. Who was the last interesting person he met? It was an obscure question. The daily, repetitive cogs had been spinning for so long that Tarron couldn't recall the last time he was authentically moved by what a stranger had to say. His mind was buzzing the same way it had during those first few months at ASU. That was when he was young and full of vigor. The lines on his face were deeper, the stress he carried in his shoulders heavier, and his back hurt. He was only 26 too. Maybe trauma was to blame.

Tarron finally turned the key into the ignition, only to be met with the sputtering cough of the combustion engine failing to fire. He turned the key several more times, only to be met with the same result.

"GOD!" Tarron shouted, pausing before he finished in a half-whisper. "Fucking dammit."

He pulled out his cell and clicked the home button to peer at the time.

01:39

The kitchen crew had gone home at least an hour ago, and Tarron had let the lone server go early as well so he could lock up without a hassle. No one to call, realistically. Most bars tend to close last. Everyone else wanted to hurry back to their families.

Tarron reached underneath the steering wheel to pop the hood and stepped outside, pulling on leather gloves before shutting the door. He peered under the hood with the small beam of light from his cell phone. He knew the battery was older, but he could've sworn he had another couple thousand miles before he needed to replace it.

He held the phone in his mouth and disconnected the clamps

on the battery, wiped the terminals with his gloves, then reattached them.

In all actuality, Tarron had very little experience with troubleshooting cars, but he figured the ole' 'try unplugging and re-plugging it in' philosophy he had followed throughout his life might prevail. Albeit, this was a '97 Hilux extended cab edition, in contrast to his internet modem at home.

"Hey man," a voice called out from behind him.

Tarron wheeled around, alarmed, and dropped his phone in the process. As he bent over to pick it up, he failed to register how close this new stranger had come to him. The snow must've worked to silence his footfalls.

"Ya got a smoke?" The stranger asked. He was dressed in a ragged green fur coat. The smell of which registered as rotten food or vomit to Tarron's nose. He fought the urge to wince and held his hand over his face before he answered.

"Nah, I actually stopped smoking a couple of months ago, man. Sorry."

"So that means ya got a pack still, in yer truck there?"

"No, I told you I don't have any. Can you leave me alone? I'm just tryin' to fix my car here."

"Maybe you should check," He reached into his coat and withdrew something, "Just to be sure."

"Hey, relax. I don't want any trouble, man," Tarron said horridly with his hands up, backing towards the truck.

The man in the tattered fur jacket held out a crude knife and grinned. "Oh, you don't want no trouble? But you don't have any smokes?"

"Listen, hey, just listen," Tarron slowly started to reach into his pocket to retrieve his wallet. "We can both walk to the corner store, and I can buy you some cigs, okay? Please just relax, okay?"

"I don't want yer fuckin' charity" The man lowered the knife slightly, "I just wanna go home" He began to tear up and wiped his face "they call me names, ya know" he paused to sniffle again, "when they leave this bar, the call me fag and spit on me."

"Hey, I'm sorry about that. I actually work here, man. Do you want to come inside and warm up, maybe?" Tarron slowly started closing the small distance between him and the man in the fur jacket. "I can get you a drink and a bowl of pistachios if ya want. Hell, you can have the whole bag."

"I don't want yer fuckin' charity!" The man screeched, swinging the knife rapidly.

Tarron barely reacted and pushed the man away from him. But as he looked down, he realized it was jutting out from his own abdomen.

The man in the fur coat rose and stood over Tarron as he fell. "I just wanted some smokes." He whimpered before disappearing.

Tarron touched the knife gingerly and looked at his hand, which was slick with blood. He could feel the snow starting to pile onto his belly.

This may be bad, he thought with a glimmer of sarcasm. His mom always said he could make the best out of a bad situation.

The knife stung a white-hot pain through his core. He attempted to rise but lost his bearing while reaching for the truck. He elected to crawl in any fashion he could around to the driver's side door. He stuck his arm out towards the handle and fumbled his grip, slipping again. He winced with pain and slowly rose to his knees, reaching again for the handle that mocked him, daringly close but still out of reach. He had most of his weight on the truck and could feel the outpour of blood rushing from his belly. He reached once again for the handle and caught it this time. With a death grip around the metal, he pulled with all his remaining strength and swung the door open.

With both hands now, he placed gloved palms on the floorboard and forced himself to stand. Grasping the steering wheel with his left hand and roof with his right, he paused to collect himself.

C'mon, man, not here. Not like this. You will not be murdered by a hobo. We gotta take Alina fishing tomorrow.

"I gotta take her fishing," Tarron said shakily before forcing himself into the driver's seat. White spots danced around his eyes as he felt his stomach begin to radiate with waves of pain. The snow continued to fall indifferently to the ground as Tarron Faust sat in the driver's seat of his Hilux, unconscious and blood slowly draining from his abdomen.

3

Talking Heads, Flaming Lips

"YOU POOR bastard. This is how you're going to make your exit, huh? Dying on a hospital table before you're 30 and right after Jack," A feminine voice spoke. Tarron trusted his ears and the context to make out the owner of the voice as Celeste.

Everything felt immensely heavy. He could hardly open his eyes, and when he did, fluorescent lights stung like a hot iron against his corneas. Time seemed odd too. Sometimes he would hear other familiar voices and tune into the conversation. In the absence of people talking to him, he felt like he was dreaming.

What remained of sensation was radiating nerves coursing through his medicated body. His hand was a ten-ton rock which he could only flex the fingers. At other times he felt pain pulsating from his abdomen. At those moments, he could make out the sound of beeps from a machine as his body wanted to shake awake from its induced slumber. When the beeps became too loud, he could hear concerned voices fill the room before a slow wave of numbness crawled over his body.

Was *this* purgatory?

Tarron couldn't recall much from Sunday school. Thoughts were fleeting, but when his brain decided to work, he would return to this musing of purgatory. Of all fates he could consider a final ending, this was one hell of an anticlimax.

More moments of clarity came, and it felt like he was going to return back to normal. His mind was filling in the blank for the future, like waking up and falling back asleep. The dream continues, but the dreamer—is blind to the fact that they are still asleep.

"This might be the worst I've ever seen you, Tarron." The same familiar voice, one that used to speak love songs to him as well as spew emotionally fueled words of rage.

Sometimes he could remember associating a memory when his body recognized the voice speaking to him.

"You don't know how heartbroken I was to get the phone call that you were in the hospital. Your daughter doesn't need to see you like this, and it looks like she may never see you at all." The same voice once again. Such a condescending sentiment. Scores of memories of arguments, conversations over a relationship, and the life once shared.

Although he did not have any sense of time, at this moment, the coma felt different. Somewhere between forever and nowhere, things started to feel ethereal. It was like the lights had been finally turned on for the show.

Curtains up and enter stage right.

He knew he was falling. The rush of adrenaline and the excitement of the act were both absent, only the forgone feeling of flying helplessly through space. Falling now still, with no end in sight or ground for him to splat upon like a children's Sunday cartoon.

He felt thralls of vertigo as the feeling shifted. He was now falling but in reverse. He moved his head to look around and saw nothing but utter darkness. He tried shouting but had no voice, he tried lifting his arms to stop, but they felt like lead attached to his body.

Everything stopped in an instant, and a blinding light shone over. Darkness left, and only pure white light remained. Tarron realized he was lying down. As he attempted to rise, the space around him shifted again. He peeked up.

A classroom. all desks pushed aside and the chalkboard blank, in an unidentified school.

Back to school... back to school.

He held his leg up and took a step forward, akin to how one walks away from a wall. A lone figure stood opposite him.

"Hey, bucko."

Jack's voice. But not Jack's face. The figure wasn't facing him. Tarron reached his arms with every ounce of strength he possessed to grab the shoulder of the figure, spinning them around. They had no face, a blank space of a skin-colored mask.

The voice of Jack continued.

"I've missed you, man. Been too long,"

Tarron opened his mouth, and still, no sound came out. He felt the world around him collapsing and his eyes getting blurry.

"What? No words for your best friend," not-Jack shouted, "WE WERE BROTHERS, TARRON. YOU OWE ME THAT MUCH. YOU OWE ME."

The figure flashed a blinding grin of white teeth as a pair of eyes appeared and danced around the face. Swirling like roaches on the floor. A nose popped up, and hair began to bubble from the top of his head.

"YOU COULDN'T PULL OUT, AND I GET DROPPED AS YOUR FRIEND? WE WERE BROTHERS, YOU AND I." not-Jack's voice beamed higher and higher in pitch, reaching a screeching tone.

Tarron reached to cover his ears, but he looked down and realized the figure embodying Jack had firm grips on his wrists. The classroom began collapsing. Panels of the floor started to slip away rapidly until the panel on which Tarron stood disappeared.

He fell. Jack's demented doppelgänger still holding fast to his wrists. They were bleeding now as 'Jack' dug his grip deeper. Wringing his fingers around back and forth until skin tore away to reveal the bone. Tarron began to screech as the pain climaxed until he felt absolutely nothing. His body dangled as he felt himself go limp. He looked up at Jack, whose devilish grin had been replaced by a somber pout. Tears began to flow from the eyes, which had finally stopped in their anatomical centers.

"I'm sorry, Jack," Tarron said, out of breath. Hearing his own voice speak but not feeling his mouth move.

"You were always jealous, weren't you?" Jack replied, suddenly releasing his grip on one of Tarron's wrists. "YOU WERE SUPPOSED TO BE THERE. INSTEAD, YOU GO FUCK ABOUT AS A DAD." Jack boomed again as Tarron felt his grip on his remaining wrist slipping.

"I'm sorry, Jack, I'm so—"

"DO NOT LET THEM BURY ME" Jack screamed as he let Tarron go.

Falling now, Tarron felt the classroom spinning faster and faster. He felt the skin peel off his face as he raced towards the void. His voice had left him once again, and he could not scream.

Tarron's eye's blinked open. He could feel the vibration of his pulse. His lifeline to the world, pounding and pumping blood throughout his body. He felt strength return to his body. Hands first, of which he made a fist. Then traveling up his arms before an ice-cold shock invigorated his lungs. He gasped faintly, fully aware of the pain in his abdomen.

Ladies and gentlemen, your main entertainment for the evening: a man is returning from the pits of hell, hastily remembering how to wiggle his toes and crinkle his nose.

His eyes blinked rapidly as he scanned the room—devouring each detail around the room in flashes of shorthand pieces of information.

Bed. Hospital. Pain. Celeste?

"Cellie!?" He gasped. His former lover, as startled as him, sat upright in her seat. Tarron paused to gaze at the women he once loved so intensely, feeling as if it were years earlier. She was as beautiful as he remembered. Serious, gray eyes contrasted by her delicate facial features and superbly dark but well-manicured eyebrows. And although her blonde hair was tucked messily into a bun, her makeup was unblemished and not forgotten. She sat cross-legged in a mini skirt and Sublime t-shirt that Tarron distinctly remembered giving to her.

He vomited suddenly and violently over the side of his bed. A nurse rushed in and started to re-attach his IV, which Tarron had accidentally ripped out. She quickly called an orderly behind her to help. In the background, an EKG machine beeped incessantly. Tarron felt his panic continue to rise as Celeste's quiet cries filled the room. The nurse injected a syringe into the IV, and Tarron slowly felt the waves of pain and frenzy flee from his body. He laid back down in bed and felt the rigid beat of his heart pound against his chest.

"Jesus Christ, Tarron. What the hell is wrong with you?" Celeste said.

"Well, if I remember right—" he began to say as he wiped his mouth and propped himself up, "I think I was… stabbed?" he finished, looking at the nurse for confirmation. She gave a modest nod.

The orderly who had just arrived in the room took one look at the vomit on the floor, laughed, and scrubbed it up quickly. Once Tarron stabilized, and the room was clean, the two departed.

"I'll give you two some privacy. Try not to die again, please, Mr. Faust." The nurse said on her way out.

"Where's Alina?" Tarron asked as the door clicked shut.

"She's with your mother, at your place. I brought her in yesterday after you gave the doctors a scare. You went septic or something. I stayed overnight while they monitored you, and your mom took her home."

Tarron peered a little closer at Celeste. She wasn't wearing a completely full face of makeup as he originally thought. The bags under her eyes were apparent.

"How was she?" He said softly.

"Scared. We were both scared. She didn't really know what was going on, but she could feel that I was worried." She sniffed. "Kids are smart like that. You can't hide much from her nowadays." She finished with a small laugh. Her eyes were reddening, and Tarron saw tears welling up. She wiped them before adding, "But you're awake now, and I'm glad you're okay. I'll let Alina know."

She rose from her chair and gathered her purse and jacket,

beginning to leave.

"Why didn't I have a say in naming her?" He interjected.

"What? Who do you mean? Alina?" Celeste replied quickly, "Nie wywołuj wilka z lasu, Tarron. Why do you want to discuss this now?"

"Don't call the wolf..." how'd the rest of that phrase go?. God, I almost forgot what it's like to hear her speak Polish, Tarron mused.

Celeste continued, "You didn't want a child. No—you did not want a child with me. You made that very clear before I got pregnant, yet now you pester me to ask why you didn't get to suggest a name for the daughter you did not want. Dupek."

Dupek...asshole. I remember that one.

Although Celeste was born in Arizona, Celestyna was born to two Polish immigrants desperate to flee their country after the fall of communism in search of new jobs and new lives. He had fallen in love the second he saw her during freshman orientation at ASU. An absolute knockout by any standard. Taller than most girls and had a devilish smile that begged you to try and say something stupid. And at that time in his life, Tarron hadn't quite learned how to be clever. Jack ended up being quicker on the draw.

It was true, too. Tarron was not wanting a child with her, but the pregnancy was a lucky result of the first time they ever slept together.

"I had names in mind. Yet you decided to name her after your mother, who you despise." Tarron shot back.

"Whom I *despise*? Tarron, what does this have to do with—" She paused, exhaling sharply. The next sentence came out slowly and concisely.

"I want you to know that I am only here because you still have me listed as your emergency contact."

Tarron opened his mouth, feeling a mix of shame and resentment along with pure disbelief.

"That's the only reason? Not the fact that the father of your child might've bled to death in a fucking parking lot." He said.

"Actually, the doctors said you nearly froze to death in your truck. You're lucky an off-duty cop found you so quickly."

Tarron sighed, exasperated. He rubbed his eyes with his palms and tried to compile anything to say. The room became quiet as he laid back in the bed, staring at the ceiling with a multitude of things racing across his mind. Celeste sat back down, motionless, weighing him with her gray eyes before looking away to avoid his gaze.

She would've rather I'd die. I knew it. It's like that question of who would cry at your funeral or who would wait to dance on your grave. The ghost of Celeste has lived in my mind so long that I had completely forgotten how much I regretted staying in a relationship with her.

But I still hate how we left it.

Had her last words to me been "never speak to me again" or "I hate you"?

"How's my mom?" Tarron asked.

"She's okay. It's been a while since Alina has seen her. She still comments on my Facebook posts, you know." Celeste replied.

Tarron was relieved at the change of subject. This was how they worked. Argue and change topics.

"I am well aware. Since she moved to Cheyenne. I haven't really seen her. She says gramma's got dementia."

"I'm sorry to hear that. And Tarron—" She paused, biting her lip.

"I heard about Jack, too." She finally said, "You've been asleep for a couple of weeks…maybe you should call his father? I know he's not the politest man, but—I don't know." Celeste finished quietly, shifting in her seat uncomfortably.

The room was quiet for a moment more before Tarron started, dodging the topic, "You can leave if you want. I can have someone pick me up whenever they say I'm good to go."

Celeste stood up slowly, gathered her purse, and stared at the ground. Tarron could see her start to tear up. Before she turned to leave, she said quietly, "I can bring Alina by as soon as you're home so you can see her. But Tarron—you nearly dying is *not* an apology. And before I forget—" she rummaged around in her pursed and retrieved a letter. "I haven't opened it, but your mom brought this from your place." Before Tarron could reply, she made her way to the door, leaving Tarron in a plastic state of dejection.

***

The letter was void of name or return address. But Tarron recognized the handwriting as soon as he opened it. Jack had sent him a letter. His stomach dropped, and he felt a wave of nausea wash over him. He lay there in bed, spinning before he managed to crawl out of his bed to retch in the toilet. He heaved until his stomach screamed, and there was nothing left to let out.

A passing nurse must have heard the sounds of his stomach and rushed into his room to help him from the bathroom back to his bed. After confirming that he was fine, she left him alone.

He reached for the letter again.

It is a sincerely bizarre and macabre thing to read someone's reasons for taking their own life. But, as he read, Tarron thought the letter sounded almost upbeat.

Tarron,

I am going to die. And it will be by my hand. I hope that in your mourning process, you will find this letter as a sort of comfort.

I wake up most days lost in a dream or a feeling like a record that keeps skipping. The only comfort that seems to come is the realization that the afterlife has escaped me. There will either be absolute nothingness or the greatest something. I don't particularly believe in hell, or heaven for that matter. You know, when Dante wrote the Inferno, he put people who committed suicide in the 7th circle of hell? Right next to murderers and tyrants. If he was correct, then I'm in for some lively company.

The God I've found has given me peace in choosing to lay my own life to rest. Energy in the universe is neither created nor destroyed. It just passes on. This is my passing on.

There was nothing left for me in my life except my own mistakes that I could not correct. Even in trying to reconnect with you—that was made remarkably clear. I am glad to have helped you on your feet, even if that meant you still lay blame on me. If you still harbor that, I would understand. Being your brother was the greatest privilege I could've asked for. I will always cherish our memories. When I pass, I hope you will not weep too much for the life that is over but for the life that I lived right beside you. I love you, Tarron.

When I take my own life, it will not be the end of my existence but my transition to the next. There's more for me on the other side. I find peace in knowing that.

Go with God,

Jack F.

P.S. I told Darian to find you, go be the brother to him that you were to me.

P.P.S. Tell Magnús and Jóhann hello for me.

Packed in a separate envelope were plane ticket vouchers for a trip from Cheyenne to Iceland and back. Tarron held them up with trembling hands and anger. This was the storm he was waiting to blow over. He wanted the grief to be over with already.

That evening he could barely stay asleep as he continued to vomit relentlessly through the night. Nausea he felt would not allow him to keep down any of the mostly liquid food they gave him. That was what he gathered from the doctor. At least, Tarron couldn't make out much of what the doctor said half the time as he had a seemingly continual morphine drip whenever the Doc came to check-in. When he asked the nurses for something solid to eat, he could read the pity in their eyes. Whatever pain medication they gave him helped, but eating made him more nauseous, and the combination of both drove him insane.

Finally, on his third conscious day, the doctor said he'd recovered enough to start eating solid food again as long as it didn't cause him to throw up more. Tarron made his way to the hospital cafeteria with the help of an orderly. The meal of the day was fried chicken with a side of mashed potatoes, the smell of which instantly had Tarron's mouth-watering.

After sitting down and beginning to eat, Tarron starred in disbelief when Darian, the same spray-tanned giant who had sat at his bar weeks ago, walked through the cafeteria doors in green scrubs. A bright red "HI My Name Is..." sticker hung on his chest.

Tarron quickly turned to the orderly who had accompanied

him. "Does that guy work here?" motioning a plastic spork towards Darian.

"Oh, big D? Yeah, his nursing class started here this past May, I think. They come in, like, twice a week. Super nice dude. Why? D'ya know him?" the orderly said with a mouth full of chicken.

"He's my best friend's little brother. He was there at my bar the night I got stabbed."

"Oh, shit, man, that's rough" He finally swallowed his food and continued, "I thought a cop brought you in?"

"No, no, no, they did. He had left a while before that. I just remember talking to him before."

Darian suddenly glanced at Tarron and made eye contact. That sixth evolutionary sense of feeling like you're being watched must've tipped him off. He smiled warmly and grabbed a bag of chips before striding over to Tarron's table.

"Dang, if it isn't Mr. Tarron, the bartender? What're you doin' here, man?" Darian asked excitedly.

"Good to see you again. But I, uh, got stabbed," Tarron said, lifting his hospital gown a bit to show the stitches.

"Wow! That looks horrible! When did this happen?" Darian said.

"The…night we met, actually. Right in the parking lot of Ozzie's. Yeah…" Tarron trailed off

Darian opened his bag of chips and began shoveling them into his mouth. He hadn't even finished chewing when he started talking again. Does everyone here talk with their mouths full? Tarron thought.

"You didn't, like, stab yourself—didja? Hari Kari-style or something?" Darian said, "I gotta know in case they need to put you on suicide watch, man. Can't have you joining my brother that quickly."

"Fuck no. But I do think I need to see him again. At the funeral, I mean."

"You're late by like…." Darian looked at his phone, which read Wednesday, "3 days. It was this past Sunday."

Tarron hung his head and stared at his lap.

"Fuck me." He finally said in a half-whisper.

"Don't be too bummed, man. Funerals are depressing. I was bummed, though, when you weren't at the bar when I popped in last night. I was gonna leave you a big tip," he winked.

"You mean like the last tip you left me?" Tarron asked, wondering for a moment if the seeds were still in his truck.

Darian put the bag of chips down, asking gravely, "You didn't lose them, did you?"

"No, of course not!" Tarron said, laughing awkwardly.

Darian immediately grinned. "Nah, I'm messin' with you. I got a bunch more seeds at home. If you did lose em', I'd be happy to give ya another baggie."

The orderly who had accompanied Tarron got up suddenly, "Hey, D. Y'all seem to have a thing going, so I'm gonna head out." He turned to Darian. "Gretchen from Oncology left me a note to meet her in the stocking room, and I definitely don't wanna miss out on that. So, I'll catch ya later."

Darian laughed, "Gretchen with the—" He motioned, cupping both hands at his chest, "you know?"

"Nah, that's Gretchen from Radiology. Gretchen from Oncology has the" the orderly motioned his hands to imitate an hourglass. "You know." He laughed gaudily.

"Oh yeah… she's cute, man. Go get 'er tiger" Darian smiled, pumping his fist.

Tarron stared at the two, dumbfounded. "What the fuck,

dude?" He asked

"What?" Darian shrugged "we have two doctors named Gretchen who work here? Gretchen from radiology is cute too, don't get me wrong."

"Never mind," Tarron sighed, "you know he wanted to be cremated." He spoke again, "your brother. He told me from time to time how weird a process he thought embalming was. Don't really know where he'd want his ashes spread, though."

"Oh, it was a closed casket. Did no one tell you how he died?" Darian said softly, his face darkening.

"No, I just know it was a suicide. What happened?"

"Shotgun," Darian said, pointing a finger gun underneath his chin, imitating a gun sound, "Just like Kurt Cobain. Fuckin' gruesome stuff."

"Jesus Christ," Tarron gasped. Again, speechless. He thought about his dream (though nightmare was more accurate) while he was unconscious.

"Hey, I know it sounds ridiculous, but before I woke from the coma, he came to me and told me he didn't want to be buried. I've broken a lot of empty promises, man, but I thought I could at least help your brother. He got me through a really hard time."

"Worse than being stabbed?" Darian asked innocently. "I dunno, man. He's six feet under. Kinda hard to cremate at that point."

Tarron stayed quiet, staring at his hands a while before Darian excused himself, stating he had to return to work.

Tarron felt nauseous again. He pushed his plate away and stuck a fork in the remaining pile of mashed potatoes. *How hard would it be to get a body exhumed and cremated, I wonder? You got that right, Darian, gruesome fuckin' stuff.*

***

Tarron didn't see Darian again until the day he checked out from the hospital. When he was walking toward the front desk to sign the outpatient forms and meet his mother, he was surprised to see the two of them in the lobby. Tarron's mother wasn't abnormally short by any means, but she was dwarfed in size next to Darian. Tarron couldn't make out what they were discussing. Whatever it was had his mom double over in laughter.

Grabbing the stack of hospital documents the desk nurse handed him, Tarron took a last look at the grand total of the hospital bill before handing his credit card over.

It might've been cheaper to die, even if I had insurance. Fuck, the one thing my dad urged me to invest in was a retirement and health insurance plan. I'll have to work overtime at the bar to make rent next month.

Or he could ask to move back in with mom. Or Celeste.

Ha, ha. Am I still high?

"You're lucky. You know," The nurse chimed in, reading his facial expression. "The surgeons were able to save you from having to use a shit bag."

Tarron looked up from the paper. "Excuse me?"

"A colostomy bag since the knife just barely punctured your colon. Usually, you see colon-cancer survivors with the shit-bag. You don't want me to tell you how bad they smell. Ugh!" she shook her head in disgust.

Tarron quickly handed back the forms to the nurse and hurried out the door before his mind could make its own conclusions about the odor of shit-bags.

As soon as he was through the double doors leading to the lobby, Tarron's mom made a beeline to him, already crying and with arms ready to smother him and re-aggravate his freshly removed stitches. Her hug was warm, and despite the tinge of pain from his abdomen, he felt comfortable in her embrace. The last time he had seen his mother was when she came to help Celeste move out.

Their hug was interrupted as Darian interjected, "I'm glad I bumped into you, Mrs. Faust! He gonna be all fine, just like I said. I gotta run up to the 3rd floor!" He turned to Tarron and clasped his shoulder. "I hope if I see you again, it's at the bar."

"God, I hope so too," Tarron replied. He hadn't even thought of when he'd return to work. His boss seemed annoyed on the phone when he told him he'd have to get someone to cover for him for a week. He also made a point to tell Tarron that despite the stabbing occurring in the bar parking lot, he couldn't seek legal action for any compensation. Tarron had to fight every urge to tell the man who employed him not to royally piss off.

Tarron's mother grasped his hand tightly as they walked through the parking lot. He felt like a small child again, fresh from getting a shot and on their way to the promised ice cream reward. She squeezed his hand tightly and looked at him.

"So that's James's other boy. Lord, he's grown up. Looks just like his father. Jack always looked more like his mother." She paused, feeling her son squeeze her hand back. "I'm sorry about Jack, hon. Did you two at least talk before… before he passed?"

"We did. Maybe a couple of months or so ago. He seemed fine? I really don't know anymore. But the letter you brought me was from him."

"What did it say?" She started, astonished. "And what about Celestyna? I know she visited you quite a bit."

Tarron frowned and waved his hand. "It was his suicide

letter, mom. I don't want to talk about it yet. As for Cellie… that's something for later too."

"Ugh, what, Tarron? You don't see me for months, and suddenly the two little boys that ran all through my house for years are either dead or dying? You think you'd at least talk to me more" She let go of his hand to grab a tissue from her purse. Tarron stumbled and caught himself, grabbing onto her shoulder.

"Sorry. I'm just frustrated with you," she said, grabbing around his waist for stability. She helped him into the car slowly and carefully shut the door behind him.

The car ride home was long and monotonous. Traffic was slowed due to snowfall. Tarron's mother tried to make more conversation, but prescription painkillers had Tarron slumped over in the passenger seat once the car started moving.

He jerked awake as soon as they parked, startling his mother. She helped him through the front door, into his bed, then slumped over herself on his couch as soon as he was settled.

Tarron lay on his bed staring at the ceiling. Celeste's words still hung in his head. Their entire conversation repeated itself on ends.

"…you nearly dying is not an apology."

She had a special way of dramatizing even the most mundane sentence into a line that telenovela writers would seethe over. That was her specialty as well—creating a space in which Tarron could hardly fill with; words, feelings, or presence otherwise.

Tarron rolled over and peeked underneath his bed to withdraw a box that contained his dress watch collection. Although "collection" was putting it elegantly. Among the 12 spaces for fancy timekeeping pieces, only three were occupied. He withdrew a silver dress watch and held it gently in his hands, reading the inscription on the back:

Our love is enough

It had been their 2-year anniversary when Celeste gave him the watch. Gifts were always the one thing they splurged on each other. Both being broke and in college was—as Jack put it: "paddling along on a semi-sinking lifeboat which is attached to a perfectly functioning boat driven by your parents. And sometimes they throw bread out to you."

Being broke, a college dropout, and having an unplanned child spoke to a different level of poverty that Tarron had become accustomed to over his time since leaving ASU. Moving back to his hometown had been Celeste's idea initially, to get support from Tarron's parents. Tarron's father's passing away and Cellie and he breaking up shortly after killed that idea much sooner than predicted.

He picked up another watch from the box. An Omega Seamaster, his father, had received as a gift from the city when he was the fire chief. His father always liked to joke that it was the fanciest and most pointless gift he had ever received. A good watch should tell the time and be durable, he reasoned. He wore it constantly, and each nick or scratch could show its wear.

Tarron took off the one from his wrist, a cheap G-shock he wore for work, and replaced it with the Seamaster.

He could feel his heart swell up and pushed back down the urge to cry right as his phone rang. He wiped his eyes and inhaled deeply before answering.

"Yeah, hello?"

"Is this Tarron Faust?" a very annoyed-sounding voice asked.

"Speaking," Tarron replied, pinning the phone between his

cheek and shoulder while he started to put away the watches.

"This is Officer Graft from Glenrock PD. We have your Hilux in our lot. Besides the bloodstains, it's in good condition. The alternator may need a look, too, but other than that, you're welcome to come by the station anytime to pick it up. Just need a form of ID and a copy of the insurance."

"Great, thanks. Is there anything else I need?" Tarron asked, waiting a second before hearing the line go dead. Dial tone.

"Have a nice day," Tarron said to himself.

He still had the watches in his hand. He placed the box back down on his bed.

The last watch in the box was 1 of 2 matching graduation presents that Tarron's dad had given him and Jack. It was a simple watch, still dressy enough to pass for formal but simple enough to where Tarron knew his dad probably picked it at first glance.

Tarron unclasped the watch on his wrist again and replaced it with this one.

***

The pancakes had left a very stale taste in his mouth. Tarron found himself lighting a cigarette and taking a long drag before waving to his mother, who had dropped him off at the police station. They had gone to a nearby cafe for breakfast at her suggestion before she headed back to Cheyenne, remarking that she had to return to take care of another helpless adult who barely spoke to her.

Tarron took another long drag from the cigarette, cursing the newfound taste of stale waffle and cigarette smoke that hung in his mouth.

The man at the front desk of the station gave him paperwork to fill out. Tarron recognized the same irritated voice from the man on the phone. This voice changed drastically as Officer Graft made the connection that Tarron was here to pick up the Hilux. He wanted to buy.

Before Tarron was out the door, the man made him an offer on the vehicle. Tarron smiled and nodded but politely declined, not before Officer Graft upped his asking price by $700.

"Listen, it's hard to find a Hilux like yours these days that's not in the hands of some Mid-east terror group with a machine gun mounted on top…Great trucks to work on. Can beat 'em' the-hell-up and still have them running the next day. Actually, one of your spark plugs was out, so I took the courtesy of replacing it myself. That alternator may need to be replaced, though…."

"Wait, wait, wait." Tarron cut him off. "You were the one who found me? Good God, man, you saved my life!"

"Yeah, yeah. All in a day's work. We found the bum who stabbed you, frozen to death, outside a liquor with your blood still covering his jacket. It's funny. I only transferred here to get away from a big-city crime like this. Anyway, how much would you take for it?" Graft said, waving his hand.

After declining the subsequent offer and explaining that one: it was his only source of transportation, and two: his father had given it to him as a college present, Graft made a point to give Tarron his personal cell number before he left.

"Just mull it over and get back to me."

Yeah, if dad hadn't given it to me and it wasn't my sole means of transportation, I might've just given it to you outright, Tarron thought as he drove out of the gates of Glenrock PD.

As he drove, he saw the light reflecting off an object on his dashboard. Reaching over, he realized it was the baggie of seeds Darian had given him.

He exhaled a sigh of relief and felt a smile form on his face. Graft was right. The blood stains weren't too bad.

4

From the Dead

THE STACK of mail that his mother had organized for him was organized into neat stacks with sticky note labels under each pile. He gathered the newspaper under one arm and combed through it as he grabbed the stack of white envelopes with his free hand, leaving alone the pile of what his mother wrote: *Bills* ☹.

He saw that his mother had also taken the liberty of circling two stories in the local paper with a red pen. One was a column on the third page that talked about his stabbing, and the other was in the obituaries section. Tarron skipped over the story about himself when he saw the name on the obit.

Jack Finnegan. Aug 16 1992-Nov 15 2018.

Glenrock HS Alum: Jack graduated Valedictorian from Glenrock high CO' in 2010. He was a State Champion in Track & Field and wrestling. He graduated with a Master's in Anthropology from Arizona State University. Jack is survived by his father, James.

45

Tarron read the line below, which stated who submitted the obituary: James Finnegan. He balled his fists and quickly felt the muscles in his arms tense.

Did his goddamn piece-of-shit Father not have time to write anything more about his deceased son?

Tarron thought about asking Darian if his father had even made an effort to attend the funeral sober. He knew he wouldn't like the answer.

From the letters pile, there were two 'sorry for your loss' cards from people Tarron vaguely remembered from high school. He figured he should at least reach out to them to say thanks, but the gesture felt empty. He threw the cards in the trash and went to bed.

***

What a treat. Getting to see two friends in one day. First, running into Tarron, back on his feet, and leaving the hospital with his delightful mother. And the aging Doctor Donald Ulrich (Veterinary doc, not MD) came in for his routine check-up and once again asked for Darian, or "that goofy, fuckin' nursing student" by name. Ulrich had taken a liking to Darian due to his innate ability to charm the over-60s of the world. It was also a chance first encounter, where the doggy doc was set up for a nasty fall off the bed—had it not been for Darian's barely sufficient reaction time. Don only came away with a bruise as Darian managed to mitigate the fall by cushioning the impact between Don and the ground with his own body.

Don was pleased to see him again. He came in pretty regularly for his arthritis and total disregard for retirement.

He built the first veterinary hospital in Casper with his own two hands and would have a stroke before someone else took it from him. Currently, Don's son had come on as a partner to shed the load.

The geriatrician at Casper Med. assured Don that a stroke would come sooner than he could pray for. Don replied with an array of curses and expletives, and the geriatrician tried to laugh it off as old folks saying the darndest things. Darian, though, spoke Don's language. The man practically lit up the first time Darian told him that he was in the Air Force. Don's favorite line is to tell people that not only was he a vet of the animal kind, but of the serve-your-country kind as well. Enlisted in the summer of '71 right out of high school into the Navy as a hospital corpsman to catch the "ass end of Nixon's war in Vietnam."

Donald Ulrich was retelling his favorite story to the nurse who was aiding him right as Darian came around the corner after being paged that his favorite patient was there.

"…I used to jump 6 feet right up in the air to get back onto the Huey! That's what we called the helicopters. They called me 'doc' back then too! I tell you—Darian!" Donald said as he saw him, outstretching his hand.

"Don!" Darian grabbed the man's hand with both of his to shake.

"I was just telling Nurse Jackie here about my time in 'Nam. She didn't believe that I could jump! I told her I'd show her right now in this gown, I—"

Darian looked at the nurse whose name tag very clearly read *Beth.* But her blonde hair, cropped short, must have made a larger impression of identity on Don than the name tag. Darian tried to smile innocently in a *sorry about him*, sort-of-way.

"I'll have her take your word for it. How about I take you back? Beth?" Darian asked. Beth gave a small nod and then strode off. Darian waited until she was out of earshot before turning to Don.

"So d'ya have the stuff, son?" Don asked in a hushed voice.

"Hm, that depends, Don, my man. Do *you?*"

"All in time, son. It's in my coat pocket in the room."

"Well, in that case…." Darian shrugged. He brought out a small, crumpled brown bag, took Don by the arm, and they walked side-by-side back to his exam room.

"How's it been with your hands?" Darian asked as they walked.

"Fuckin' terrible. John doesn't let me write up reports anymore 'cause my handwriting is *illegible.* I tell him, 'Then have the nurses do it, and I'll sign, for chrissakes' my name is on the building, after all. He thinks I can't even grip the goddamned pen anymore. I want to wring his neck, some days."

"You're too hard on him. He's your son, Don. It's his name too."

"And his pansy ass is only two years out of Vet school! Spent too much time with his mother, that boy."

"And how is Marlene?"

"Oh, she's great. Her hands are worse than mine, though. Can barely hold my prick in bed, so I tell her, 'Don't rip it off, woman. Use your mouth, how abouts'?" Don cackled.

Darian smiled at the old libertine. They walked inside the exam room; Darian closed the door behind them and shut the blinds.

"Heads up," Darian said, tossing Don the brown bag as soon

as he sat down on the bed.

"Ahhh, my real medicine," the man withdrew the contents. A large orange pill bottle with a plastic bag containing 14 grams of dried *Psilocybe cubensis*, locally grown and ethically sourced. A smiley face sticker reading *Happy tripping!* was placed on the other side of the bottle.

"Hundred, just like last time?" Don said, withdrawing his wallet and a small vial from his coat jacket hanging adjacent.

"Half off," Darian smiled, "wouldn't charge you the full price, especially with the phenyl."

"PPA is dirt cheap in comparison," Don argued, placing both the five $20 bills into Darian's palm and holding up the vial "let me do this favor for you."

"If you insist," Darian said, ironically rolling his eyes. Don reminded him of his great-aunt in this fashion.

"'fraid I do!" Don laughed. He stood up and began to redress himself. Darian turned around awkwardly to give him some privacy. Old men had a certain proclivity to not give a fuck if their dicks were out.

"You gonna keep dealing once you graduate?" Don asked as he pulled up his slacks.

"Uh, we'll see. I know there's a light at the end of the tunnel, but it's hard to see it sometimes."

"A'int that the damned truth."

***

When Tarron awoke, the sun was just barely bleeding through the blinds—making its descent to twilight.

Everything hurt. The prescribed drugs had worked their very best in concealing the painful protest from all of Tarron's organs and flesh, but now the numbness was gone. In its stead was a dizzying, aching pain that started to radiate from his abdomen to his head. He felt as if the hemispheres of his brain were tectonic plates grinding away at each other.

The pain medication the doctor had given him was just about gone. Three pills were left in the orange bottle. He didn't know if this was a tactic to prevent him from overdosing accidentally or an early incentive to get the prescription refilled. He sat up on the bed and pried open the cap, and poured two pills out into his hand.

Right before he tossed them into his mouth, a pounding on his front door broke the silence. He returned the pills to the bottle and swung his legs over the bed. His legs, however, had other plans as the blood rushed to his head, and they gave out on him. Tarron crashed into his nightstand and swore loudly. The unknown guest continued their onslaught of knocking at the door.

"Coming! Coming, fuckin' hell. Hold on a minute," Tarron called as he pushed himself to his knees and made his second attempt at becoming bipedal. He shook his head, then each leg rapidly, and made his way to the door. He swung it open, and his legs were attacked again, viciously by the tiny hugging arms of his daughter. She let out an excited "papa!" and continued to squeeze.

"Hello, Tarron. Please make an attempt not to swear in front of our daughter. I can barely handle her picking up words. I don't try to teach her in Polish," Celeste said, making her way past Tarron and sitting down at the bar in the kitchenette.

"Do you have anything to drink?" She asked, pulling a small make-up mirror out of her purse. Alina continued to hang on to Tarron's legs as he walked, koala-style. He smiled, realizing how deeply he had missed her.

Probably better I didn't take the pills; Cellie would've never let me hear the end of it if I forgot they were coming today, He thought.

"There's a couple of beers in the fridge and a bottle of Jäger if ya want," He replied, grabbing Alina by the arms and swinging her up to his shoulder. She giggled endlessly and made herself comfortable sitting on his deltoid. Tarron ignored the touch of pain in his gut as she swung her legs back and forth.

"Daddy, I'm your parrot, hee hee. Raaawwwk!" She cried.

"And I'm a pirate looking for mom's booty, argggg!" He replied. Celeste looked up from her make-up mirror and glared.

"Do you have anything to mix with the Jäger?" She asked, putting away her mirror. It would seem that all the fine details of her make-up were in order.

Tarron looked at her with a half-shrug, "I have mountain dew?"

"That sounds terrible" Celeste pursed her lips, mulling it over. "Fine, Jäger and dew."

Their visit was the most pleasant evening Tarron could recall since Celeste, and he had initially moved to Wyoming together. They drank several more Jäger and Dew's, finishing both bottles, played with Alina until she was exhausted, then put on Ice Age 4 at her behest. Both parents knew she would be asleep 15 minutes into the film. Halfway through, Tarron caught Celeste blinking her eyes shut as well. She had stretched out and made herself comfortable on the extended part of his sectional sofa.

"You and her can go sleep in my bed if you want. I can take the couch," he said softly, nudging her shoulder, careful not to wake Alina, who had fallen asleep on his lap.

Celeste blinked several times; then once hard and reached her arms up, yawned, and sat up. "We should go," she checked her phone, "it's late, and I need to finish some paperwork at the office before the holidays...." She trailed off.

"You're definitely in no condition to drive. Y'all can stay the night."

"That's okay—" She rubbed her temple. "No, you're right. Thank you." She was silent for a long time, and Tarron had thought she had fallen asleep again. His own eyes were growing heavy when Celeste broke the silence again suddenly.

"Do you wanna talk about what happened that night?"

Tarron remained silent. Internally, he wasn't sure if he had pushed away all memory of getting stabbed or if the compounding grief had forced him to forget it like a really unhealthy self-defense mechanism. He had no desire to talk about anything. Not the stabbing, Jack taking his own life, or the pair of tickets to Iceland he left behind. Tarron wanted to simply relax here, in this moment. It was something close to peace.

"Or about Jack?" she prodded again. Tarron clenched his jaw, silently wondering if she could read his mind as well as his face. He felt his eyes tear up and fought to be somewhat stoic.

"Or not... I'm sorry I brought it up." She responded again. They continued to watch the movie, and Tarron felt himself start to relax once more.

"You know, this is her favorite Ice Age," Celeste said, trying to defuse the tension.

"I'm more of an *Ice Age 2* guy myself," he replied quickly.

"No *dupek*, she has me put this movie on nearly every damn day. She knows it line by line."

Tarron waited for her to continue, unsure if she was going to or if it was his turn to contribute to the conversation.

She stayed silent, and Tarron watched the three animated mammoths on the screen: one mama mammoth, a papa, and the little daughter named Peaches. Tarron made the connection and immediately felt redundant.

"Oh…they're a family," He thought out loud. "Fuck, that's rough" he sucked in air through his teeth, "I'm sorry" He quickly added, "I just meant—"

"It's okay." She stopped him. She slowly ran her hand over his shoulder. "You know—you don't have to take the couch," her hand touched his "I remember your bed being big enough for the three of us."

"What would Ian think?" He blurted, instantly regretting the words as they exited his mouth.

Celeste frowned, pulling her hand away. "You just have to say something, didn't you?" She rose from the couch and started towards his bedroom. "You're fine on the couch, right?" she remarked before shutting the door. She popped it open again.

"Ian doesn't need liquor to get me into bed," she said. Closing the door once more.

Alina quietly groaned and rolled over in his lap. Her curly hair spilled across her face. Tarron brushed it behind her ears, then grabbed a blanket to cover her up. He hung his head back and let it rest atop the top of the couch.

"No, Ian just pays for everything with lawyer money and makes you resent me more." He sighed. He closed his eyes and awaited sleep, silently praying it would be dreamless

5

Good Days Bad Days

THE RUSHING river, harmony of birdsong, and sway of trees had a quiet way of lulling Tarron into serenity. He felt each note of nature's symphony reverberate, and the pull of the river surround him. Only the occasional question about 'if she was doing this right' from Alina pulled him away from his daydream.

The green fishing waders he had bought for his daughter were a bit too big around her torso, so she didn't dare venture far from shore. Tarron, though, stood in the middle of a shallow bend in the river, showing her the proper way to cast a line. His father had taught him fly-fishing when he was about 5, so he made a goal to do the same—Alina was just a month shy of her 5th birthday. Tarron, similarly, was a month away from 27. He always loved that they shared a birth month and was hoping to be able to plan something special for her 5th.

"Alright, Lina', keep your wrist straight. Imagine the rod is a big, long paintbrush, and you have to flick the paint off the end quickly—no, not too fast. Just fast enough to stop it at the end of your cast. Watch me" Tarron brought his pole back with practiced hands and flicked the line back into the water, exaggerating his motions slightly to show Alina the proper technique. She watched with wide eyes before trying again.

"There ya go—good!" Tarron said.

"When do we get a fish, dad?" Alina asked.

Ah, the dreaded question. Only a matter of time now before she gets bored. Better come up with something before she asks to go back home, he mused.

"A good fisherman, or fisher-woman, is patient. You have to cast your line
a bunch and wait for the fish to bite," Tarron stated. Echoing, with less crude language, a similar lesson passed down from his father.

Alina put on a youthful face of determination, and Tarron saw her focus more on the small mechanics of her cast. For four almost-5-years-old she had marvelous concentration. Tarron felt a tender feeling of pride in passing down a lesson that was passed down to him.

This sentiment lasted about 20 fish-less minutes before Alina loudly declared: "I'm cold. Can we go home, dad?" Tarron opened his mouth to answer as soon as he noticed Alina's line suddenly go taut.

He quickly called to her: "Reel it in, Lina'! You got one! Careful!"

She tugged at her pole and grabbed the line as Tarron waded over to her to lend a hand. Before he could get to her, Tarron watched his daughter fall flat on her face into the water.

"SHIT!" he yelled.

He dropped his own rod and waded quicker to Alina. He pulled her up by the shoulders and saw her rod still in her hands. She wiped her face off with the crook of her elbow and continued to try and reel in her catch.

Tarron put his hands on his hips and grinned. Martin Faust would be proud. She fought with the fish for several minutes, back and forth, as her father encouraged her. Suddenly the line slackened completely, and Alina turned to her father in confusion. The look on her face said it all.

"Oh no. I'm sorry, chicken, the fish must've gotten away." He saw her eyes well up with tears as she sniffled back a cry. He wrapped an arm around her and knelt down into the stream.

"Hey, hey. It's okay. We can always come again. Now that mom let us. You had a really good cast! I'm so proud of you, Alina." Tarron praised, continuing, "we can get some ice cream on the way home. You earned it."

Alina looked up and smiled, wiping away a tear "Really, dad?"

Yes, baby, just don't tell your mother, he thought. Reassuring her out loud, he grabbed her fishing rod, reeled the rest in, and grabbed his own from the riverbed. He took his daughter's hand with his free hand, and they walked out of the steam together.

His Hilux was parked a short walk away. He tossed the fishing gear in the bed of the truck and secured Alina in the passenger seat. Celeste had forgotten to give him the car seat, so he silently prayed they didn't run into any trouble on their way home. It was only Saturday afternoon, and he wasn't meeting back with Celeste until Sunday evening. Best not to press his luck.

They stopped at the gas station a stone's throw from Tarron's house. Tarron halted the car and hopped out. He got drumsticks, Alina's favorite. Returning to the car, he reminded her to try her best not to drip any of the ice cream on the front seat.

Once they were home and parked, Alina exited the vehicle and ran into the house, leaving her dad to put away all the fishing gear in the shed. She plopped herself on the couch and grabbed the remote to turn on the TV. Tarron could glimpse the TV through the window and saw that she was again putting on Ice Age 4. He finished organizing all the fishing gear, closed his shed door, and headed inside to join her.

"This really is your favorite one, huh?" he said, draping his jacket on the car and unlatching his waders. Alina responded with a quiet "yes, dad" without looking up from the television.

Tarron put himself in between the screen and his daughter and looked down. She craned her neck to look around him.

"' Lina, c'mon, ya gotta change into normal clothes. You're getting the couch wet," he said sternly. Alina looked down at the damp marks that outlined her legs on the couch and slowly reached her legs down to hop off. As Tarron led her by the hand to help her change into dry clothes, she didn't take her eyes off the TV. After putting her in a T-shirt and pants, Tarron put a towel down where she previously sat and collapsed into his chair. Alina made her way on top of the towel.

"You really like this movie, huh?" he asked.

"I like the ma-moths," she said softly.

Tarron sank into his armchair and let his head fall back. He couldn't quite figure out how constant watching and rewatching of the same show was addicting to kids. Then again, he could recall his own mother claiming how she couldn't go the day without putting on Sesame Street—or hear baby Tarron's cries of protest.

The movie had progressed a bit further than the point that Tarron remembered himself fumbling about getting into bed with Celeste last night. She had left without a word this morning, slamming his front door, which woke him from his spot on the couch.

Tarron looked at his daughter locked into her trance of bewilderment with the television and wondered, as all separated parents do if she could give him some insightful drama about her mother's current boyfriend.

"Hey Lina', does mom ever argue with Ian?" He asked, adding, "like, are they ever yelling at each other?"

"Ummm, argue? Sometimes?" she turned her head towards her dad, but her eyes were still focused on the screen.

"Yeah, like," Tarron broke off, scratching his beard, "is mom ever sad after talking to him? Also—" He continued, "don't tell mom I asked, okay? Pinky swear?" He paused the movie on the TV and then held out his little finger. Alina broke her disposition with the TV and returned the gesture.

"I—" Tarron started, holding his opposing hand in front of his heart as they had done many times before.

"I—" Alina repeated, mirroring her dad.

"Pinky, swear not to tell."

"Pinky swear." She echoed, crossing her heart. Their secret.

"Okay," Tarron smiled. "So…?" He asked patiently.

"Sometimes, mommy cries. Sometimes Ian is loud. And he doesn't let me watch Ice Age."

"That monster," Tarron gasped. "Well, you know you can always watch Ice Age here. Your mom still uses my Netflix, anyway."

"Okay, dad."

"How is Ian loud? Is he loud to mommy?"

"At first. Then she cries, and he gets quiet. It makes me scared."

"If you're ever scared, you go ahead and call me, okay?" He

picked up a pen and scratch paper lying on the coffee table and scribbled down his home phone and cell. "I know mommy also has these numbers, but I want you to keep this safe just in case you need to call me."

He handed the paper to Alina, who looked up at her father, nodded then folded it slowly to place it in her tiny pants pocket.

"I love you 'Lina."

"Mmhmm." She replied, staring at the screen again, waiting for the animation to continue.

Tarron pressed play again to resume the movie. He figured his method of toddler interrogation could only hold her attention for so long. Alina hadn't voiced anything realistically new to Tarron.

Pre-dating his stabbing and best friend's suicide, Tarron occasionally found himself with an open bottle and his phone in his hand past 2 AM. Usually texting or calling Celeste. The conversations never seemed to last long, but when they did, she would humor him with a certain uncertainty in her words. Last night had given Tarron a bit of hope, albeit that hope was undercut by the slamming of his door this morning.

"I don't like Ian," Alina said.

"Me either, chicken. Me either."

Alina stretched out on the couch and yawned. "When mom comes to pick me up, I'll ask if you can come too" she closed her eyes and rested her head on the armrest of the sectional.

"I'd like that," Tarron remarked.

His phone started to buzz. The caller ID read: CELLIE WALCZAK. "Ah, speaking of which… hey, what's up?"

"Hey Tarron, it's Ian. Celestyna and I are coming by later today to pick up Alina. Just a head's up."

Tarron rose from his armchair and walked to his bedroom,

closing the door behind him. "Wait, what? This is my weekend. Did something happen?"

"Nah, we're just going on a day out. Alina finished school, and I got time off from work. Anyway, yeah, just have her ready. We'll be by around 1. Thanks, champ."

"Wait, no—why didn't she call me why—" the line went dead, and Tarron pulled the phone away from his face slowly. Feeling agitation rise within him, he sat down on his bed and began to type out a future message to Celeste. The contents of which were filled with a number of expletives and sarcasm before he deleted the entire text and threw his phone on the bed, exiting the room. He sat down next to Alina and wrapped an arm around her. She settled in his embrace and made herself comfy.

"Hey, your mom is coming by to get you today."

"Oh, okay. I can ask her about you coming with us!" She repeated.

"Maybe not this time. We can see about next week. I, uh, have to go to work."

"Aw, okay, daddy. Does your tummy hurt?"

Tarron reached his palm down and ran his fingers along the scarred tissue slowly. At certain points, he could feel the smallest burning sensation meet his fingertips. But the wound was healing nicely, according to the doctor.

"Sometimes. I have my days."

Alina reached into a pocket of her pants and retrieved something from its contents. She opened her small balled fist to him, opening it up to offer a blue Jolly-Rancher candy.

"Here! Mom gives me these when I get a cut. I like to keep them in my shorts just in case!" She said cheerfully.

Tarron grabbed the candy and put it in his pockets carefully.

"Thanks, chicken. I'll save it for when I have a really bad day."

The papa mammoth onscreen appeared to be fighting a band of dinosaur pirates to free his mammoth family with the help of a whale. Tarron watched the animation with fascination, remarking how far the movie franchise had come.

***

Tarron decided that only in the United States, where healthcare was almost more of a burden than the actual injury, would a person go through what he had and still clock in for work the next day he was able.

He felt stupid but helpless at the same time. It gave him time to think about the Iceland tickets and Jack's letter. He didn't want to tell Cellie about it yet.

The letter that the tickets came with had ruined that for him.

The tickets seemed like a literal "call to adventure," as his high school English teacher, Miss Emily, liked to call it. But instead, he decided to return to his regularly scheduled program—sans the capitalism-sponsored coma-cerial break.

Dreadfully sorry I let you down, Miss Emily. I have to pay medical bills.

The bar was in full swing, buzzing with energy. It was Sunday evening, and primetime football demanded worship. He had work to do, and the years of an emotionally distant lover, recently widowed mother, and dead best friend hadn't left him much time to mourn his own personal ego death. He simply didn't have the time for...

"You alright, there, fella?" An older man seated at the bar suddenly asked.

Tarron felt himself mentally check back into the conscious world around him. He slung his rag across his shoulder and sighed. Please stow all emotional baggage and prepare to get the show on the road.

"Yeah, I'm fine. Can I get you anything?"

Back to auto-pilot. Serve drinks. Clean spills. Send orders to the kitchen. Clean spills. Bronco's win. More drinks. Crowds start to leave. Tarron checked the time: 9:30 PM. We close at 11. Thank God. Only 30 more minutes until it was 10, then 30 minutes after that, he could cut people off. Then a short drive home and a good night's rest.

A quick shout from behind him caused Tarron to wheel around on his heels.

"Bartender!" The voice cried out.

Darian, all six foot seven, eight, or maybe even nine of him. Same bronzed skin and messy brown hair tucked under knit beanie reminiscent of Sherpa's. His smile beamed from across the bar, and Tarron made his way over to him.

"Tarron! Great to see ya' man. How's it back?" He bellowed, grabbing Tarron's hand with both of his own to shake.

"Great man, yeah. It's a bitch to get up some days, but I've been able to work all week. Can I get you something to drink?"

Darian stroked his chin and scrunched his eyebrows, appearing to think very deeply over the routine question. Tarron spied the beginnings of a colorful tattoo sleeve peeking out under Darian's jacket. He hadn't noticed that on their first encounter.

"Do you have anything that's not beer?" Darian asked.

"Um… we have a couple of ciders on tap? They're local."

"Tap?"

Tarron chuckled firstly but read Darian's expression, who was completely serious. "On tap. Like that means I can pour it from these spouts behind me…." He explained.

"Ah!" Darian cried, "Then I will have one of those. Shop local, right? He asked.

"Definitely. The owner and his son make deliveries to here and the diner across town. Also, can I see your ID before I forget?"

Darian handed over the plastic card and then held up his head with both hands, resting his elbows on the bar. "I love that! Reminds me of back home in Tahoe. This old couple would go around the neighborhood with a basket from their garden. Ma loved that stuff."

Tarron peered at the ID. Two curious things stuck out to him immediately. He saw that Darian had taken his mother's last name, McConnell. He had heard before of women reverting to their maiden names after a divorce before, but for Darian to go through the same trouble…

The birth date on the ID was just as curious. It stood out to him in that he only could recall it by way of its macabre. Darian had turned 21 the night Tarron first met him. Another thing he hadn't noticed before.

As he brought the glass to the man, he placed a napkin at the base. He then grabbed a bowl of pistachios from underneath, where they were kept in a large bucket. Ready to be scooped up by the gallon or bowl-full.

"Whatcha reading this time?" Tarron asked as he placed the glass & bowl down to the right of Darian's elbows.

"This, friend, is *The Brothers Karamazov* by the late Fyodor Dostoevsky." He said, closing the book onto the bar and picking up his glass.

"Polish guy? What's it about?" Tarron prodded.

"Russian. One of the most important Russian authors to live. He actually died four months after the book was published, sorta like his swan song. It's about these brothers, and they bicker a lot over women and money, then one of them kills the father, but I haven't found out who, though, yet. Interesting stuff." He put the book down and grabbed his glass.

"Will you toast with me?" He asked.

The question, by force of habit, prompted Tarron to look around for his non-existent drink.

"Uh, I don't typically drink while I'm at work, man." He hesitated.

"I thought that's a bartender's thing? Besides, I don't even know if I'll like what you just poured me."

"Sure, then." Tarron turned and grabbed a 16-ounce glass. He filled it with seltzer water. "What are we toasting to?"

"To you, friend. Back on your feet. Back from the dead. Cheers!"

The glasses met, clinking and Tarron sipped on the seltzer water. Darian drank hard into his cider, tipping it more, and downed the entire glass. He set it down and exhaled sharply.

"Ah! Not bad!" He began, "I wanted to try other drinks tonight. If you'll have me. I'm fascinated by the liquors of other cultures. The more I read, it seems every culture has its own booze or drug.

"They actually theorize that drugs might've been the catalyst for evolution. The 'stoned ape theory. Ha! I actually love 'shrooms, though don't tell the hospital…." Darian began to trail off.

Tarron noticed an obese, angry looking-man trudging up to the corner of the bar and started to wave him down.

Darian didn't seem to take note of the man and continued excitedly. "… and that was the first time I tried ketamine!"

Tarron held up a hand, signaling to Darian that he indeed

was listening but needed to put a pin in their conversation.

"Just… hold that thought, man." Tarron took a step towards the obese man before halting and turning once more to Darian

"Wait, did you say mushrooms? Like magic mushrooms?" Darian opened his mouth and held up his index finger, ready to rattle off before Tarron stopped him again. "Actually, no, sorry. Just hold that thought. For one second, please."

Darian lowered his eyebrows and then smiled, bringing his book back up to the counter. Tarron was nearly halfway there when the grumpy-looking man opened his mouth to heckle him. The smell coming from the man's mouth already reeked of vodka. Tarron quickly decided to give him the nonalcoholic beer Ozzie's had, regardless of what he ordered. And if he escalated, then it would be twice in one month that Tarron would have to throw someone out. "Jeezus, finally. Is this the kind of service I can expect in this shitstaintown?" The obese man wailed, "All I wanted was a fuckin' beer, man."

Tarron's clenched his jaw. He had lost the shock value of rude or drunk customers very early on to working at Ozzie's when he was a teen. He began to disingenuously take the man's drink order and ignored every other word out of his mouth, being either an insult or a swear. People around began to stare. He obviously wasn't local.

Tarron desperately wanted to avoid another bar fight as well, if at all possible, for the last shift of his first week back.

The angry, obese man took his "beer" and stared at the bowl of pistachios with a sense of spiteful bewilderment as Tarron placed it on the counter.

"The fuck is this shit?" the man asked after taking a drink.

Tarron's heart jumped for a second.

"Who eats pistachios at a bar?" the man continued. He then

picked up the bowl of green-shelled nuts in astonishment. Then, suddenly regurgitated onto the bartop. The patrons nearest to him fled like victims from a burning theater. Vomit perforated its smell at the same speed, and Tarron fought his own urge to gag.

"ALRIGHT. THE BAR'S CLOSED. EVERYONE OUT." He shouted. Several heads snapped to him with faces of concern to gauge if this was some sort of joke. Only the jukebox and sounds of the puker gurgling his beer were audible. The bar had been mostly cleared out following the game. Only his regulars were left, and they'd understand.

"OUT!" Tarron affirmed. Before tossing a nod at Darian. *Not you, you stay.*

One brave soul put an arm around the overweight drunkard and helped him out as well. The kindness of strangers in strange times.

Tarron got to work. Clearing the tables and wiping the puke up with a rag.

He saw Darian rise from his stool.

"Darian, you're fine," he said quickly.

"Oh, I'm just moving. I can only deal with the smell of puke for so long. Brings back bad memories."

"Don't wait up. I wanna finish our conversation."

"But of course," Darian answered with a grin.

He was done in around ten minutes, but the ache in his legs from working the previous 9 hours made it feel like eons. He walked towards the opposite end of the bar that Darian had relocated to.

"Tarron, I'm beginning to think I bring you bad luck when it comes to other bar patrons," Darian remarked, placing his book back into his lap and then looking at his cider. He lowered the glass and pointed it towards Tarron.

"More?" The empty glass inaudibly seemed to say.

"You want another one, or is that your way of saying you're tired of holding an empty glass?"

"Uno mas, por favor." He requested in very Anglo-Americanized Spanish.

Tarron replaced the empty glass with a fresh, clean one and filled it practically to the brim with Glenrock Brewing's finest apple cider. As he handed it to Darian, a thought which was previously stuck in the back of his head made its way to the speak-without-thinking portion of Tarron's brain. "You still do shrooms?" He blurted out.

Darian's cider was inches from his mouth. He paused, grinned, and placed the glass back down firmly with enough force to splash the cider onto Tarron's apron.

"Now that's what I like to hear. Yes, in fact, I do, from time to time. What would ya like to know?"

Tarron took a deep breath and scratched the back of his head, trying now to conjure the words to politely ask someone he realistically barely knows if he could help him trip balls.

"I don't know," He lied. "I was talking to the doc a couple of days ago, and he had mentioned something about people micro-dosing, or whatever that's called… I've never even tried anything other than alcohol…." He began to trail off. "Well, the one and only time I tried weed, I burnt off part of my beard trying to light the joint."

Darian took a long drink from his glass, waving his hand and inviting Tarron to keep talking.

"Or something… I don't kno—" Tarron stammered.

"Man, you've got to stop sayin' that! Uncertainty is a mind killer!" Darian said, placing his glass down for emphasis.

"Check it: when the CIA leaked LSD to the hippies in the 60s, you know what happened? The summer of love, man! If any of those hippie pioneers kept doubting what they could experience by way of something other than what the government deems legal, then we would never be where we're at today. Any music you like, any of it at all. Guaranfuckin-teed that those musicians were high on something. There's no progress in the world of art without the opening of one's mind."

"You got a lot of big ideas for a nurse, I'll admit."

Darian leaned back a bit. "Nursing student… But yeahhhh, like I said, don't tell the Medical Dept at Casper. Ha-ha." He grinned. "Plus, I haven't even been there for a year. Jack was the one who convinced me to go back to school, ya know."

At the mention of Jack's name, Tarron felt the last ominous lines of Jack's suicide note. The postscript had such simple instructions in the form of a request.

"Go be the big brother to him that you were to me." Weird how he phrased that. I always felt like I was the one who looked up to him. If this goofy, impossibly tall boy is your blood, though, Jack, I'll try to do right by him.

"Jack… that's right, so you've said." Tarron lost his train of thought and decided to switch gears, "Do you want a nightcap before I cash out the register? I realize that only half of the people I kicked out probably paid their tabs. So…"

"Well, in that case… Do y'all happen to have mead? That was one of the drinks I wanted to try. It was the drink of choice for ancient Vikings."

"Hm…mead, we may. I'd have to look. Be right back."

"Mhm." Darian acknowledged before strolling over to the wall of cuckoo clocks. Examining each one closely.

Tarron walked to the liquor shelf and scanned the bottles.

Nope, nope, nope, honey tequila? No, not that, either. Who even carries mead? Well, actually, Oz had a taste for things like that.

Tarron's eyes landed on a dusty, unopened bottle. The label had diminished some since he had last seen it. Bingo.

Years ago, as barbacks, he and Jack had snuck drinks of all but every bottle in the place. "Just so we know what kind of alcohol we like when someone asks us at parties," Jack had said. As if they needed a better reason. The bottle of mead, though, they had not dared to touch as normally... normally...

Oz kept it in his office. That's right. That new owner kid must've put it here when he cleared out the office. Fucker.

He cracked the bottle open and let it breathe on the countertop. The smell of honey filled the air as he retrieved clean whiskey glasses.

"Ah, so you're sharing this drink with me?" Darian grinned.

Tarron picked up his glass and raised it: "To dead friends and to new ones."

"Oh, that's dark. But I'll drink to that."

The glasses clinked, and Tarron sucked down the liquor. It burned gently and sweetly. He exhaled fire out of his nose. He watched Darian sip delicately at first. Then again, tipping the glass back before downing it like a shot. The kid's a natural.

"Another?" Tarron suggested, "Or is there another you wanted to try?"

"Nah, man, I can get out your hair. But—are you hungry? There's a 24-hour dinner near my house."

"Where? Casper? No, I gotta get home. Trying to get back into an actual workflow."

"It's right outside the city. 10 minutes there, I promise. Plus—" he dug out his wallet and laid a couple of bills out on the table, "Let's say you owe me one. I'll drive!" Darian strode to the door before Tarron could answer, calling out, "It's the blue jeep with stickers on the back!"

Tarron sighed and grabbed the glass Darian had left. He began to scrub down the bar top vivaciously, disinfecting it twice. He then counted the tips and tallied the sales. Locking up the money from the cash register coupled with receipts in a manila folder destined for a filing cabinet. All things and vomit considered—it was a good night for tips. Hourly wages be damned. He actually would be able to make next month's rent and bills.

He shut off the overhead lights to the bar, and darkness enshrouded the room, save for the jukebox's neon glow. The sole source of life in the room. Its rack of CDs seemed to give him a toothy grin from across the way and say, *"Be careful. You don't know what's out there."*

"Shut up, jukebox."

The bar was closed and not of his concern anymore. He shut the door and locked it behind him.

He half-heartedly expected the parking lot to be empty when he walked over, but Darian whistled loudly and waved as soon as he saw Tarron round the corner. Tarron waved back and headed over to the vehicle.

When Darian mentioned stickers, Tarron half-expected a collection of 'Life is Good' or 'Not All Who Wander Are Lost'-type statements decorating the back window. In their stead was a United States Air Force sticker; a black-and-white text bubble reading IRAQ, and next to it: a cartoon gunship firing down on stick figures with the caption "No one cares about your stick figure family."

"Cute," Tarron remarked, catching Darian's attention and

pointing at the stickers.

"Oh, these?" Darian laughed, "Been meaning to take them off for a while.

Just keep forgetting, ya know?"

"Did you go overseas? I thought you were in school to be a nurse?"

"GI bill, my man. I had enough credits from my time in and from when I took dual-credit classes in high school. The nursing program at Casper college teams up with the Hospital in town to get you experience, and if they like you during clinicals, they'll ask to hire you once you finish your degree."

"Wow. Good for you, man. What'd you do in the Air Force?" Tarron asked awkwardly. He had remembered asking the same question to other vets who had come into the bar in the past but more as a conversational bit. People were more likely to tip and buy more drinks when you seemed interested in their lives. But in this instance, Tarron found himself genuinely curious.

"Was on an AC-130," Darian said quietly, jabbing his thumb at the sticker raining death upon the stick figures on the window. "Flew around. Shot some stuff. Let's go. I'm freezing."

"Sure, you should be driving?" Tarron asked as he hopped into the vehicle, nervously pressing the lock button on his key fob to triple-check that his own truck was locked.

"Trust me, T—I've driven through a lot worse conditions." Darian grinned. He reached over and slowly turned the dial on the radio clockwise. Tarron remarked that although he was placing a lot of blind trust in someone, he learned more and more about him as minutes passed, and he had a strange sense of security in Darian's certainty.

The deejay for 107.7 KRQU proudly announced their 11 o'clock zero commercial hours were commencing. The song began, and the quiet details of a vinyl record being spun up filled the airwaves. Tarron sat back in his seat and momentarily basked in the sound quality the speaker system in the jeep produced. The song playing was a live rendition of Heart's Crazy on You. Tarron found himself shutting his eyes and sinking into his seat with the acoustic guitar chords lulling him to sleep.

He felt as though he had just momentarily shut his eyes when the car shuddered to a halt.

"Hey man, we're here. See, I told ya, less than 10 minutes." Darian said as he removed the keys and killed the engine.

Tarron rubbed his eyes with both hands and sat up in his seat to look out the windshield. It was a chrome-covered diner reminiscent of the retro 60's architecture every restaurant of similar intentions was built upon. Neon light strips that spelled out the restaurant name Classics, checkerboard pattern exterior, and nostalgic decorations. Blinking several times, he read the diner's sign which boldly proclaimed its 'to-die-for patty melt' and $4 malts.

"So…shall we?" Darian asked as he exited the jeep. Tarron followed suit and hopped out of the passenger side, stretching his legs as Darian impatiently waited.

"Let's go, old man. Well, I guess you're not that old," Darian called out as he strode towards the double door-ed entrance to the diner, holding one of the doors open with a broad smile across his face.

6

In the Cradle of Stars

CAREFUL ATTENTION to maintaining a 60's theme seemed to stop at the door of Classics. The inside was virtually indistinguishable from any chain Denny's or ma & pa breakfast shop. The sole retaining factor that reminded Tarron that he and Darian were in such a restaurant was the bright teal blouse and skirt their waitress donned. The restaurant's upholstery was a similar color. She was an older woman, maybe in her 40s, who, given the occupation, either had been here for a long while or just started because she needed the money.

She led them to a booth and handed them laminated menus. The lines on her face suggested a history of taking food orders from people who were too rude to realize that she was also a human being. Tarron decided she had probably been here a while and made a mental note to tip amply as a token of appreciation from one to another in the service business. Although Tarron thought she probably didn't have the luxury of kicking out drunks who overstayed their welcome.

"What's good here?" Tarron asked once they were seated.

"Oh, man!" Darian leaned forward and laid the menu down

on the table. "Let's see… I've had just about everything. Been trying out something new every time I stop by." He started listing out entrees along with his own personal, five-second review, which ranged from: 'fuckin' loved it' to 'would politely throw away, so the chef didn't feel bad if he saw it sent back.'

At the end of his listings, Tarron still didn't know what to order. The waitress had made her rounds to other tables and was now heading back to their booth. Tarron sighed, scratched his beard then made a panicked order for the patty to melt.

He didn't feel hungry, but after a garrulous shift, he had a backlog of other feelings that needed addressing. Chiefly his feet. He half-heartedly wondered if expensive in-soles were worth it.

Darian had been talking the entire time he had pondered this, and he felt an undertone of embarrassment that he hadn't been listening,

"Yeah, man." He replied once Darian finished his sentence, not really knowing what to say to a dialogue he hadn't mentally been present for.

"You were mentioning something about mushrooms?" Darian prompted.

"Uh, *mushrooms?*"

"Psilocybin. Magic mushrooms. You had asked me if I still did shrooms when we were at the bar right after that guy was a dick to you and threw up.

It was pretty neat when you threw everyone out."

"I… I think I was just at the end of my rope there. Glad to have made a friend, though."

"Are we friends?" Darian asked innocently in between gulps of ice water.

"I mean… yeah! It's not like we just met. But then again, I

just found out you were in the Air Force, which was a total surprise, but…." He trailed off and shrugged. "I'd have a beer with ya." He quickly added.

"Awe, well, thanks, T." Darian agreed, placing his hand on his chest "me, I don't like beer, but I'd gladly share a cider with you, which—I found out tonight I like it!"

"God, you're young. There was a lot of underage drinking that went on at the behest of your brother and myself. We were broke, of course, so we drank a lot of cheap beer. But our roommates were Icelandic, see—they had bottles of this liquor from Iceland that sometimes tasted terrible. But, like, after one or two shots, it wasn't bad. Like black licorice."

"Whoa, whoa. I know it gets a bad rap, but I actually like black licorice," Darian contested, laughing. Tarron joined him in a short laugh before the conversation grew quiet.

"So… shrooms?" Darian prompted, breaking the silence. An inviting smile crept on his face.

***

The patty melt truly was to die for. The meat was cooked to perfection, and the cheese was a savory, melted mess. A friend had told Tarron once that the best meat for a good patty melt or Philly cheese steak was cheap, bottom-shelf meat—and that it needed to be prepared by a grumpy short-order cook who claimed to be from Brooklyn. Tarron wasn't too sure of the chances of a New York-born chef in rural Wyoming, but he had enough faith in the sandwich to picture such a character behind the grill.

Tarron also had a chronic habit of forgetting to eat right until the smell of food painfully reminded him of the emptiness in his stomach. He practically swallowed the first half of his patty melt before the waitress returned to refill their drinks.

He forced himself to slow down and took another bite. The taste brought him back to Friday afternoons in high school after track practice when his dad would take him and Jack for food afterward.

He'd gotten to a point where he didn't want to repress any more memories. He knew everything in some way or another might remind him of Jack, so he tried to at least surrender to the notion. He was, after all, having dinner with Jack's little brother.

The nightmare he endured in his coma still haunted him. Responsibility to fulfill a dying man's last wish seemed a decent enough thing to do for any decent enough person. Meeting Darian and coming close to death all in the same night gave Tarron the idea that it was some sort of sign, should he choose to take it, from a higher power.

Shiva, Zeus, or Jehovah? The universe, maybe? Religion didn't have as big a place in his heart as when he was a tot in Sunday school.

Disenfranchised. That was the correct word for it.

But I am alive to see the next day. And able to eat a patty melt. Tarron put the sandwich down and wiped his hands.

"Lose your appetite that quickly?" Darian asked.

"Just—thinking…I'm luckier than most. I guess I could say. A lot of people will go their entire lives without ever being in a coma because of getting' stabbed. That a whole lot of other people get stabbed or shot every day and don't make it—I'm just… thankful. But I don't know what I should do. Everything almost seems like a waste. I barely was able to make enough money this week because the bar is understaffed."

"Is that healthy?"

"You know," Tarron started, picking up the patty melt again, "probably not. But I don't think I have it in me to find another job so quickly. Besides, I like working there most of the time. Get to meet new people."

"You make up reasons to continue working there 'cause you're comfortable. Change is like jumping into a Jacuzzi or an ice bath. A change from where you're comfortable at now and what's unknown."

"Why in the world would you wanna take a bath in ice?" Tarron laughed.

"Sore muscles usually. Masochism. Take your pick" he took a bite of his food and swallowed, "It's a matter of if you to wait and take that step whenever you feel ready. Or if you want something to give you a nudge.

"Answers to these kinds of questions of should 'I wait for a sign' or 'take a leap' aren't always as straightforward as we'd like. There's only so much you can spend your time doing in this life. Time is… what you make of it. Like here, at this moment," he held up a fork with a piece of meat on it, "this cow lived and died in its own time. Eventually, making its journey from calf—eating grass every day a simple existence. To being slaughtered a served to me, fried like chicken. And is—" he took a bite and slowly chewed, "very fuckin' delicious."

"I… I don't follow, man. You had, and then you lost me."

"Humans just have a funny way of how we perceive time. See—the earth is on her own time. A sort of" he waved his hands in the air searching for the right word "biological rhythm just makes sense. The sun gives off energy and life, plants soak up that energy, animals eat the plants, and we eat the animals, and so on and so on. Nature has no set agenda or goals. Life is…" he paused, starting to stare at the ceiling, hands still in the air for thought. Tarron momentarily followed his gaze and realized Darian wasn't staring at an object, just lost in reflection.

"Yeah, man?" He prompted.

"Life is a miracle indifferent to whether we live or die. So, we owe it to ourselves to live. Despite the odds."

Tarron clenched his jaw and returned to his sandwich. Not wanting to seem rude, he offered a comment that reflected some level of regard for his new friend's five-minute philosophy lesson.

"I appreciate the advice, Darian."

They finished their food in comfortable silence. Darian raised his hand and flagged down the waitress, then fished something out of his jacket pocket and laid them on the table. Tarron made them out to be two tea packets.

"Can we get two cups of hot water with lemons and honey on the side? Then the check whenever you get a chance, please?" He smiled, then pulled out several bills from his wallet and handed them to the lady. "Also, this is for you." Darian tipped the woman $20.

"That was very generous of you," Tarron remarked.

"She looks like a hardworking lady. Besides, I bet she just wants to go home."

Tarron looked down at the two tea packets. The aroma coming from them was faint but strong enough to reach his nostrils. Not any herbs he was familiar with.

A nudge towards being comfortable with being uncomfortable. He hadn't thought of taking hallucinogenic drugs to be as easy as a sip of tea.

"Is that it?" he asked.

"How do you take your tea, Tarron? Honey and sugar? Lemon?"

Tarron ignored the question, "So is that a yes? I didn't know you could take shrooms like this."

Darian simply grinned. Tarron resounded to keep his mouth shut for the time being. The waitress returned carrying two mugs with resounding steam coming from the top. Tarron felt his heart quicken in tempo. He'd bet money that Darian had some axiom or wise words to summarize that feeling. Tarron felt himself fidgeting with his hands briefly and stuck them in his pockets.

He felt his cell phone start to buzz. Several texts from his boss.

Oh, what fresh hell? He thought to himself.

Evidently, he had assaulted a man this evening at the bar. A very wealthy man that was so verily furious with his treatment at the bar in this "shit-stained-town' that he placed several calls until he got a hold of the young man who owned Ozzie's.

His employer was not pleased in the slightest. Tarron read the texts with cold apathy. He had nothing to say. Even words of cynicism and frustration escaped him. He returned the cell phone to his pocket as the waitress returned to the table holding the ticket for their meal. Tarron reached to grab it first and pulled out his wallet.

"My treat. In exchange for the philosophy lecture." He declared.

"That's very generous of you. But you never answered me. You take your tea plain or—?"

"Surprise me, bud." Tarron replied, handing the waitress the check along with his debit card "Hey, if this doesn't work the first swipe, just wipe it off. Old card, ya know," He added before she walked away. He watched Darian prepare the tea with practice and skilled movements. Placing a slice of lemon followed by one of the tea bags in the mug. He then proceeded to tear open four packs of honey and squirt the contents in as well. He stirred the cup slowly, then returned it to the small saucer and slid it across the table to Tarron. He repeated the same process for his own mug and held it out to toast.

"Bil-'áfya, T" he brought the mug to his mouth and drank. Tarron felt the beating in his chest slow its pace. He brought his own mug up to drink and slowly let the tea roll over his tongue in the same fashion he had been taught to enjoy whiskey rather than simply drink it. The honey and lemon had each worked to mask the subtle bitter taste of the liquid. It was still bitter but not unpleasant. He took another drink slowly so as to not scald his mouth.

"What was that you said for a toast?" Tarron audibly wondered as he placed the mug back in its saucer.

"Bil-'áfya, to health, basically. It's something our interpreter would say before meals in Iraq. He was Kuwaiti, I think. Nice guy, had a lot of stories of growing up under Saddam Hussein. His father had fought against the invasion of Kuwait in the 90s, and he always would say how poetic it was that he inherited a war to fight in."

"That's sad. There's so much fighting there. We've been at war in the Middle East since I was in elementary school, I think. Forever wars, I heard them called. I don't know how those people live through it all."

"Well, sometimes they don't," Darian spoke, barely audible.

Tarron took another drink of tea. And another. Letting the liquid again roll over his tongue. Its flavor was beginning to grow on him, although he didn't yet feel any earth-shattering effects. He relaxed and took in the aroma. And as he continued to drink—Tarron Faust's mind detached from the mortal coil and checked itself out to roam freely amongst the stars. He placed the cup back on the saucer.

In his head, he pictured Alice in Wonderland. *Drink me!*

At some point, a voice called out to him. Anchoring his unbound floating consciousness back to his body. He fluttered his eyes open. The words were escaping Darian's lips though the sound of them reached his ears at their own pace. The meaning of the words made its journey to Tarron's brain. His frontal lobe was no longer in control.

"…a book I read about Arithmophobia." The sound echoed from Darian's mouth.

Tarron felt every sensation of touch from every square inch of his skin. He could feel the polyester thread of his shirt touch his skin. His leg hair brushed against his blue jeans.

He was supposed to reply to Darian now. The last word he had said was repeated a dozen times over as an echo. It did not make any sense to Tarron.

What was the word?

Arithmo—phobia? The fear of what? What am I afraid of?

"What's that?" He felt himself mumble. His memory shot back to the first instance he met Darian. Those were the first words he uttered to him. Words of confusion. Accurately describing his quiet uncertainty in every situation he found himself in with Darian.

Anxiety started to crawl up. As if something terrible was imminent. But this was his friend. This was Jack's brother. There's no reason to be tentative around him. Darian's voice continued to resonate around Tarron's head.

"The fear of numbers. Arithmophobia. It's a funny concept. There are numbers everywhere, ya know? Nature is full of its own arithmetic. That's where that word comes from too. The

Greek word arithmētikē. The art of counting—I think that's kinda poetic to call it art."

How does he know so much about nothing? Tarron felt himself say inside his head. He realized he was not speaking.

"How do you know so much?" He spoke aloud.

"I get curious. I look things up." Darian shrugged. "How are you feeling?"

Feelingfeelingfeelingfeeling

How am I feeling?

Tarron tuned his ears to the swell of the music playing. A beautiful symphony of depressingly beautiful notes from a wailing guitar. He felt as though he understood why George Harrison wrote While My Guitar Gently Weeps. The instrument itself was a medium for pain. Tarron told himself that wasn't the song currently playing. His brain process, though, was: thought.

Mouth.

"Is this the Beatles?" He asked Darian.

"Don't be pretentious—" Darian said with a hint of disgust "this, sir, is Funkadelic's, Maggot Brain."

Maggots? Tarron thought.

"It's so—it's so sad, man. Haunting, but the best thing I've ever heard."

"When they were in the studio, the lead singer told the guitarist, Eddie Hazel, 'play it like your mom just died, picture the day, how you feel, and everything inside you.' Then he played the greatest damn guitar solo known to man."

Tarron shut his eyes and rubbed them hard with the flat edge of his hands. When he opened, a brilliant shift of color met him. He realized they had been sitting in Darian's jeep.

I hope Darian got my credit card.

Darian had indeed taken his friend's credit card back from the waitress and taken the liberty to sit his friend in the passenger seat of his jeep. He had a fair amount of experience in trip-sitting. That was the proper term for it; to lead or prevent a friend from a bad trip. Only Darian did not believe in a bad trip. He believed that people were already influenced heavily by what lay heavy on their conscience. They may realize this from time to time by way of dreams at night.

What some people see when tripping is dependent on their emotional ties to personal trauma. All of your best and worst emotional baggage out on display top you. In that sense, it was conscious dreaming. A retreat to the recess of your mind to fight what demons you may have—if you have them. Darian had gone strides to befriend them. Nietzsche had said that the danger in killing your demons was that you sometimes kill off the best parts of yourself.

Work on the ego for the ego to work for you. Only thereafter can you achieve anything. Or something along those lines.

Far-out man.

Most of these insightful tidbits had been taught to Darian (or similarly rambled on about, more accurately) by a Navy SEAL in his thirties Darian had befriended while in Iraq, Chief Malcolm "Mac" Bradley. This was the man who guided Darian's path in the wonders of psychedelics as a means of coping with the trauma of war.

War forces men and women to kill each other, and the toll which follows is a demand for why. That toll drove Darian to a dark, dark place. When he met Chief Bradley, he found a little light. Mac Bradley went on to be dishonorably discharged several years later after making the news too many times. But not before teaching Darian how to tend the earth and reconvene personal meaning. He was not his job.

There was an informal debate within the Air Force between Darian's former job as an aerial door gunner and those who piloted unmanned-drone for the ease at which an operator took the life of a target. That's all they were: targets. A simple way to dehumanize the life you're about to take. Weapons that are discharged at the press of buttons. The loss of human life was just an impact on a screen and a verbal report acknowledged by your fellow airman.

Goodbye to the dearly departed. Fire for effect.

Darian was explaining all this to Tarron, who lay motionless in the passenger seat of the Jeep, save for the darting of his eyes bath and forth. Tarron was listening but not that intently. What had caught his full attention was the dazzling overture by the constellations above. The last few weeks had been so filled with storm clouds, but the stars had finally come out tonight to dance. A calculated waltz like the characters in Tolstoy's War and Peace, a play Celeste had dragged him to years ago, carried out with graceful steps. He felt a newfound appreciation for the play. Although the light emitted from the Jeep's headlights was drowning out the shine.

"Can ya turn your lights off?" He mumbled to Darian.

"Can't do that, chief, gotta drive."

"But the stars." Tarron insisted

"Are they talking to you?" Darian asked, to which Tarron nodded his head slowly in earnest.

"Then pull over and turn the lights off. I shall." He concluded. Glenrock was still only a faint glow on the horizon. Darian had decided to take the scenic route back. When he pulled to the side of the road and shut off the lights, the stars glimmered in agreement. The waxing crescent moon did not dare outshine its celestial brethren. Tarron thanked it for its contribution.

Darian undid the cover to his jeep so his companion could view the stars above more easily. He made sure the heaters were on since Tarron probably wasn't aware of the cold bite of December, which crept into the idling jeep. As he finished unfurling the cover to the jeep, he heard Tarron grumble, "goodnight, moon." He chuckled to himself and pulled a blanket from the back seat to cover Tarron.

The single measured gram of mushrooms in his own system did little in terms of psychedelic visuals. Darian had been micro-dosing the drug daily for around a year now. He was still in awe of how smaller doses compared to the high dosages he had been introduced to the drug on. A high dosage Tarron was currently riding out on. Chief Bradley's mantra on the dosage was a simple axiom he remembered fondly: *a little to kill your daily demons, but a lot to kill your Self.*

He always liked to hear people's take on one's self and one's ego and how they tied back to one's physical being. He made sure to record the most interesting responses in a notebook. Most came from some of the younger terminal cancer patients he came across at the hospital. The kids usually had a wicked sense of humor.

"Who else would dare stare death in the face and laugh with such reckless abandon?" Darian declared to himself. The piece of prose pulled Tarron from the astral performance he was watching above.

"That's beautiful, man. Is that poetry?" Tarron asked. He had his hands gripped on the tops of the blanket, similar to a child. Darian hadn't even noticed that his friend had extended the car seat fully.

"Nah, just something I've been thinkin' about. How're you

feeling, T?"

"The stars are dancing. It's wonderful. It's a waltz, I think."

"Are they telling you anything?"

Anythinganythinganything

They're telling me everything. Tarron thought. He reached down and felt for his cell phone in his pocket. Retrieving it, he scrolled through his contact list for what felt like an obscene amount of time, searching for the correct name. The pixels on screen were barely cooperating in Tarron's eyes. To Darian, his companion appeared to be staring at the phone quite intensely without interacting with it.

An idea of genius-level magnitude popped into Tarron's head on how to sort out the mess he was looking at.

"Siri, call my boss."

"Woah, is that what you're sure you want right now, man?" Darian contested and reached over to take the phone. Tarron pulled the hand, holding the device away slightly as the phone's voice command software obeyed the words spoken to it and began to dial. He lowered his eyelids and nodded. Darian relaxed and then gave an 'okay, I give up' gesture.

"Hey, yeah, it's me. Yeah, no, I don't know what time it is. No, shut up and listen. I quit." He ended the call decidedly and pulled the blanket back over his torso. "Can ya take me back Darian? Gotta see my daughter in the morning. I'm unemployed now."

"So, I've heard, man. Good for you. What's the plan now?"

Tarron didn't respond. Darian repeated the question and then leaned over, slightly concerned. He could hear the man lightly snoring. He chuckled to himself and then fished around for his wallet to return the man's debit card before he forgot.

As he started to return the wallet to Tarron's pocket, a

Polaroid photo fell out from it onto the console. Darian picked up the photo inquisitively and held it up. It depicted a smiling Tarron holding a newborn swaddled tightly with her mother holding the camera out to capture the three of them. He carefully placed the photo back into the wallet and returned it to Tarron's pocket, then re-covered the jeep.

"I'll get ya back, friend. Doncha worry."

The last notes of Maggot Brain droned out as the song faded to resounding silence. Darian let the dead air hang for a moment before changing the radio station.

7

Dreams and Theater

HE WAS back at the diner. The same booth and same meal. He could smell the patty melt on the plate below him. As he reached down to bring the sandwich to his open mouth, he noticed his company. She did not appear to pay him any mind. She was a beautiful young woman with jet black curls cut short. Her face was hidden by a makeup mirror that looked familiar to Tarron.

"Cellie?" He stammered.

The makeup mirror shut. Green eyes looked through him with a deadpan stare. Green eyes she got from her grandfather.

Alina?

"Chicken, you're all grown up," he added. Alina glared at him and ignored the comment, continuing down another tangent.

"So, I'm leaving for Tempe tomorrow," she said with disdain "was there anything you wanted to do?"

"Tempe? For what?"

"For college?"

Tarron continued to stare back blankly at her.

"This is how you're gonna be? You've been horrible since

mom left!" She cried, rising from the booth. "You can—you can fuck off!" She added and stormed away. Tarron rose to follow her. He followed her to a corridor of the diner leading to the restroom. He stopped himself as she entered the lady's bathroom. Taking a look at the closed door, he sighed to himself. Dramatic escape may have been an inherited trait.

Maybe I should give her some space.

The world began to fall away. Tile rose from the floor, and sheetrock burst from the walls. The hallway fell beneath him and began spinning around in a kaleidoscope fashion. Screaming, Tarron turned around and retreated to the door in front of him.

He tore open the handle to the women's restroom to reveal a dimly lit hallway. Linoleum floors and gray dotted curtains hung from the ceiling to conceal hospital beds. Wisps of human shapes wandered aimlessly from bed to bed. Alina appeared behind one of the curtains, and Tarron broke into a sprint to meet her. She saw him then turned to run as well, ripping curtains down behind her.

"Alina!" Tarron cried out.

He gained on her. As he ran, he burst through the wisps and heard buzzing when they dissipated. He continued to run, but his daughter was faster. He nearly tripped over the curtains she had pulled free and then stumbled down completely, crashing into a bed. He rolled over to his side and grabbed the side of the hospital bed to lift himself up.

Cold fingers from a bony hand gripped his wrist. Ripping his hand free, Tarron stumbled backward and rose to his feet. He could not see the face of the figure that had grabbed him. He looked upon the decrepit figure. To his horror, his own face stared back at him. The color was drained from the face, but it still bared his resemblance. He felt his heart pound out of his chest. His knife wound pulsated with every beat. Blood quickly spread from it and dampened his shirt. The same bloody wound appeared on the figure in the bed. He reached to stop the blood flowing from the wound when his own voice called out to him.

"You cannot save them and yourself. But you cannot afford to lose them all." the voice boomed. He heard it emanate from his doppelganger's mouth, and he felt the words echoing in his head, splitting his eardrums and bloodying them.

"Why am I here?" He felt himself say.

"You determine our path," it answered.

"Our? Who are you?" Tarron demanded. The face in the hospital bed twisted. Lips curling back, revealing rotten teeth and blackened gums. It howled with laughter.

"I am you." It screeched. The face continued to twist. Lines of skin wrinkled around the face and molded its features. "I am your failures." It said, wearing the face of his father. It morphed again to the face of Celeste, "I am your love" the face darkened as dark red blood spooled along the crown of Celeste's head and screamed again, "I am your hate!"

Tarron grabbed his own head tight to cover his ears and collapsed to the ground. He shut his eyes and could still hear the echoes of the booming voice.

It reverberated louder until reaching a deafening level.

Silence.

When he opened his eyes, he was standing in the middle of a river. A much younger Alina was at his side. The sun was out, and snow fell from a gray sky. He reached down to his stomach and felt for his scar. Still there. He reached for his daughter's hand, and she took it warmly. She held out her other hand to capture the snow as it fell. Tarron felt a sense of calm wash over him. He raised his head to the sky to open his mouth and stick out his tongue.

***

Darian looked over at Tarron. He appeared to be sticking his tongue out. His eyes were still closed, however. They had been parked for a couple of minutes, and Darian had held off from waking him. He shrugged; it was about that time.

"Hey, what happened, buddy? Any good dreams?" Darian asked inquisitively.

"Wha—?"

"Dude? Duuuude?"

"Oh, Woah. Hello. God, no. Thank you but also fuck you." He said all at once with mild, panicked sarcasm.

Darian shrugged. "Hey now, like I said before we started—if there's something on your mind, then the shrooms will show you. What's left is for you to decide how to take it."

"I think…I think I learned something. It was horrible and exhilarating at the same time. I do think I'm still high, though. Do you think you could stay with me for a while? I'm particularly terrified of falling out of my body again and maybe out of bed too."

"Yeah, no, you are definitely still high, man. My shift doesn't start at the hospital for another 3 hours. I was just gonna head back home and read."

Tarron checked his watch. "Christ, you go in at 4 in the morning?"

"It's not too bad—I used to work the graveyard shift before. But that was when I was a lab tech instead of in my clinicals."

"That still sounds terrible."

"Don't you routinely close the bar at like 2?"

"Yeah, and then I sleep for 12 hours. Why?"

"Nothing. You good to drive home?"

"Definitely not. I am terrified I may fall out of my body on the way home."

"I can follow you if that'd make you comfortable?"

"That's very kind of you, Darian."

Tarron agreed that he was still high as he got behind the wheel of his Hilux. He had a small amount of fear of admitting to Darian that he wasn't completely okay to drive home. It was something that made him feel a tad incompetent. They drove home at the blistering speed of 20 miles per hour. He was grateful for it. The wind had started to pick up nastily, driving a freezing breeze like a knife through the air.

The ten-minute drive took about twenty, but Darian didn't mind.

Upon arriving and parking, Darian was surprised when his friend came up to his window rather than go inside his home. "You still hungry?" Tarron asked.

"Yeah, kinda. How'd you know?"

"I don't really know anything right now, but I'm sorta afraid to go to sleep until I'm sober."

"Aw, dude. You don't have to worry."

"Can you make sure I don't die?"

"Love to."

The two walked inside the house. Darian made his way to the bar at the kitchenette and sat down. Tarron seemed to move in slow motion, taking his time locking the door behind him, walking towards the fridge, and staring intensely into it before withdrawing a Tupperware container full of food and placing it in the microwave. He also took out a gallon jug of milk and poured a glass. Darian sat down and studied the chess set Tarron had out on display.

"Thank you, kindly." Darian smiled as Tarron placed the glass down in front of him. "You play?" He added.

"I recall how the game of chess works. Yes."

"Would you like to play?"

Tarron returned the milk carton to the fridge, withdrew a Coor's banquet, and took a seat on the barstool across from Darian.

"You can play white. On your move." Tarron said, cracking open the beer. He clicked the red button of the chess timer with the bottom of the can and then took a long sip.

Darian smirked and moved his pawn to D4. Hitting the timer, back to Tarron.

"So, how was your first trip, man?" Darian said.

"Not sure yet. Ask me when it's done. Still kinda waiting to crash and burn terribly." Tarron responded. Knight to F6, timer click, back to Darian.

"Well… fuck. I'd hate for your first to be your worst." He responded. Wasting no time, bishop to G5. Back to Tarron. The timer continued to tick monotonously. Darian took a swig of milk.

"I had a dream I was with my daughter. Only she was grown up. And she wasn't happy with me." Pawn to C6, Tarron barely knew what he was doing. Only making sure he moved his pieces in accordance with the rules of chess.

"Oh shit, did she say anything to you or like do anything?" Darian asked, curiosity rising. His hand hovered over his pieces. Although he didn't mind losing, he was trying to gauge whatever the hell Tarron's strategy was. He had played a multitude of games while deployed. It was one among other things he learned to pass the time.

"She just wasn't happy. It makes me feel like I have to patch that relationship up before it goes sour. Like, right now, the little girl loves me. But her mom… eh" He trailed off, still waiting on Darian's move.

"Hey now, it's alright. It's your first trip. You just gotta get comfortable with your mental state."

"I think I'm coming down now. Is that what you'd call it?"

"Yeah, exactly. Psychedelics are like… an elevator. The trip to the top—you take it and peak, right? Most people see what the shrooms are trying to show them. That can be influenced a ton by what you're thinking of at the time. Either consciously or subconsciously. Like some people think you can conjure up your own visuals if you focus hard enough—the thing is, it's hard as hell to focus when you're tripping. And that's not the point. You have to release." He finished, finally deciding on a move: pawn to E3. Immediately after he released his touch on the piece, he began to pray that Tarron didn't catch his mistake. He cursed under his breath. So much for chess strategy.

Tarron rubbed his temple again and covered his eyes. He whimpered, "I think I'm a terrible father."

"Aw, man, don't say that. Are you and the mom…" He waved his hand around, searching for the right phrase "…not on the best of terms?"

"Complicated" may have begun to describe the terms he figured he and Celeste were on. Who else lives alone and only got weekends with their daughter?

Tarron thought back to the breakup. It went a little like this:

He had just been hired at Ozzie's, despite Celeste's protests that being a bartender was not a sustainable job to raise a child on. He then made allusions that having a dual-income home would make things easier with money. She fired back that if she wasn't knocked up, she would be working the job she wanted. Plates were thrown, and round and round they went. Building off much of the unresolved arguments never given closure. One fight to end them all.

"We're separated. I was gonna marry her, though, at one point." Tarron finally said. He had briefly forgotten the chess game that lay before them. He lazily moved his queen to A5 and hit the timer, Darian's move.

"I was married once," Darian stated, taking a sip of his milk.

"Was? What happened? If you don't mind my asking."

"It's okay. I mean… it's not, but I just lie and tell people it is. Anyways, she just passed away while I was overseas. Car accident. Best damn two years of my life, though."

Tarron stood up, walked towards Darian, and wrapped his arms around him in a bear hug. Darian, surprised, smiled and embraced him back. He then reached around and turned off the chess timer. The continuous ticking was driving him insane.

"Ho-lee-shit, man." Tarron said as he returned to his chair, "You've been through hell and back, and you're only just starting your 20s. Here I am talking about me fucking up my relationship."

"I—I…made my peace within the last year. When she first passed, though, there used to be a lot of bad days, and I'd just try to focus on work. Throwing myself into maintenance or working out. My commander had initially given me emergency leave for a month to like… go home for the funeral and everything. But I didn't know how to live normally with things back home. So, I requested a flight back to my unit in Iraq the next week.

"Sometimes work was too much, and I'd want to sit and

unpack what just happened after we'd get back from missions. But then I'd wanna unpack losing Scarlet. It all just started to mesh together when we finished the deployment. Even more when I got out, but… eventually, it got easier. There started to be fewer bad days and more just 'OK' days. Lots of shrooms and other drugs in the process of that, though, don't get me wrong." He added. He had gotten caught up in remembrance and conversation. Looking at the board, he realized Tarron had checkmated him.

The microwave dinged loudly behind him, and Tarron whirled his head around.

"Food's ready!" He announced. He rose from the table and left Darian to wonder how he had lost a chess match so quickly against a guy high on a heroic dose of psilocybin. Tarron brought him the Tupperware container and a fork. Darian tore into the food eagerly.

"I had a bad stint after my father died, which led to Celeste walking out on me with Alina, our daughter. But your brother was the one to get me out of that hole, actually." Tarron said.

"I think he told me about that. He said he was visiting home, trying to make peace with our dad, but he came across you and decided you were more important. I don't blame him—our dad was a piece of shit."

"Amen, brother. Jack stayed at our house a lot while growing up. Here's to Jack" Tarron raised his beer. Darian's glass clinked against the can deftly.

"You had said he didn't want to be buried. Was that, like, a big thing to him?" Darian asked.

Flashes of Tarron's coma-induced nightmare appeared before him. The tormented and faceless Jack who had screamed at him.

"He saw a PBS special once about the process of embalming." Tarron began to recall "When he told me about it, we went to my mom about it. You see, she had worked as a coroner for a while before marrying my dad and having me. Her answer grossed us out just that the body stays like that for so long and doesn't decompose normally.

"And so, this one time at this party when we were both obliterated, this girl that our roommate was dating started this game. She called it the 'best worst-case scenario.' Basically, it went like this: what is the worst realistic way for you to die, and what would be the best? Before anyone even answered, Jack looked at me and went, *'Tarron...'* and he grabbed my face with both hands to show me he was serious, *'Tarron, buddy, I need you to make sure I get cremated. You gotta. If I die first, you have to'.* And I promised him then I would."

"Can't deny a drunk man's promise. Of course." Darian said. "What was your best, worst-case?" He asked.

"Hmm. My worst was dying alone from alcohol poisoning. And my best was...." Tarron zoned out, staring at the chessboard, searching deep in his memory bank. "...was dying on a ski trip with my future grandchildren after they dared me to hit the halfpipe. I would do the sickest 540 iron cross to octo grab you've ever seen in your life. Then I would plummet back down to earth and die instantly. Dying is tragic no matter which way you spin it. Might as well have my grandkids would remember me as a legend."

"Wouldn't they be extremely traumatized?"

"I mean... I wasn't." He said flatly before realizing there was an additional needed explanation. "I uh... watched my dad have a heart attack on the slopes. He passed away later in the hospital. So, as aforementioned, I drank myself close to death.

Someone told me at the funeral *'at least he died doing what he loved. And next to someone who loved him'.* Go-fuckin figure."

Darian was silent for some time. An inquisitive look took hold of his face as he began rapping his fingers along the side of his glass. The chessboard lay still between them. Tarron thought he heard his friend mutter to himself, but he wasn't altogether sure—he was still trying to decide if the chess pieces were vibrating on their own or if he imagined it.

"Is that a landline?" Darian pointed out, suddenly, "I didn't even think people still had those." Pointing at the phone hanging up on the wall behind Tarron.

"Ha. Ha. Most people here do. Cell service isn't the greatest during storms. Mine's been unplugged for a bit after Jack passed and then after I got back from the hospital… too full of messages from people I don't care for," Tarron continued to ramble.

The tapping on the glass ceased, and a smile crept across Darian's face as he extended his arm to grasp Tarron's shoulder. Tarron, surprised, closed his mouth and looked at him suddenly.

"Yea, man…?" he probed.

"Wanna get his body?" Darian asked innocently.

"What?"

"Jack's body. I think I can help you can keep that promise."

"How? Isn't that—like, illegal? Exhuming a body? Or, I guess you're related to him, so? What do you mean, dude?" Tarron rambled.

"Tomorrow or later tonight, I suppose. Let's meet up. Wear some clothes; you can get dirty." Darian stated as he rose from the barstool and headed towards the door.

"Wait! What about the game Darian? It's still your move!"

Tarron called to him.

"Look at the board, shithead!" Darian called back. He opened up the door to Tarron's small home and disappeared into the wind like an apparition.

Tarron looked down; he had surprised himself, check and mate.

***

There was a myriad of ways in which Darian initially had envisioned murdering his father. The plan had gone through quite a metamorphosis over the years. Plan, though, was putting it empirically. Enough time in the medical field had revealed to him the method—but the timing and ambition had still been left subject for an internal discussion. Though it was originally pure hate that had been his driving force, he now only felt loathsome contempt. He figured that had changed around the time he got out of the Air Force. He had been part of a crew that had taken dozens of lives over dozens of fire support missions, and the idea of killing one more who really deserved it had not seemed to be a question of 'should.' It was something that needed to be done before he could lay his estranged brother to final rest, too.

But this was a far more intimate act of taking life. Growing up with his mother in Lake Tahoe, he had only heard mentions of his father. Mostly from other relatives and always with disdain. It wasn't until he graduated high school that his mother sat him down and told him the real reason they had left his father and Jack behind. She told the story with such horrid sincerity that he did not doubt a single word. She was the woman who had lovingly raised him, after all. When he reconnected with Jack, however, two sides of the story came together, and the estranged brothers shared a bond over a traumatic event childhood innocence made sure they forgot.

He had landed on the method. A simple, non-violent act with enough poetic ambiance to whet his childhood fury and give him an ample amount of plausible deniability in the case an autopsy pointed fingers toward foul play. Sometimes he figured why more of those in the medical field weren't murderers. He had met enough narcissist doctors with maniacal egos to fit the bill of a serial killer. But the oath was to *do no harm.* An oath of which he had not officially sworn himself to. After getting his discharge from the Air Force, he had more than his fill of doing harm, but the old bastard needed to be put down—mercifully.

Darian sat in his Jeep a few blocks down from his father's house. The light from a lone street lamp shone over his car among the overcast darkness of night. No moon was out, and the stars were hidden. He opened a small gray shaving kit bag that he had brought his supplies in to check the syringe and Phenylpropanolamine (PPA). A compound usually found in decongestants and medications advertised as a new amazing weight loss component by way of appetite suppressant. It got banned by the FDA some years back due to its tendency to cause strokes. Though use on humans was found to be dangerous, it still had uses to help treat elderly dogs who had trouble pissing.

The small amount Don gave him earlier that day was concentrated enough to act directly on those tenancies under ideal circumstances. Darian bemoaned, lying to the man about needing the PPA for his mother's fictional Great Dane with a problem of urinary incontinence, but they didn't carry the drug in regular hospitals anymore. If it was all the same to Doctor Ulrich, Darian settled to make it up to the old man somehow—given that he lasted as long.

His nerves were kicking in. A jitter he hadn't felt since the anxious jolts that would ride his conscious mind on fire missions. It wouldn't be until the AC-130 was high in the sky that he would start to settle down. He knew nearly every one of his fellow crew members leaned heavily on downers or muscle relaxers every time they went out. Everyone sans the pilots, but he figured they had their own secret methods of coping.

He looked over all the things he had brought inside the shaving kit bag. Two syringes (one for backup), the lone vial of PPA, nitrile sanitary gloves, and a shot of epinephrine just in case he fucked up the initial dosage. He zipped the bag shut, then grabbed hold of the real-enough-looking airsoft gun that was supposed to model a Glock 19. He had removed the orange-red tip from the toy gun easily with acetone and ample patience. To the untrained eye, it looked about as real as one would gamble their life for. The darkness and the inebriated state of his father would work to make his eyes all the more untrained. He tucked the toy gun into his waistband, then opened the door of the jeep to step out, pulling a bandanna over his face as he went and briefly wondered how bank robbers managed to function in these. A lone bark from a distant dog echoed in the darkness.

***

Tarron hadn't remembered dozing off during his marathon of internet videos. The lull of his phone came to an end when the battery died, and his room became quiet. He sniffled loudly and sat up in his bed. His coat and jeans were still on. He strode to his desk chair to shed the coat and sat down in it. The envelope containing Jack's swan song letter and parting gift of tickets to Iceland seemed to lay there innocuously, unaware of the emotional weight it carried printed on paper. He withdrew the letter and read it again. He read it and re-read it. He poured over every line searching for some double-depth meaning behind the words. Something that suggested it was an elaborate ruse to lure Tarron out to Iceland, where Jack was alive and waiting. He could picture him waving him down and smiling, beer in hand, inviting him to sit and stay awhile now that he had made the journey. Magnus, Johann, and even Darian are all in on it to get Tarron out there. To leave the hole, he dug himself in.

If his unfinished time as an undergrad at ASU had taught him anything, it was that the harder you search for the intrinsic meaning behind things, the foggier it becomes. Especially in the austere case of your best friend's suicide letter. What came with adulthood was accepting the fact that miracles are only in the movies and in the bible, dreams change and never come true, and politicians always lie.

It could be possible; Jack always had the darkest sense of humor. And he never shied away from suicide jokes, He thought with a grimace.

But in this case, it *wasn't* a joke? What then? Good God, Tarron was firmly entrapped back in denial. Miss Grief had made her rearing head once more at the remnants of his mushroom escapade.

He thought about Darian's suggestion. It wasn't insane at face value. Only semi-retarded in the planning. Dig up a grave? That sounded like an unnecessary risk. Couldn't they file for exhumation or something? Everything was so bloody frustrating.

"I will lay you to the rest you deserve, buddy. If it kills me."

He said aloud to the empty room.

***

Darian had to force himself to walk soundly to his childhood home. The anxiety turned to excitement as he got nearer and nearer. The porch light illuminated the front door of the one-story house. He made his way to the south end of the building and walked along the fence until he reached a large potted fern he remembered from his colorfully painful childhood, many occasions of hiding behind it. Said fern was also his father's choice hiding spot for a spare key. Something he and Jack had learned when they successfully hid from the man and had to let themselves back in after he gave up looking.

The flaw in his perfect plan began to unravel to Darian when the realization set in that the key was not in its familiar spot. He had placed too much stock in his father, keeping the key in the same spot after all these years. He felt around aimlessly and dug handfuls of dirt, searching for the key unsuccessfully.

Stupid.

Fuck it. Stick to the plan

He quickly looked around and pulled a loose brick from the porch floor. He weighed the brick in his hands and loaded up his arm, ready to throw. When a light flicked on behind the curtains of the window, he was ready to shatter. He dropped to the ground quickly and crawled backward until his head was just underneath the windowsill. Nervously he pulled out the air pistol and gripped it tightly. He first heard the familiar drawl of his father's voice accompanied by a female one, much younger and more excited. He felt himself shake with the thought of his disgusting, wife-beating, deadbeat father bedding a desperate young girl who was probably clueless to the type of disgusting she chose to go home with this night.

There was not much time left in the early morning to come back. He knew if he didn't have the nerve to pull off his ambition now that he would never return. He crouched and made his way back to the fence and silently walked back to his jeep. He would wait.

8

Dawn Therapy

THE YOUNG lady of the night Darian's father had the company of failed to light her cigarette three times. Darian's patience was being tested when, on the fourth attempt, it took light. She took a drag and exhaled, the smoke rising slowly into the air. She began to walk toward Darian's Jeep. He tightened his jaw as his pulse sped up, then gripped the fake pistol sitting in the console of the car. The young woman reached into her purse suddenly, and Darian instinctively jolted to bring the air pistol up in a false hope of protection. The woman retracted her hand from the purse with a set of keys in hand and clicked the lock button. Darian heard the beep of a sedan parked across the street from his truck and immediately sunk down in his seat, praying he wasn't seen.

The boys on the team probably would've given me a mountain of shit for that. Times o' ah, they are a-changin.'

Darian's last iota of his patience strained like a substitute teacher waiting for the class as the young woman fumbled with her keys getting into her vehicle. The vehicle started with a groan, and she swerved onto the sidewalk as she drove off.

He halfheartedly wondered if she had any intuitive knowledge. She just finished fucking a dead man.

Always leave them wanting more? Was that the phrase?

Darian asked himself as he exited the jeep. A fake gun in his waistband and in his left hand a bag full of very real needles, filled with a drug that helped dogs piss or an old bastard has a stroke.

He moved silently back along the fence and once more to the front door, which had been left unlocked from the young lady's exit. Darian gripped the doorknob and eased it clockwise to open. The door opened with a betraying creak in its hinges. Darian quickly pulled it open and hurried inside. The living room was dark, with the only light bleeding in from the adjacent bedroom. On the opposite side of the room, the sliding glass door leading to the back patio was cracked open. Darian crossed the room slowly, his feet muffled by the carpet. He could sparsely make out a shadowed figure occupying the lawn chair to the right of the glass door. Darian watched the figure's hands reach for a pack of cigarettes on the side table and light one up. The glowing end illuminated James Finnegan wrinkled face. Darian placed his hand on the handle of the glass door and eased it open.

The motion sensor porch lights kicked on at the opening of the door. James rose quickly from his lawn chair, cigarette hanging from the corner of his mouth and a bottle of Jack Daniels in his left hand.

"Hey, pops." Darian sighed, pulling the bandanna down from his face and holding up the air gun. "What're we drinking?

The question caught James off guard, and he sat back down in his chair. Seemingly ignorant to the gun currently pointed at his face.

Fuck, I can't tell if the old bastard knows it's a fake, or he's already too drunk enough to call my bluff.

James remained silent and held the bottle up to take a long swig. Sighing loudly, he pulled it away from his lips and brought it down with force, drops spilling as it hit the ground.

"Yeah. I figured you'd come around one of these days. Lose one of my boys to be reunited with the other who I didn't care for." James began, pausing to take a drag and exhaling the smoke with a heavy cough.

The words Darian had formed over the last decade of all the things he had wanted to say or shout at his father fled. Every ounce of anger and resentment was forgotten or only in hiding. Here was the man who ruined his marriage and tormented Darian's mother to the point of a psychotic break. Enough to move across the country, taking with her the son who was too young to be influenced by anyone other than the women who birthed him. His grip tightened around the grip of the pistol.

"You know how to use that thing?" James remarked, pointing with the end of his cigarette before tapping the ash off it.

The comment broke the mental block silencing Darian. It was said with such disdain and mockery to pull him back to his entire reason for coming back to the roots of his childhood.

"Not really. They only taught me to shoot in Bootcamp."

"Bootcamp?" James cackled at the notion.

"That was a few years ago when I joined the Air Force. You'd know that if you decided to be in our life instead of beating my mother." Darian said, the tone in his voice shifting. James' smile disappeared.

"Instead of beating her so badly, she ended up in the hospital," Darian continued, "the doctors told her she had bruised ribs, but that wasn't as important as what else she lost. You'd've remembered, too, if you didn't drink so Goddamn much what you took from her, what you took from Jack and me. You didn't care for *any* of us. At this point, I'm not even sure how you get women to sleep with you with how vile of a man you are. Drink up, pops. It's gonna be a long night for you."

Darian noticed redness in James' eyes as the man remained silent. Clenching his jaw before taking another drag from his cigarette. He opened his mouth, and Darian immediately cut him off, rushing toward his father. Shoving the pistol in front of his face and gripping the man's shoulder.

"I said drink, fucker!" Darian hissed.

James fumbled his free arm around, reaching for the bottle of whiskey. Finding it, he brought the bottle up.

"Slowly," Darian added, backing away while still holding the pistol up. James brought the bottle to his mouth and drank.

Was he starting to cry? Darian thought, *He knows this is a joke, right?*

"Son…" James began.

"NO! You do not have the luxury to call me that. You stopped being a father the moment you decided to lay hands on my mother. You—"

"D—Darian…" James stammered, "What's in the bag?" his eyes darting to the grey shaving bag Darian set on the ground.

"PPA. Phenylpropanolamine. Just a drug that is used to help with appetite suppression. Now it's only used on doggies. They found out too much of it causes strokes in human patients" He paused, seeing the realization widen his father's eyes. "Especially human patients with a history of alcoholism. That's what I learned in nursing school, at least."

"I—I didn't know."

"Didn't know what?!" Darian erupted. "That I'm even in

nursing school? That you're a piece of shit, father? That your oldest son died knowing he'd never be able to make peace with you? And that's why I'm here, actually."

"To make peace—?" James asked, bewildered.

"No fucker. To put you down."

"I didn't know she was *pregnant*," James whispered, barely audible, hanging his head down.

"What was that?" Darian asked, rising to his feet once more.

"I didn't know she was pregnant!" James repeated loudly. His reddened eyes began to swell with tears, and he buried his face in his hands. "I'm sorry, Darian. I'm sorry. I'm so sorry—please just, don't kill me." He sobbed, rambling on, "I know I was hard on you and Jack, but it was to make you strong. I woulda never laid a hand on your mother if I'd've known. For chrissakes, I'm no murderer. No baby killer. Jesus, fuck. How—how did I ever…Why did she never tell me? Why—?"

The evil that Darian had been preparing to encounter face to face for so many years, after vowing to face, was weeping like a child. He had not expected this response in every iteration of the plan he was to follow. It was almost hilarious. The difficulty in preparing for contingencies in a murder plot didn't allow room for the terrible bastard who was supposed to be murdered actually turning out to be not so terrible of a bastard after all. How was he supposed to continue in good conscious?

"You're crying now? Crying?!" Darian sighed and began to pace. Bringing both hands to the back of his head. Air gun still gripped in his left. He stopped and brought the arms down. His father flinched as the gun was pointed again at his face.

"What are you so jumpy for? This—?" Darian motioned with the pistol, not wanting to lose any leverage he had, "Nevermind.

I should be going."

James shrank into his seat and continued labored breathing in between sobs. Darian tipped the man's face up with the pistol to look him in the eyes. The lines of his face and salt & pepper scruff lining his jaw-line aged him so. It was not the face of evil that had haunted his nightmares months after he and his mother moved away. He was pathetic! Who cries at his age? It's almost as if the decades of bottling up emotion and *being a man* was starting to tear at him. That or the spousal abuse.

Darian grabbed the gray shaving bag and rose to his feet. James let out another fearful yelp and held his hands before his face defensively.

"Chill," Darian said softly. He turned and began to walk into the house before stopping suddenly. He wheeled around in his heel and leaned up against the doorframe.

"Wait, shit. Before I go. Where's Jack? That was like, the entire reason I changed my mind about coming here." He asked.

"Jack? Well, he's—he's dead." James hesitated.

"Yeah, no shit, dude. Where's his body buried? I didn't go to the funeral. You forgot to invite me."

"He's buried at the—at the—"

"Stop." Darian knelt down and put a hand on James' shoulder, who flinched at the touch.

"Take a deep breath. And spit it out. Kinda on a time-crunch here."

James heaved as he inhaled deeply. Darian didn't need a stethoscope to feel the effort the old man's diaphragm was going through to push air through his weathered lungs.

"He's buried at Saint Colmcille's. The cemetery near the

church."

"Thanks, pops. Be seeing you." Darian called out as he turned around and strutted back into the house, out the front door, and into his jeep. He had no bloody clue who or where Saint Colmcille was, but he figured it wasn't *too* important. He needed to maintain enough dramatic flair as he exited.

As soon as he was sure his son had driven away, James rushed to his kitchen for the phone. The 911 operator who responded to the call would later remark that the call was short, and the only audible sounds were whimpers before disconnecting after ten seconds. A police unit was called to investigate as per procedure, but a unit never arrived. Glenrock PD was short that night, with all available units responding to calls pertaining to an overturned truck on the highway.

James Finnegan sat in his bedroom for a long time after Darian's departure. Cradling the bottle of whiskey between his legs before finally finishing it and praying to forget the night. As he got to the bottom of the bottle, the strongest urge to dig up photos before his wife had left possessed him. He frantically searched through boxes of photo albums. Overturning his desk and ripping out every cabinet in desperation. He eventually came upon an envelope of unframed photos from the local Walgreens. To his dismay, most photos had some degree of water damage. Among the surviving photographs one depicted a much younger, smiling version of himself holding a newborn with his firstborn next to him, staring in awe at his new baby brother. James staggered to sleep in his bed, half-clothed, the bottle still in hand, still clutching the photograph.

***

The cell phone was ringing, and his head was pounding. Tarron sat up to stretch and felt the same familiar pops and creaks that reminded him he was a tad closer to 30 than he liked to admit publicly. Feeling a tinge of pain, he slowly ran his hand over the scar on his abdomen. Sans vertigo, he figured the morning pains he had felt from his wound were getting less intense, almost entirely gone.

The phone continued to ring. He groaned and leaned over to his bedside table to answer, then laid back down as he brought the device to his ear.

"Hello?" He yawned.

"Daddy! We almost died!" the voice cried. Tarron sat back up.

"What happened, chicken? Are you okay?" He asked, exasperated. He had stood quickly and began moving towards his dresser to put on clean clothes, pinning the phone between his cheek and shoulder.

Before his daughter could answer him, he heard the faint sounds of the phone being taken from her. Celeste's voice filled the speakers.

"*Give me that.* Hey, sorry, we're fine. I promise. But we were on the way to your house, and I hit a patch of black ice. No, I'm alright, the car's just a bit dented, and Alina's shook up. Also, there's a flat. Anyway, I hate to ask, but do you think you could come to pick us up?"

Tarron breathed a sigh of relief. In the back of his mind, he almost felt grateful for an opportunity to swoop to the rescue of Celeste and their daughter. In light of last night's nightmare. "Yeah, definitely! I can change the tired too if ya need. Wouldn't be the first time I've changed out a flat on your car."

"Oh—well, no, it's okay." Celeste paused. "We were actually in Ian's car. He already called to have it towed. He's very specific about the maintenance on his Benz."

"Oh," Tarron started, dejected. He inhaled quickly and let any feelings of jealousy wash over and out of him before opening his mouth to speak again.

"Okay, well, I can still come to pick y'all up. It's only" He checked his watch "930, anyway. Why don't we go get some breakfast?"

He knew Alina must have been in earshot of the phone. Enough to hear the word "breakfast." He could hear the echo of her giggling and begging her mom to say yes to the offer. Breakfast foods happened to be the 4-almost-5-year old's absolute, most favorite kind of foods. The sounds dimmed by Celeste's pulling the phone away from her face to chide the young girl. Tarron waited patiently, grinning, and pictured the scene in his head.

Celeste brought the phone back. "Yeah, that's fine." She said plainly.

"I'll be there in 10. Don't worry!" He grabbed the keys sitting on his nightstand, then began to pull on a pair of boots and a coat and rushed out the door. The Hilux started with a growl, and he silently prayed to any automobile deity that was listening to bless his vehicle for another trip without any *major* issues. And if they did—he promised to be a good noodle. In the name of the car-father, car-son, and car-spirit, amen.

As he drove, the radio hummed quietly. Blondie's Heart of Glass came on, and Tarron smiled, turning up the volume. He found himself singing along in his own off-key falsetto but not really caring. By the time he neared the side of the road where Celeste had told him to rendezvous, the last few lines of the song finished. He did not see Ian's Mercedes-Benz but instead a Police truck with the officer outside waving him down. He slowed down and pulled up behind. Celeste and Alina hopped out of the back.

Alina rushed to her dad, and Tarron knelt down to swoop her up, holding her in one arm as the police officer made eye contact and grinned.

"Well, I'll be damned. I knew I recognized that Hilux. How're ya now?" Robert Graft beamed, outstretching his hand. Tarron returned the gesture. Celeste strode right past Tarron coldly and opened the passenger side door to his truck. His stomach tightened.

A warmer welcome from a guy I barely know than my baby momma. Go-fucking figure, He thought, turning back to Officer Graft.

Well, I guess he did save my life. Or was that the work of the doctors? That's a philosophical question for Darian.

"Truck's still not for sale, unfortunately. But thanks for taking care of..." *my family,* Tarron stopped himself from saying, "These two," he finished.

"Just doing my job." He replied humbly.

"He let me turn on the siren, Daddy!" Alina boasted.

Tarron chuckled. "He did?" He gently squeezed his daughter's sides enough to make her giggle. "So's that mean you're gonna be a cop now when you grow up?"

"Heehee. No!" She said in-between laughing. Graft smiled as well.

She doesn't even seem rattled by the accident. Now her mother, on the other hand... Tarron mused.

"Tarron, can we leave?" Celeste called from the truck, holding her hand out the window. Tarron turned and waved as to say I'm coming.

"Well, thanks again, Officer. I'll see ya around."

"Please, call me Bob. And I do mean call me. I'll add another $250 to my original offer for the truck." He replied, handing Tarron a business card. Tarron tucked the card into his back pocket.

"That's very kind of you. But I don't see myself selling any time, so—" Tarron was cut off by the sudden honk from his own truck's horn and turned to see Celeste again waving her hands. Let's go! Tarron clenched his jaw and let Alina down to walk beside him.

"Sorry about that." He added.

"I get it" Hank held up and tapped his left-hand ring finger. "Wives."

Before Tarron could correct the man, he heard another sharp honk from the truck. He grabbed Alina's hand and started walking towards the vehicle, waving at Bob before turning around completely.

"Jesus Christ. Is patience a foreign concept to her?" He mumbled.

"Is mommy mad?" Alina looked up and asked before they reached the truck. Tarron looked at his daughter with uncertainty and shrugged before opening the Hilux's passenger side door to the woman in question. He lifted Alina up and handed her off to Celeste before closing the door and running around to the driver's side. Celeste was silent as he started the truck and held Alina in her lap.

"She can sit in the middle seat. It's safe." Tarron suggested, turning the key in the ignition and merging onto the road.

"You mean on the faded bloodstain?" Celeste replied, "It's okay. I'll hold her."

Alina looked up at her dad for a response, and he winked at her, mouthing the words 'sorry chicken'. Before Tarron could think of a way to address the previous few minutes, Celeste beat him to the punch.

"I'm not in the mood if you want to argue. It's already been a day." She professed. Quickly adding, "I am sorry. I bet you think I'm a huge bitch now." Upon hearing the word "bitch", Alina looked up, shocked. Her mouth in a surprised O. Celeste looked down. "Sorry Alina, *zamknij uszy*" *Close your ears*. Alina put cupped hands over her ears and pouted.

"She picking up more Polski?" Tarron asked.

"A little more every day, I guess." She paused and pursed her lips. "Do you really care which language speaks?" she shot back.

Tarron hit the brakes of the truck and slowly pulled off to the side of the road. Celeste looked at him inquisitively. As the truck stopped, he put it in park and rubbed his eyes.

"Alright. What's up? What gives?" He asked.

"Nothing," Celeste answered.

"There's not nothing. It's never just nothing. I pick you up after you wrecked your boyfriend's car, and there's not even a 'thank you.' I was genuinely hoping to be able to talk to you today without worrying about what to say or being afraid to say anything in front of our daughter."

"I didn't wreck the car!" She snapped back.

"Okay. And?" Tarron retorted, holding up both hands. A familiar uncomfortable feeling in his gut from past spats returned to him. He tightened his grip on the steering wheel.

"Take us home," Celeste mumbled.

"What?"

"I said TAKE US HOME!" she hissed. Despite covering her ears, Alina was still observing the back-and-forth between her parents and began to sob silently. Tarron, seeing this, coddled her shoulders and started to console her. Celeste then began to sob as well. Tarron looked up and saw the tears begin to stream from her eyes and felt his throat catch.

Throughout their entire relationship, the emotional distance—he would reason, was the largest contributing factor to their breaking up. He did have a tendency to play dumb when he knew he shouldn't.

He also never knew what to do when she was upset. He couldn't figure out how he upset her or what the problem was, or how he should deal with it. Or deal with her. Frustration always followed like thunder to escalate.

"Now, why are you crying?" He began. Celeste's reddened eyes stared back at him. Her eyeliner was beginning to run.

Catharsis hit him like a train.

I never needed to 'deal' with her. Just be there for her. She didn't need me to solve all her problems. She just needed me on her side.

"Hey. It's okay. It's okay, I'm sorry," he said softly. He reached up and delicately placed a hand on her shoulder tentatively.

When she didn't brush him away, he pulled her in close. She rested her head on his shoulder. He hugged Alina, wrapping his other arm around them both.

"I know there's a lot we need to work through if I'm gonna continue to be in your and Alina's lives. I never want to be at a place where I couldn't talk to you."

"That's all I've wanted lately," Celeste said before clearing her throat. "I know with Jack dying and you getting out of the hospital that it's been rough. I understand that, but today you are coming because of an accident. It just feels like I've been wasting away." Celeste sniffled.

"Are you happy?" Tarron asked bluntly.

"What? I—I mean, it's been okay for the most part, and

things with Ian are mostly okay."

I didn't even mention Ian, Tarron thought. "Mostly? How's that?" He said aloud.

"We had…" she paused, gathering her words, "a spat, I guess. Over you, actually."

"I should be so honored," Tarron said with mild sarcasm. Celeste rolled her eyes. "No, really, what was the matter with me?" He added.

"It was something where, when you think you know a person so well, then they just say one thing that leaves you so shocked."

"Ian being this person?" Tarron interjected.

"Yes. You had just been admitted to the hospital, and they called me about it—since, well, you know. But Ian picked up my phone and didn't even tell me who had called after. I didn't know what had happened to you for hours. It was your mom who frantically texted me at almost 2 in the morning.

"When I confronted Ian about it, he just said, 'I didn't think it was something to waste your time over.' And we argued back and forth. I said you're still Alina's father. He said he thinks you were the worst thing to happen to me. It just was a lot of yelling." She started tearing up again. Tarron held her a little closer.

"Do you still keep napkins in here?" she said as she moved to open the glove box of the truck.

"No, not since we stopped, uh. Well, you know…."

Stopped having sex in my truck like deprived teens in high school, he thought.

Her nervous laughter at the realization of what he left unsaid broke the tension. She wiped her face with a sleeve.

"Don't be gross," she sniffled, nodding towards their daughter.

Tarron smiled nervously and shrugged his shoulders. The memory was better left played out in his head.

The three of them sat in the truck for a minute, quietly watching the sun begin to peek out from the gray storm clouds that had formed.

Breaking the silence, Alina declared, very decisively, that she was hungry, and her parents both shared a laugh. She looked up with the confusion of a toddler not in on the joke and repeated herself.

"Me too kurczaczku. Let's go get some pancakes," Celeste replied.

"Hey, I know a place. On the way to your house, too." Tarron said as he turned the key in the ignition.

***

Alina loved the decorations on the outside of Classics. Apparently, every time she and Celeste drove home from Tarron's, she would beg to go there because "it looks tasty, dad!"

Walking up to the restaurant for the second time in twenty-four hours felt surreal. Tarron could sparsely remember the taste of the patty melt. The mushroom tea had left a bigger imprint on his tongue, as well as his psyche.

The entire drug trip felt like just that—a hell-bending, *Fear and Loathing in Las Vegas*-style trip. Mostly in a good way, barring the premonition/nightmare about his daughter. Here they were, a dozen years early to what went on in his inebriated mind. They even sat in the same booth; it provided a nice view of the snow-topped Casper Mountain, which was beginning to peak out over the clouds.

They ordered pancakes, as they had come to do. With extra whipped cream and strawberries for Alina to make up for the harrowing car accident, she'd just experienced.

Tarron was grateful that they were being served by a different waitress. He knew it was probably highly unlikely for the same lady to work midnight to 11 am the next day, but crazier things had happened. Or it will happen.

A great example: digging up your best friend's grave with his estranged little brother so you could cremate his remains and spread the ashes... somewhere.

Iceland? I mean, I have the tickets already. I wonder if Jack meant that extra ticket for Cellie to join me. But then we'd have to buy one for Alina—or leave her with my mom. I guess going with Darian would only be right... still—Iceland?

Besides dealing with Darian, Tarron had a lot on his mind during breakfast, and he figured Celeste could read it on his face. She always could. He did his best to try and distract himself before figuring out what he wanted to say.

Celeste, on the other hand, was already running scenarios A through Z of what-the-fuck had gotten into the man she called her ex-boyfriend (that or "Alina's father"). She saw a shift from his normal body language all throughout breakfast. Her first thought was that anyone who was as close to death as Tarron was probably had their own "come-to-Jesus" moment.

"What's that, hon'?" Celeste asked.

"Huh? Oh, nothing. Just thinking about Jack." Tarron realized he must have been muttering.

"You would've hated the funeral," Celeste replied before taking a sip of coffee.

Tarron set his silverware down on the table, dumbfounded.

"You went? His dad didn't even invite me or tell me anything."

"I did. Do you remember Diana? From the dorms? She lived

a couple of rooms down from me."

"Dee-ana…" Tarron racked his brain. "Oh, the Spanish foreign exchange student?"

"Uh-huh. She and Jack were sleeping together for a while after you got me pregnant. I guess it was pretty serious because he proposed to her at some point. They were supposed to get married a few months… after he passed." Celeste trailed off, looking out the window. Tarron noticed her eyes were red again, but no tears had formed yet. He grabbed her hand from across the table, and she squeezed it back.

"Did she reach out to you or?"

"Oh!" Celeste shook her head and retraced her train of thought. "Yes. She did on Facebook and then over the phone. The weirdest thing, though, was she never, at any point, seemed sad. Like, even a bit. Her fiancé had just passed away, and she didn't even cry at the funeral. It just seemed so bizarre."

"People handle grief differently?" Tarron suggested.

"What she was handling didn't seem to be grief at all. And she came with a bunch of friends that no one seemed to know except her. They all dressed the same too. Head to toe black with accents of oxblood red. Creepy necklaces, too. Like a red *Złe oko*. I didn't hang around for long."

"Ah, the zley oh-ko. Your mom used to wear one, right? Remind me again of the superstition around it?"

Besides the evil-eye magic that your parents failed to explain to me already, He narrated to himself

"She wore a normal, well—traditional, blue one. Definitely not red. And it's not a superstition Tarron." She paused, taking a shaky drink of her coffee. "Those people had evil or something around them." She decided.

There was a slew of other mysticisms that Tarron remembered Celeste's parents practicing: avoid eye contact with the one you felt ill intentions from, don't count pierogi while still in the pot, the number 7 was un-lucky, and incessant jokes that Celeste fell for Jack then Tarron so easily because she was born in May—Venus' month.

"Ya think they were in a cult?" Tarron blurted.

"Hush. Don't say that, Tarron. Gives me the chills." Celeste shuddered.

Perturbed from the absolute mess on her plate of pancake, chopped fruit, and syrup, Alina looked up inquisitively. A mix of strawberry and syrup stains at the corners of her mouth made her look slightly feral.

"What's a cult, mommy?" She asked. Celeste glared at Tarron, see what you make me do? Her eyes seemed to say.

"A cult, kurczaczku," Celeste began, cleaning the stains on Alina's face with a napkin she dipped in water, "is a group of stinky people who have too much time on their hands."

"Like Mormons," Tarron added. Celeste glared again but smiled and rolled her eyes.

"Mormons. Mor-man's. Hee-hee." Alina cried delightedly as she put another forkful of pancakes into her mouth.

It wasn't too far off for Jack to be involved with such things. Mormons, no, but a weird group of Satanists or perhaps even followers of an ancient Aztec vampire god, definitely. He was always interested in taboo and the occult when he and Tarron grew up. But that interest never seemed to proceed past a scholarly infatuation. Jack started off his college career at ASU as an astrophysics major, jumped briefly to pre-law, then landed happily in anthropology. And fell in love with the field.

Tarron reminded himself to ask Darian if he talked to his brother much about school—and about Diana as well.

There was that scratching in the back of his head, begging him to doubt that the suicide was a simple black-and-white matter. The same scratching that had driven him to have hope when he saw the Iceland tickets.

Miracles don't happen in real life. And friends don't come back from the dead.

As that thought made its way through Tarron's mind, he glanced at Alina. She was barely eating her plate of pancakes anymore as much as playing with the remains. Her life which he had helped bring into this world, was by accident. Life was a gift. Alina was a miracle, regardless of the relationship he had with her mother. He swore that he would do everything in his power to make sure his child would be happy and healthy.

Two attributes that characterize the good life—are happy and healthy. What didn't occur to Tarron as simply was the fact that he and Celeste were, firstmost, neither happy nor healthy.

Well, maybe she was the latter. But together, they were far from married or financially stable. All of these qualities Tarron's father emphasized were crucial to starting a family.

9

Temper, Temper

AFTER LEAVING his father's house, Darian drove. He drove home to his apartment in Casper, changed clothes, packed away all the unused equipment from the botched patricide then decided to immediately walk back out the door. There was still a plan to be hatched about digging up his dearly deceased brother. Darian figured he'd drive until he couldn't stand it any longer. At which the plan would come to him. At which point he'd meet Tarron later tonight, and at which point he'd have the rest figured out from there.

So, he drove. Music blaring. Energy drink in one hand and steering wheel in the other. He headed east back towards Glenrock and kept going. Eventually, he turned off the main road and drove until the paved road ended. With the music loud enough, he simultaneously tried to ignore the voice in his head begging to know why he didn't carry out the murder and scream back at it why it didn't matter. And why he was already jumping to the next plan after failing the previous one.

The music was loud, but the Id was louder. It demanded an explanation and blood. The order of which did not matter.

Darian revved the engine, and the speedometer climbed, kicking up a plume of dirt in his rearview mirror. The road jutted, bent, and gave way to small indents every so often, and he felt his adrenaline spike as he rounded the turns. He wasn't worried. The jeep was practically made for this. He turned the volume nob louder before it read MAX. He slammed the steering wheel with the flat of his palm repeatedly, then took another swig of the energy drink. Empty.

Of all the bullshit I've had the misfortune to deal with in this miserable life and the peace I've made with it. So elegantly terrible. I couldn't even finish my dear old pops. He was a miserable sort.

Grunting, he crushed the can and flung it from the jeep with a scream and instant regret.

Now that wasn't very nature friendly. He reminded himself. He slammed on the brakes and skidded the jeep into the roadside ditch. The wave of dust caught up to him. As he released his grip on the steering wheel, he realized his hands were shaking. He put the jeep in park and hopped out to retrieve the litter.

It did not want to be found. He continued to walk, head-down, desperate to find the piece of litter. But despite the amount of other miscellaneous other pieces of trash he had found along the way, the can he had flung would not be another one. The sun blazed in the sky and warmed his skin. He had already walked some distance from his jeep and needed a break.

The energy buzz from the mushrooms he had started out the night with had begun to waiver after leaving his father's house. He briefly wondered if he should stop at a gas station for another energy drink. His caffeine tolerance had waned some since he left the Air Force but only to be duly reintroduced when he started working graveyard shifts at the hospital; a single energy drink at this point would be but a pick-me-up, and he didn't dare re-start his tobacco habit to supplement. He exhaled loudly.

Welp. Back to business, shall we? Strutting back into the jeep, he went on a desperate mental search for purpose. He drove. Desperate for logistics rather than ideas of grandeur. But for once in a very long time, Darian was at a loss for ideas. He felt terrible for lying to Tarron, although it was more leading-on than lying, he figured. If only there were more books on the matter. But: *How to Exhume a Body for Dummies* probably wasn't in any section of your local Barnes and Noble if there were even a Barnes and Noble remotely close to here.

Barnes and Noble be damned. Darian would write the guide himself. That way, he broke the rules he laid out for himself instead of somebody else's.

Alright, Darian. Think, motherfucker, THINK!

Step one: obtain legal permission. The morality behind that step was a point of contention. Did the state of Wyoming care much about two morally gray tax-payers digging up a body? He was his brother, in any case. Maybe the law wouldn't care if it was family who carried out the act. Especially if the body being dug would've much preferred to be lit aflame and ashes spread. A more than noble cause he felt more than obligated to help out. As a peculiar sort of necromantic-lorax, he and Tarron shall speak for the deceased, and the deceased wants to be dust.

He had to find the damn body first. Prying any more than the name of the cemetery from his terrified father would've been another endeavor on its own last night. Would it look unprofessional if he took Tarron to the graveyard and they searched for the gravesite? He wasn't posing as any sort of professionally hired exhume-er, so most likely not. In this case, an entire book on how-to wasn't needed—just a pamphlet on the next step.

How to cremate a body that has since been embalmed. The chemistry classes Darian took as an undergrad told him that the fluids inside his brother's body *probably* needed to be drained to avoid a very angry crematorium operator. A large, unsure emphasis on "probably" as he was scratching his head over what chemicals those were.

Oh, what was one of the dumb jokes my o-chem professor would say? Formaldehyde? More like casual-dehyde. That's the bugger, Darian chuckled to himself.

Avoidance of a crematorium operator altogether would most preferable in this situation. Put breaking-and-entering on top of gravedigging for the list of charges and call it a day. In any last resort, Darian figured they could give Jack a Viking funeral in Iceland. Albeit he had no idea on how to build a longship, had very little experience with a bow and arrow, and doubted it would be any easier to transport a dead body through customs without any paperwork whatsoever. Ideas, ideas; none good, all improbable.

Step Two: Dig, baby, dig. And pray you don't get caught.

Nearing the entrance back onto the main paved road, Darian decided to pull over again to jot these road thoughts down in his pocketbook. Pausing once to think of the final step in this grisly business.

Steps three and four: light that sum' bitch aflame and collect the ashes. Overall, probably the easiest step.

Darian continued onto the main street of Glenrock. The city was beginning to wake up, and the sounds of civilization clamored on. Minor construction on a pothole to his left, a lady jogging with headphones, oblivious to the world around her, to his right. A man walking his dog crosses the street in front of him.

Darian had a thought.

People get their dogs cremated, don't they? Paging Doctor Ulrich. Urgent matter at hand, sir.

***

An invitation inside after dropping the two of them off at the door was a surprise. It was Ian's house, after all. Celeste and Alina only lived there after moving out of Tarron's place.

Walking into the house felt foreign and cold, like stepping into a well, manicured garden from which the owner was absent. The monotone walls were a stark white with an occasional abstract painting. Black furniture contrasted the walls, straight from a uber-modern, minimalist catalog.

Celeste set her purse down on a barstool and disappeared into one of the rooms further down the hallway. Alina retreated to a corner. To her right was a sliding glass door that led to a backyard, where her toys were strewn about. Her toys and drawings on the floor provided the only bit of color and chaos in the systematically organized living room. Tarron sat at a barstool adjacent, examining the kitchen. The fridge was a monstrously large monolith panel of gleaming silver. All the supporting appliances gleamed in a matching color.

A single framed portrait of Ian and Celeste was on the white marble island countertop. Tarron picked it up curiously. As he did, Celeste reemerged from the bedroom. She quickly changed into a simple pair of black sweatpants and a tank top. Her hair was expertly and messily tucked into a bun. Glancing up, Tarron realized she was not wearing a bra. She leaned in next to him before sitting down.

He blinked. In a single instant, the mix of perfume and beauty products that made up her personal aroma transported him back six years. He was standing in the tiny college dorm room he and Jack shared. In his hand was a red solo cup full of cheap beer, mostly foam. Before he was at a heavily graffitied beer pong table with cups set up, she was leaning in to hand him the ball that had just bounced astray. She wasn't Celeste then; she was simply Jack's girlfriend. But even that title was transient with Jack's track record. Maybe that's why Tarron didn't feel guilty looking at her cleavage then. He knew he felt a tinge of guilt now. His eyes darted back to the picture frame in his hand. Her voice snapped him back into focus.

"I hate that photo. He was the one who pressed me to take pictures, and of all the ones we took that day, he decided to frame that one. 'Lina's not even in it, and I hate how my face looks."

"Hmm. Seems to me that's just how your face looks." Tarron shot back "*Spierdalaj.*" She swore at him while laughing, *fuck off.*

Tarron smiled. Her laugh seemed genuine.

"Careful, as you said, the little one'll hear you. But probably better to have her swearing in Polski than English, just in case her teacher hears it."

Celeste rubbed her temple timorously. "Her teacher is a heathen witch of a woman who's at risk of a stroke at any moment. I mean, seriously, Tarron, this woman must be made of sentient maggots. Nothing else would allow a human that old and decrepit to teach children."

"That's the most colorful description I've ever heard to describe an old person."

"Maggots, Tarron, maggots—I swear."

The two shared a laugh. Tarron placed his hand on her thigh experimentally. She grasped it with her own. Tarron began to feel his brain cease to have cognitive thoughts, only arousal and exhaustion. The mix of the two drove him to open his mouth.

Quick! Think of something clever.

"This house is a bit much. Don't ya think? Ian watch American Psycho too many times?"

She pulled her hand away slowly and crossed her arms, then began to bite at her thumbnail. Tarron slowly withdrew his hand as well.

"You're not wrong—actually," She finally said, "I made the exact same joke one day, in passing really, and he stopped and looked me dead in the eyes and said 'people really don't begin to understand to the real point of that movie.' Can't begin to tell you how much it creeped me out."

He's your nutcase of a sugar daddy, Tarron wanted to say.

Tarron's cell phone began to vibrate and bailed him out of having to reply. He fished it from his pocket and mouthed 'sorry' before answering.

"Yeah—" he started. An uncanny voice cut him off.

"T man! Big T! Tee ran-o-saurus-rex. What are you doing right now?"

"I—, uh Darian, this really isn't—"

"Must not be important then. Moving on! I've had a thought, well—a collection of them, really. Wait—what time is it? Noon—good lord. I've been up for 36 hours. Also, not important."

"Darian! Slow down. What's up? Why'd you call me?"

"Hold on" The sounds of rummaging around filled the speaker. Tarron was sure Darian also dropped his phone one or two times.

Celeste's face had a creeping look of concern, and she held her hands up as if to prod an explanation. Tarron pulled the phone from his face quickly to whisper the words 'Jack's little brother.' At that, Celeste scrunched her eyebrows in further confusion. Tarron matched her confused look momentarily.

Then it clicked.

How did I fail to mention that I met Jack's little brother? The night I was stabbed too.

"You still there?" Darian prompted.

"Yeah! Still here," Tarron piped while rising from his seat. He pressed the mute button on his phone as Darian began to ramble on.

"Sorry. I'll be right back. Explain later." He apologized to Celeste before walking towards the sliding door. He anxiously fumbled with the lock while Darian continued to ramble on. His words seemed to string onto each other in excited succession. The lock on the sliding door refused to unlatch as well, only adding to Tarron's unease.

Darian continued: "All I had to do was threaten my dad! And that's when we'll take the body to this friend, I know! He's more of an acquaintance that I made at the hospital, but he owes me a favor or two. It'safunnystoryactually, howwemet. Theguyisaveternarianwho—. Hey, are you still listening?" Tarron's hands continued to wrestle with the lock. He made an attempt to force the door open, then fiddled with the lock again—all to no avail.

"Turn the knob left, and there's another lock on the top!" Celeste yelled. Finally, Tarron got the door open. He stepped out and shut the door behind him.

"Yeah! Darian, I am still listening. Darian. Darian?" He

quickly tapped the phone screen to unmute himself.

"I'm here. Yeah, sounds great. Where do you want to meet?" He prompted, without really knowing what he had agreed to. Anything to shut Darian up at this point. That may have been rude, but in hindsight, he was already going over in his head how he was going to explain this all to Celeste.

"Place is called Saint Colmcille cemetery. It's in Glenrock near the church. The one on—"

"The one on the main street," they said in unison. "Yeah, got it. What time?" Tarron finished.

"The sun goes down around seven, so how about midnight? Great time to dig a grave, I think. Also, I have to go to bed, or I may actually tear my eyes out slowly. See ya!"

The phone line went dead. Tarron placed the device back in his pocket and held both arms behind his head. The sound of the sliding glass door shutting made Tarron jump, and he turned around sharply.

"Christ! Just me, Tarron. No one else it could be. Now—what was that? Or who, rather," Celeste said.

Tarron took a deep breath. Any and all last-minute explanations fled his mind. Time to wing it.

"He's...Jack's...little brother. Darian, their parents divorced when he was young, as you may know—"

"No, actually." Celeste crossed her arms. "Jack neglected to tell me a lot about his family. All he said was he grew up with you and didn't talk to his dad much anymore. I figured his parents were divorced. Or that his mother died. Either way, I never tried to pry much."

Oh? That makes this explanation a lot less painless in that case. He sighed in relief.

"Oh. I see." He paused, collecting himself. "Well, yes and no.

Their mom moved and took Darian to Lake Tahoe after they divorced, and Jack stayed with his dad—obviously. Did you not see Darian at the funeral?"

"If I did, I didn't recognize him. Jack's dad was sitting with some skinny blonde thing that looked about half his age."

Sounds about right for Mr. Finnegan. So that's a no. You damn sure would've recognized him

"What? You're mumbling again." Celeste remarked.

"I said his face would definitely have stuck out in your head. He's a carbon copy of Mr. Finnegan. Taller though. Skinnier too. But the same eyes. Same husky blue eyes."

"You know, when I first met you and Jack, I was sure you two were brothers. The way you acted and just how you interacted with each other. And you made me think you were! It wasn't until I started dating Jack did he ever flat-out say you and he weren't actually related. It made it confusing as hell when he ever would talk about his 'brother' 'cause' I figured he always meant you."

Tarron felt his chest swell up and started to fight choked breaths. He didn't want to cry in front of Celeste. Not here, at least. God forbid Ian to walk in and make his own assumptions. He wasn't expecting Celeste's words to cut so deeply and bring back memories.

Another thing people fail to mention when someone dies: You wouldn't be as sad if there was nothing to miss, nothing to remember. But the fact that you are sad now because of memories, good or bad as they may be, was the fact that they were a part of how you remember that lost person. All of which served to make the loss feel so much heavier.

At one point, they were brothers. Many points, in fact. All the way up until Jack and Celeste stopped dating, and Tarron let alcohol get the better of him. The outcome of which led to the end of his and Jack's friendship and Alina's birth nine months later. Tarron looked at her now, through the glass door sitting with her toys. Determinedly scribbling a crayon on a piece of paper.

She looked up and smiled and waved. "Hi, daddy." Her muted voice said.

The tears came. He broke down. He felt Celeste's hand on his back through heavy heaves. He never figured himself for an ugly crier, but the floodgates were open, and there was no stopping this much bottled-up, manic grief.

***

Recounting the remainder of his and Darian's encounters went over a lot smoother than Tarron could have expected. After bawling his eyes out harder than when his childhood dog got run over by a semi-truck, Tarron sat down, put on Ice Age 4 to distract their daughter, took a deep breath, and told Celeste mostly everything from start to finish. Only omitting the dream, he experienced after passing out in Darian's jeep and the half-cocked plan for Jack's body. He tried to include all of Darian's quirks as well as the footnotes of the conversations they shared.

Throughout, Tarron tried to read Celeste's facial expression to get a gauge of if she thought this was as ridiculous as he felt.

When he finished, she had only two questions, and the first was only for clarification.

"So, Darian works at the hospital?"

"He's a nursing student. That's my understanding."

"Ah. Okay," She replied, "And he offers you this mushroom tea, and you just…drink it? With no second thoughts? Didn't they put you on medication for your stab wound?"

"I...uh. Well," Tarron scratched his head, then interlaced his hands behind it.

'I wasn't really thinking' probably isn't a good answer here. He thought.

"I'm not easily convinced. You know me—I'll admit to being stubborn at times—" Tarron paused as Celeste cackled at his statement before covering her mouth and motioning for him to continue.

"...but Darian. He persuaded me without even really trying. Maybe I was more curious than desperate. I've already gone down that path of being a fuckin' drunk when my dad died, then when you left... and well...I just needed a bit of reassurance that being sad wasn't just the ground state for me. That I could be happy again." He finished, lowering his hands back down, and started nervously clasping and unclasping his watch. It was 4 in the afternoon.

"I get it. But hey—impulsivity is not a good look for you." Celeste paused, "Isn't that the watch your father got you?" She asked quietly.

Tarron paused in-between, clasping. "It is. I'm surprised you remember." He spoke. He held it up delicately and handed it to Celeste. She took it and ran her finger delicately across the watch face before handing it back.

"Of course, I remember. Have you filled more of that little box like you had wanted to?"

"No. Same three watches in there. This one and dad's old Seamaster," He paused, biting his cheek nervously, "and the anniversary one you got me."

"Now that I am surprised to hear. I thought you had rid yourself of everything pertaining to me."

Tarron exhaled out of his nose and looked over towards

Alina sitting on the couch. He nodded and said, "it ain't as easy as one hopes." Celeste narrowed her eyes and hit his leg.

There it was again. A false flag of hope that led Tarron to think everything, at this moment, was just fine between the two of them. If he closed his eyes and imagined hard enough, this was the big house with a backyard they had always dreamed about. And sitting happily on the couch was their—completely planned out and not-out-of-wedlock, child. He even imagined a dog. Celeste loved Doberman's.

The opening and closing of the front door snapped him back.

He came in loudly, pulling off a tie and setting a leather briefcase on the bar top without looking at Tarron.

"Couldn't believe the day I've had hon', good lord. I—" Ian finally turned around and made eye contact with Tarron. The man's demeanor changed slightly, defensively. Tarron felt a sudden tightness in his chest. He began to fiddle with the clasp of his watch again.

This was Ian's house, and he did not like unexpected visitors, especially the sort who undermined his primal hierarchy. Bitter, idiotic masculinity. Tarron stopped fiddling with the watch and tightly balled his fist.

"Didn't know we had company. Can I get you something to drink, Tarron? We're out of whiskey, though. I know that's your usual drink of choice. Or was it Coors?" Ian asked.

"No, thank you." Tarron shot back sharply.

"Ah? Kicking the ole' habit, I see. Good for you." Tarron stood up quickly. He felt the tightness in his chest change into a white-hot ball of hate. He studied the man who stood before him. He stared back at him with a grin. It said *come on, hurt me, show them that bit of ugly inside of you. You know you want to.*

And, oh, how he did want, with every ounce of his being.

A logical voice reminded Tarron that Ian had connections in the police department. Cops were frequent fliers for divorce, and Ian had made sure to put a number of them in his back pocket, or so Celeste had told him. He knew what to say to the right people to make sure Tarron would never see his daughter again.

Where was the harm of a single punch? Maybe more than once, repeatedly. To the face or to the bastard's perfect jawline. Hell, maybe he could knock a few teeth out before Celeste stopped him. Ruin that perfect smile and redecorate the white walls with some crimson red. Ian was a man cut from a different cloth. He liked nice things, wore a white collar, and looked down at those who wore one of blue. Men like this had never been punched in the face, so Tarron's dad would say.

Celeste looked up and recognized the look in Tarron's eyes. She stood quickly as well, rounding her way to Ian. She grasped his hand and hugged him. Deliberately putting herself in between him and Tarron.

"He was just dropping Alina off, doll." She piped, standing on her tip-toes to kiss the man on the cheek.

Tarron became briefly aware of the cortisol in his veins and unclenched his fists. He tried to compose himself and felt his temper die down slightly. A hateful weight had relieved itself from his shoulders, and he physically felt lighter.

"I was just leaving." Tarron corrected.

He turned around and made his way to Alina, who had the TV remote in her hands. He knelt down and hugged her. Bye, bye Chicken.

"I'll walk you out," Celeste said.

Tarron hugged Alina tightly and then followed Celeste to the door.

"Be seeing you," Ian called out from behind him. Tarron lifted one hand in a half-hearted wave. Celeste was waiting patiently by the open door. Tarron shrugged on his coat and stepped through the threshold. She closed the door behind them both unexpectedly and began to huff.

"How about waiting until our daughter isn't in the same goddamned room before you start an entire domestic dispute?"

Tarron stayed silent. He didn't have anything to offer in his defense. She was exactly right; no sixth sense or mindreading was necessary to know the violent thoughts he was harboring. He turned to walk towards his truck.

"Oh, what? Nothing to say for yourself?" She called out.

"I have to go meet Darian later." He grumbled.

"Stop mumbling! What's more important to you right now? Seeing your new drug buddy or talking about what the fuck just happened in there."

"Nothing happened!" Tarron said and continued walking.

"Oh, bullshit. You know, I thought something was different with you today, Tarron. I really did, and for the better too. Even though your crazy-ass is trying new drugs instead of pissing yourself drunk, you're making me fucking laugh again and actually being a good father. And what else aren't you telling me? Jack had a whole-ass brother? I know you, and he had a mountain of unresolved shit, but—"

"That's what I'm trying to fix!" Tarron wheeled around and held his arms up.

Tarron searched for the words to say while rubbing his temple. The snow underfoot cracked and shifted, and as he looked down at his feet. He figured he'd skip the buildup and just get to the conclusion. Hopefully, the shock value would do it for her.

"We're gonna go spread Jack's ashes in Iceland."

"Excuse me?" Celeste replied, immediately taken aback.

"He didn't want to be buried. So, I'm gonna spread his ashes at the one place we always wanted to go. Call it a set-up for a dammed—Hallmark movie or something, but right now, there's nothing else that really makes any sense to me other than that. So, I'd really appreciate it if—"

Celeste closed the distance between them and threw her arms around Tarron in an embrace. Before he could say anything, she kissed him. He held her for a moment and decided to kiss back before pulling away.

Jesus Christ, woman, could you give me any more mixed of a signal?

He pulled away and tucked his hands into his back pockets, feeling his cheeks swell and blush. If the past 36 hours had proved anything to him, he shouldn't be too shocked that Celeste just kissed him outside her boyfriend's house.

"What the fuck was that?" He said.

"For luck," She smiled "now leave."

He left.

10

That's a Letdown

WINDS HOWLED, rattling tree branches against the windows of Darian's jeep. The sound jaunted him into focus, and he realized he had been dozing off. He had his seat adjusted low enough to be comfortable to lie back and watch the road without also pinching the muscles in his back. He squinted and tried to rub the blurriness out of his eyes to make out the numbers on the car clock: 23:49.

Tarron was late to being early. It would seem. The practice of being 15 minutes early to anything was something that had been beaten into Darian during boot camp, briefly forgotten while starting college, and bitterly revisited once he started clinicals for his nursing program.

Hurry up and wait. Don't be late.

St. Colmcille's church was located just at the edge of town with a wide-open field behind it. In front, though, was a newly built residential area; houses packed together tightly in suburbia.

The church predated the houses by nearly a century. It had its own quiet, oral history that sparse few Glenrock residents could remember. Those old enough who could—usually referred to it as 'the mick-church,' as it was built and attended by the descendants of Irish immigrants who had been in

Wyoming since the civil war. It was a simple church, typical midwestern. White with a large steeple. The paint had begun to chip at the corners. A dusty bulletin advertised Sunday service as well as: PRAYER IS POWER.

Darian wasn't surprised his dad buried Jack at an Irish church. James Finnegan presented himself as extremely proud of his heritage.

The one positive story Darian's mother did tell him about his father was of their first meeting. It was in one of the several dozen Irish pubs in New York. She was going to school at the time, and James, a boatswain's mate third class in the Navy, had come to Manhattan for fleet week. He had told her some corny pickup line, and she made fun of him for being from a state that no one knew existed.

That story always made Darian feel conflicted. On the one hand, he wanted to be proud of his parentage and where he came from but on the other: the child abuse.

He exited his jeep and started to nervously peel the stickers off shovels he had recently purchased. And continued to wait.

More memories came to mind of shoveling the driveway free of snow as a part of his weekly chores in the winter. He had grown to both love and hate the snow in Lake Tahoe for the work it brought him, but the absolute beauty that came with it made the work not as bad. Wyoming snow just didn't do it for him. It was harsh and unforgiving.

Headlights in the distance blinked into existence, and Darian looked at his phone again. He had missed the texts from Tarron that announced his, now imminent, arrival.

The rationale was that they weren't desecrating a grave, per se. They were moving their brother to his preferred resting place. As well as aiding Tarron to achieve some solace. The guy struck Darian as needing a hand in that department. He recognized the sort of hopelessness that Tarron tried to hide from him. It became more apparent after the mushroom tea escapade.

Tarron's truck parked behind him, and Darian strode over to meet the man. Before Tarron cut the power to the truck, the headlights illuminated the overgrown weeds that hung along the church fence. Darian made a mental note to inquire to St. Colmcille himself as to why his cemetery was so poorly maintained.

Tarron hopped out of the truck and met him. He was wearing a tan Carhartt jacket and carrying a camping lantern. He had a subtle look of concern on his face. Darian clasped his shoulder in reassurance, and they began to walk without a word. When they approached the gate of the cemetery, Tarron broke the silence.

"You know, in high school, we used to come by this place and do donuts in the dirt fields across the street. That was before they put all these houses up, too." He remarked, "One time somebody must have called the cops on us, and when they showed up, everyone just about scattered. Jack and I were barely able to get away in his little beat-up Honda civic. Scared the shit out of us both."

"You and he really got into some crazy stuff back in the day, huh?"

Tarron nodded. *You don't know half of it. Or maybe you do. I wonder how many stories Jack told you,* he thought.

"So where is he?" Tarron said aloud.

"Just keep a lookout for a gravesite that's missing grass on top. He wasn't buried long enough for it to grow back," Darian responded sharply

"That may be a bit hard. I don't know if you've noticed," Tarron shone his camp light in a sweeping motion, "but most of these graves are missing grass."

He was right. The cemetery had definitely seen better days. And if not better than, at the least, greener days. The field that surrounded them was just as dusty as the vacant lots across the street from the church. Patches of grass were tinted an unhealthy grey as well as far and few between.

"Okay. So, in that case, look for dirt that is a different shade of brown than the dirt around it." He huffed. Tarron shrugged and stayed silent.

They continued up the main path. Flashlights panned back and forth across gravestones as they went. After passing two dozen rows, they neared the edge of the cemetery.

They had been searching for almost half an hour. Midnight was closely passing.

Nothing.

"Let's circle back," Darian started to say and began to press past Tarron, who had trailed a step behind him.

As he did, Tarron put a hand on his shoulder to halt the man. He didn't have to read too deep into Darian's demeanor to tell there was something off. Half of Tarron's job as a bartender was recognizing how to read people. This was a skill he learned involuntarily through a slew of people telling him how they felt before he even asked.

"Let's say… we don't find Jack. What then?"

"Then we go back through until we do. But in the meantime," Darian half smiled and reached into his back pocket to retrieve a can of chewing tobacco. Tarron watched him flick the can with a practiced motion, open it, pinch a collection of the wintergreen-scented mulch, and pack it into his lip. He then took a seat on the ground, resting his back against a large, crucifix-shaped tombstone. Tarron set the camp light down and took a seat next to him. Patiently waiting for the man to open up. He knew sometimes people don't like to be prodded. They'll preach on their own time.

"Tried to kick this habit after I got out. Bad for the gums and hard to keep a spitter around in a hospital", Darian started.

"My dad dipped all my life. He got a lot of flak from other guys in his station for going into calls with a lip in." Tarron replied.

"Firefighter?"

"Yup. Thirty-one years. After his heart attack, I'd visit him in the hospital, and he'd sneak spitting into one of those little dixie cups when my mother wasn't looking. He'd make me laugh in that way—winking to me if I caught him…Christ, I miss that man."

Tarron didn't mean to ramble on, but he realized midway through he couldn't remember the last time he had told anyone about how his father died. His mother was too grief-stricken at the time, and he never was too keen on laying his own grief on Celeste.

"Whadda ya think you miss most about him?" Darian asked innocently.

The question took Tarron by surprise. He hung his head back and racked his brain for an honest answer.

"Maybe our fishing trips? I tried to pass that tradition on to my daughter. Maybe that's another thing, too—the way he would hold my little girl on his lap and make her laugh. He was just an amazing father growing up, and he was an even better grandpa to Alina. I swear, when I told him and my mom that I knocked Celeste up, he smiled immediately and only pretended to be disappointed, for mom's sake."

When he finished the story, Tarron saw the shadow of the lamplight shine a furrowed look on Darian's face.

"I talked to my dad last night," he said.

"Oh?" Tarron made an attempt to hide any shock in his voice. "How is James? Haven't seen him since the day Jack and I left for college, actually"

"Dying slowly," Darian said quietly.

"What's that?" Tarron asked.

"Uh," Darian cleared his throat, "He uh. He's fine. He was drinking a lot. Surprised to hear from me."

Tarron's suspicion was confirmed. Celeste didn't see him at the funeral, and the fact that James was surprised to see his son suggested he probably wasn't even aware he was in the same state. Ergo, there was something Darian wasn't saying or hiding. Tarron may have been filling in the blank a little excessively, but he needed to know more.

"Did you go see him after you got off work?"

Darian turned his head and spit. Tarron could smell the artificial wintergreen stench in the air and held back gagging.

"No, I uh—called last night."

"Oh, before you came to the bar… Or after you left my place?"

"After. I mean—why does it matter, dude?"

Time to go on the offensive, Tarron thought to himself.

"What aren't you telling me, Darian?"

"Just trust me, alright." He stood up, brushing the dirt from his jeans. "C'mon, let's find Jack and get to work before something happens."

Tarron rose as well. He knew he should leave it be. He didn't feel confident enough to start interrogating him. The drug trip had jump-started their complicated friendship, but, collectively, he'd only known the man a week.

"Let's move laterally, you take the left field, and I'll go right. We'll cover more ground that way." Darian decided, pushing past Tarron.

"Darian."

Darian spun around quickly on his heels and held his arms stretched out in a T. Tarron felt a catch in his throat and his heart drop. What was even more unsettling was the wide grin on Darian's face.

"What, dude?! What do you want to tell me, Tarron? That you think something's wrong? That you think this is a bad idea? In all honesty, *it probably fucking is.* But hey, what else but a risk to make your life interesting? You especially."

"You're on edge. And I *know* something's wrong because why the hell are we searching for Jack's grave in the first place? Weren't you at the funeral? Are you completely lying to me, or do you have some angle to waste my time?"

"I think you can do that all by yourself, there," Darian replied with malice.

"The fuck is that supposed to mean?" Tarron shot back. He pressed forward until he was less than a foot from Darian's chest. His patience was spent, and his blood was simmering after being jerked around earlier by Celeste's asshat of a boyfriend. And at that moment, Darian could match the sentiment.

"Do you want to hit me, big man? Is there something bothering you? Cause I promise you that I'm not the one," Darian prodded.

"I don't like being lied to," Tarron replied slowly through a clenched jaw and gritted teeth. He locked his gaze with Darian. He was begging for a try. Just an inclination that would give him the push to tackle him. The man was not the demon he wanted to face, but he was the next best thing. A feeling that Darian also shared. And in that particular moment, neither knew that their fight was not with each other. It was unrelated pain and aggression that they were bringing to a head.

Darian pulled his head back and forcefully brought it down against Tarron's skull. Shock reverberated through his brain, but his adrenaline spiked in the same instant. The blow caught Tarron off guard and staggered him. He took a couple of steps backward, gingerly touching the impact point on his temple, aghast. Darian advanced and reared back to kick him in the chest. The blow connected soundly, and Tarron doubled over.

"Oh, you wanna hit me, Tarron? Have-at-thee, you miserable shit!"

Tarron grunted and sat up. He sprang forward and wrapped up Darian in a near-perfect form tackle. His high school football coach would be proud. Tarron figured he had 20 or so pounds on the man but Darian went down much quicker than he could've anticipated. The two tumbled over and rolled several feet backward between the tombstones. Tarron dug his heel into the ground to stop their momentum and ended up atop Darian's chest.

He brought his fist down across Darian's cheek and felt the sharp crack of cheekbone against his knuckles. Then again, with his left hand balled into a fist.

Darian's head turned sharply with the blow. Blood had started to run from a small cut under his orbital. He brought his knee quickly to Tarron's coccyx, then elbowed him across his jaw. Tarron grunted and fell to his side. Darian followed and started hammering blows across his skull. He hit him again, and when Tarron didn't move again to writhe or retaliate, Darian rolled off him. He let his head go slack, and the back of his head hit the grave marker.

Tarron rolled over, breathing heavily, groaning, and clutching his head.

He sat up and plopped down next to Darian before pulling out the pack of Marlboro Reds from his back pocket. The pack was dented and crushed, as were most of the cigarettes inside. Tarron picked out the one with the least damage. As he pulled it out of the pack, Tarron saw that the tip was just hanging on by the rolling paper, about to break off. He snorted, flicked the broken end off, and lit the cigarette.

He caught Darian's small grin from the corner of his eye.

"Fuck you. Yeah, I tried to quit, too. Here I am." Tarron confessed.

Darian didn't respond. He pulled out the dip can once more and repeated the process of packing his bottom lip with the tobacco.

"I definitely just swallowed the lip of tobacco I had in while we were fighting." He told Tarron before spitting.

"That was... really dumb. Why did we even just do that, man?" Tarron asked.

"I haven't slept in a while, and you looked like you needed to get some demons out, so I thought we could roll a bit. Good for the muscles. But now everything smells and tastes like wintergreen."

The two looked at each other for a moment, then started to chuckle slightly. It rose to full-on belly laughter, and Tarron doubled over, grasping his side.

"Oh, it hurts. You got me good with that kick, dude."

"Oh fuck… did I hit your scar?" Darian asked gravely

"No, no, no. Right center in the gut. Great shot, man."

"You had some good ones too, don't shortchange yourself. Haven't been beaten like that since I was a child."

Tarron quickly let out a hollow laugh and quickly grimaced when he realized what Darian was referring to. He took another drag of his cigarette before responding.

"You fell hard when I tackled you. I didn't think you could've been that light with the height you have on me."

"I definitely used to be heavier, I'll admit. I think I started dropping pounds about a year ago. It's just been steady since I got diagnosed. That's the reason I didn't want to go to the funeral and why we're out here lost."

"I can understand that you wouldn't want to see your dad after all this time. But diagnosed with what, man?"

"Cancer, Tarron."

Tarron tried to prevent the cigarette from falling from his mouth. Darian took this as a cue to explain himself.

"Yeah, yeah, I know. Why didn't I tell you?" He mimicked, "It's just a lot to lay on someone you just met. Plus, I originally was gonna let you know after we did all this. I can understand if you don't exactly trust me now."

"That's… that's not even my first question, actually. Cancer? Really? Good lord, what kind? And how are you even able to work at the hospital when you're on chemo?".

"Ah, okay—so that's the fun thing, they don't know, and I'm not." Darian spits tobacco juice again before finishing, "it's breast cancer."

The perplexed look on Tarron's face invited Darian to elaborate. He held up his hands and shrugged.

"Angiosarcoma, it's in the lining of the blood vessels of my chest, so it's breast cancer. Apparently, men are one in ten cancer diagnostics. I had my doubts, too—I barely even could respond when the Air Force doctor told me. Like, I knew a few guys who got cancer and had the same job as me. I thought that if I did end up with it, it would be like… I don't know, skin cancer? Something more believable. Or even one that's more survivable, at least."

"How long ago did you get diagnosed, or wait a minute, so is that why you got out? Like a medical discharge, or whatever it's called?"

Darian stayed silent. He'd tell Tarron the rest once they found Jack's grave. His mind started to drift with unpleasant thoughts, and he inhaled deeply, remembering a meditation technique also passed on to him by Chief Bradley.

Tarron read the look on his face and just continued to smoke.

Darian stood up and dusted himself off. He outstretched his hand to Tarron, who took and began to do the same. Tarron took another short drag of his cigarette. As he started to flick it, something caught his eye.

Land—somewhat cleared. And a headstone that was not as grime laden as the rest. Tarron shone his lamp towards it and squinted. Darian followed his gaze, and they shared a moment of mutual understanding.

"Do you think—?"

"It has to be."

They ran towards the sight, leaping over headstones and nearly tripping in excitement. And as they reached the grave, there read the dearly departed:

JACK WILLIAM FINNEGAN

Both men grew silent as they began to unearth the gravesite.

In for a penny, in for a corpse.

And so, they dug. And dug. With the effort of desperate grave robbers, ironically more concerned with the fate of the body rather than anything it was buried with. The hole grew deeper and deeper. Before long, they were both standing waists deep. They began to take turns digging as neither could fit in the hole and dig at the same time.

"So, the spray tan? Is that to hide the fact that, um, you know…" Tarron probed, breaking the silence that lay in between his shovel strikes.

"Actually, I did it on a whim and really liked it.…" He started, taking a deep breath. "It's actually a funny story, so I was shacked up with this girl after I got the whole cancer news. And I was totally awkward in high school, right? But maybe something about knowing I had a death sentence gave me confidence. So, we get back to the shitty apartment I was staying in at the time and start going at it—"

Tarron held up his hand in protest. "Spare me details."

"Right… gotcha, sorry," Darian continued, unperturbed, "so the apartment I live in had these really old school outlets. Like from the '50s or some shit. So, I had to use adapters to live like in this century, right? And this girl decided to plug her e-cigarette into one" He held up his hands in earnest. "I know, I know, it must be what's popular for sorority girls or whatever. So, she plugs it in and leaves for the bathroom. I'm piss-drunk already, didn't know if I had mentioned that. Don't even know how I managed to get home.…"

"The point, dude.…" Tarron exhaled quietly, striking his shovel into the ground. Darian continued, briefly acknowledging the comment.

"So, I see that she's plugged her e-cig into the wrong outlet.

So, I, the gentleman that I am, attempt to unplug it and put it in one that works. But I grab the damn thing and electrocute the shit out of myself. Pass out, wake up, I'm naked, I look up, and the girl is on top of me, tits out."

"So…what? She, like, raped you? Is that the point of this story?"

"No, dude. What? It wasn't like that. C'mon, man."

"Darian, you can't consent if you're unconscious. That woman raped you." He paused digging and looked up to Darian to mock concern. "Are you like okay, do you wanna talk about it? I know I shouldn't be laughing right now, but I can't stop."

Darian chuckled and played along. "Well, not only did she rape me, but I later found out she gave me chlamydia."

"Oh, you poor, stupid bastard." Tarron enunciated, striking the shovel down with each word, "WHAT. DOES. THIS. HAVE. TO. DO. WITH. SPRAY-TANS?"

"I'm getting there! So, afterward were just sitting there. Laying in it. And we just get into conversation. She was totally a cool gal. She was going to UC Berkley for… architecture, art, or something, and she talks about how some kids who came to Berkley from the Midwest got spray tans to fit in with the rest of the California kids. And I thought, hey, what the heck. I'm originally from the Midwest and need to fit in with the Cali kids. And am also gonna need to hide the fact that I'm dying. So, yeah."

"That was a lovely story, Darian. I feel so much closer to you now." Tarron teased, continuing, "I originally thought it was pretty well done, wherever you got it at. The thing is—you're in Glenrock, goddamn, Wyoming, where everyone's damn near as pale as milk. You may even get mistaken for Arapaho."

"I truly admire native Americans. So, I wouldn't be mad."

"I don't think you'd be the one mad in that situation, but what do I know?"

Darian looked up with heartfelt appreciation in his eyes. Besides the Air Force doctor who diagnosed and discharged him, Tarron was the only person he had talked to about his cancer. The spray tan felt like his version of do-rags that he saw bald or balding chemo patients wear.

"What did your family think? Or mom, I mean," Tarron asked before he continued to shovel dirt.

Darian remained silent. He had been putting off telling his mother entirely. They hadn't talked much since his wife died and even less so since he left the Air Force. The longer he put it off, the more anxiety built inside him.

He felt a lump in his throat. He was about to tell Tarron that she didn't know, and he was one of the only people he had told. Before he opened his mouth, Tarron brought down his shovel with a loud, resounding clunk. He struck the spot again to be sure, and the sound echoed once more. Darian hopped down and looked at Tarron.

In minutes they had the entire top of the casket un-earthed.

"Ready?" Darian asked after clearing his throat.

"No. Fuck. I guess" Tarron held his breath.

Gore he was prepared to see. Images flashed through his head of how

Jack's body would look. If Darian's word rang true concerning the nature of his death, Tarron was fully anticipating seeing the worst. Without a face to ID him, they'd have to trust the grave marker and circumstance that it was, indeed, the body of Jack Finnegan.

He braced himself. He and Darian both grabbed ahold of the casket doors to open them completely.

In it lay Jack William Finnegan, immediately and remarkably identifiable by his very intact skull and very intact face. The eyes peacefully closed, and light powder applied to give color to the corpses' cheeks.

Tarron felt his stomach twist inexorably. His grip on the casket door loosened completely. It fell open fully and creaked loudly. His hands fiddled around nervously to the Marlboro's in his back pocket.

He wasn't as lucky this time in the selection of unbroken cigarettes. Finding none, his fingers picked something else tucked in his back pocket. He brought it out and realized it was the blue Jolly-Rancher that Alina had given him.

He almost could laugh. He unwrapped the candy and popped it into his mouth. Only after, when the ringing in his ears died out, did he realize Darian had been speaking.

"…holy shit, I thought he shot himself? And what's that in his hands?" Darian asked as he moved closer to examine.

It was the second thing Tarron had immediately noticed when he opened the coffin. It came as equal in consternation as Jack's unscathed face.

In his hands was a necklace, which at first glance, one may have dismissed as simply a rosary. But Tarron saw no cross dangling at the end of it. Instead, he saw a small pendant.

Tarron stayed seated in place. He had an answer to Darian's question but none of his own. The necklace being grasped by the deceased body of his best friend was the same as described by Celeste earlier that day.

Like her mother used to wear.

But definitely not the same regular blue.

In his hands was an ebony black pendant with a crimson red eye that almost seemed to glow in the center.

11

Ashe is Our Purist Form

IN TARRON'S opinion, the older gentleman who let them into the animal crematorium did not have as many questions as you may expect one to have when two men walk in carrying a dead body-shaped trash bag at 2 in the morning. Darian seemed to know the man well enough for that bit to be an impasse, apparently.

Tarron had far too many other questions of his own clouding his judgment. Every new event was something beyond surreal—to a point where he was telling himself it was all normal. It must've been a dormant survival instinct kicking in to keep him sane. That—or he was in shock. For some reason, the voice of his internal monologue began to sound like Steve from Blue's Clues, narrating each event as though to a child.

We're going over to take Jack to a veterinary hospital. Yes, of course, you know the Vet who runs it, Darian. You two are great friends. Oh no—it seems we can't possibly fit Jack's body in the burn chamber. Whatever shall we do?

Tarron had jokingly proposed that they saw Jack in half. Just to see what Darian's reaction would be to such a suggestion when they both realized it was the only way the body was going to fit into the smaller cremation chamber normally suited for canines.

"No, that wouldn't work. We don't have a proper bone saw. Or time." He had said flatly.

Of course. A bone saw. Silly me.

Broken limbs and bodily contortion will have to do.

Darian's anatomy knowledge helped him break Jack's arms and legs in the right places, but with the first crack of Jack's shoulder joint Tarron could spot a small look of surprise on Darian's face. As if to say, *'oh, that actually worked, neat.'* He was about to comment how this bluntness might make him more suited for the morgue rather than a hospital dealing with live patients.

He held his tongue. His brain reminded him that Darian's situation wasn't quite that simple. That he may never finish his degree before his cancer becomes harder to hide.

That first crack, too, violent as it was, churned his stomach worse than any food poisoning he'd experienced. When Tarron was eight years old, he distinctly remembered the sound of breaking his radius when he fell from his bike and braced himself with outstretched hands. He had long forgotten the pain of that incident—but the sharp, peculiar sound of it breaking was forever ingrained in his head.

Tarron excused himself from the room to go wait in the main building. The crematory was housed in a separate building, unattached to the veterinary clinic. Before excusing himself to return home, Dr. Ulrich had felt the need to explain the reason for this:

"I originally had the crematorium consolidated into the main clinic. Thought I could offer folk the convenience of euthanizing and cremating their dog all in one place. But I didn't account for the smell. Most places tell ya that a cremated body smells similar to charred pork. And at nicer places, you can't tell 'cause of fancy ventilation systems—but can't fool an animal that has fifty times the number of receptors in their nose than humans! Dogs began freakin' out when their owners brought them in. It really hurt business, and I started losing clients. The setup for the crematorium was already bleeding me money as is, so I moved it to a separate building outside."

There was something peculiar about watching Jack's limbs flail around as Darian forced them free of their sockets that made Tarron sick as well, maybe not quite as frantic as the dogs who could smell the scent of death—but close.

He hadn't anticipated the waiting around in the lobby of the main building to torment him even more. He was anxious and impatient.

The clinic appeared as typical as any for the place to take your ailing canine or feline friend. A slew of signs hung in the waiting room reminding clients to book appointments using their new app for seamless scheduling. Another sign showed a blonde lady holding her similarly blonde golden retriever. The caption read, How to tell your dog has worms. He read every sign over—there was an absence of trashy magazines for him to sift through instead.

Any patience he had in reserve was gone. It had been at least an hour. He got up and reentered the crematorium.

The fluorescent lights held an ominous glow inside the building, and the peculiar smell in the air made Tarron scowl. Darian saw the look on his face and offered him a blue surgical mask. Tarron accepted it graciously.

"Sorry about that. Forgot to mention how bad formaldehyde

can be." Darian emphasized, pointing at a dish he had placed to the side to catch the excess fluid. He continued to work on Jack's legs and hips.

The cremation chamber itself allowed for a dog as large as a Great Dane to be reduced to ash. The problem was the clearance and length. They figured folding a regular-sized person effectively in half would solve this issue. Darian himself had even climbed into the chamber to get a gauge of how much a human body would need to be contorted to make it work.

Tarron would've offered assistance if Darian had asked, but he wanted to go without having to handle the body.

In between breaking the limbs, Tarron had heard Darian mumbling under his breath about how much longer the process would all take.

"...normally takes bout' 3 hours... but we're working with half the power... and that's if the flames are to the same temp."

CRACK

"...and then we have to process the ash...does Don have all the supplies?"

CRACK

Darian finished separating Jack's tibia from the hip socket. It was the last limb that needed to be adjusted before they attempted to stuff the body into the chamber.

"All done?" Tarron asked modestly.

"You should get some sleep, T. It's gonna take about six or so hours for the body to fully cremate. You can help me with the ashes when it's done."

Tarron looked down at his watch. It read out: 1:58 AM. All at once, his muscles realized how much they should ache after the fight with Darian and the excavation of the grave. He wasn't gonna argue with an open invitation to rest.

"Yeah, I can manage that, I think." He responded.

"Don has a couch in his office. And don't worry about knocking. He left me the keys and instructions so I wouldn't burn down the place. He had to get back home to his basset hound."

Tarron nodded and started towards the exit before Darian called out to him again.

"Hey, before you go, can you take that?" He jabbed his thumb at the box they had filled with Jack's suit and the other things he had on him.

A chill suddenly rushed over Tarron at the thought of it. He swallowed his cowardice quickly and nodded again at Darian. He wasn't going to argue this matter either. But lord knows he wanted to be as far away from that pendant as he could. Celeste's superstitions were creeping upon him, and he was trying to protect himself from any-and-all hoodoo, devilry, or occult juju possible.

More pressing a matter, though; he wanted answers to however or whoever put Jack in the ground. The pendant, inauspiciously, was a start. Tracking down Diana, the alleged fiancé, was as well.

It sounded crazy. But if he had any inclination…it would be that if he waited around long enough—crazy would find him. All he had to do was relax and let it.

He walked over to Jack's body and laid his hand on his old friend's dislocated shoulder. The body was cold and frigid to his fingertips. He felt goosebumps rise along his arm and a small shake followed throughout his core. Jack himself was long gone. This body barely paralleled what he was in life. Laying unnaturally with limbs at odd angles, color completely drained from his face.

Jack Finnegan, the university track star who could shotgun a beer, educate you on the Buddhist dharma, and tell you why Shrek 2 was the best sequel to ever exist, all in one breath. His best friend in the world. One he had grown with.

And his same friend whom he abandoned over squabbles about a girl.

Nope, nope, nope. Forgive yourself, motherfucker. Get over it. Focus on what's important right now. Tarron told himself. Time to start asking the right questions.

Did Jack fly too close to the sun in his study of cults? Or was Diana somewhere to blame?

There had been a running motto in their dorm room regarding questionable female companions. Elucidated by their own Magnus's hook-up-gone-wrong story:

The girl had simple requests when the night began… but as it ended Tarron remembered Magnus pulling him and Jack aside to ask what the girl meant by 'tossing his salad.'

"Is the girl asking me if I am a vegetarian? Is this an American thing?"

Jack and Tarron didn't answer their friend's question. Booze and uncontrollable laughter inebriated them. The thought of Magnus going home with the girl and finding out for himself firsthand what she meant made them laugh even harder.

And he did. It became one of the most referred-to inside jokes between them. *"Ask Magnus how he likes his salad."*

The lesson was simple: one would be wise to avoid sleeping with any and all questionable women, if possible. However, the phrase in practice was less elegant. Spelled out on a banner and hung proudly in their dorm room.

"Don't stick your dick in crazy."

I guess that worked out well for the both of us, huh, Jack?' Tarron thought. *Although, I think I'll take Celeste's specific flavor of crazy over whatever it was that got you here.*

Did he want to know? Would an answer be satisfying enough to explain why he couldn't apologize to Jack for cutting him out of his life over something petty?

Tarron walked into Don Ulrich's office. It was cozy, by all means. His desk was simple but made from beautiful mahogany or cherry, maybe birch. Tarron knew his dad could've told him which. A matching bookcase stood tall to the left. On the wall hung an analog clock, ticking away. Behind the desk was a tall brown leather chair. Donald Ulrich VMD is embroidered on the headrest. Perpendicular to the desk, a black suede couch lined the wall invitingly. An old photo of a young Don in a camo-green military uniform hung next to his diploma.

This is how a man's office should look, Tarron thought. He sat at the desk chair and began to sift through the box, and withdrew the blank pendant. It felt dull and cold in the palm of his hand. He ran his thumb over the beady red eye in the center. A terrible feeling inside him crept up as he looked at it. He understood the obsession Tolkien's characters had with the One Ring. The magic came from his own belief that something evil this way had come or would come. And had taken his friend.

Darian's enthusiastically booming voice came into earshot as he rounded the corner. Tarron quickly shoved the pendant into his pocket.

"So yeah, he's all set up and burnin' away. By my best guess, it'll be about 5-ish hours before we can collect the ashes and get him outta here. It was a bitch to get his whole body in there, but I didn't think he'd mind be contorted like a Jacob's ladder."

"Darian, I have to say… doesn't this all seem like some of the most messed up shit?"

"Pardon?"

"I feel like I'm going to go clinically insane unless I actually address it out loud. Let's just like… backtrack a bit, okay? We just dug up, transported, and pretty much mutilated the dead body of your brother—who, I know you didn't know too well, but he was one of the closest people to me for a majority of my life…" Tarron trailed off, losing his train of thought. "Yeah, no. That just about covers it." He finished. Darian yawned before sitting down next to Tarron and clasped his shoulder.

"The evil we commit in the name of necessity often begets any answer any red-blooded American could come up with. See, I stopped asking why God is cruel and just started wondering what I should do next to make life less dreary. If that includes breaking a cadaver's arms to help someone out—then hell, I'm happy to be the one.

"Fate has it that the cadaver and I share DNA, 'magine that. And it also just so happens that that 'someone' is my new best friend."

"Well…thanks, Darian, I'm uh," he scratched his head, looking for the right combination of words, "I'm more than grateful you walked into my bar that night. Maybe even grateful for getting stabbed. Who knows?"

Darian was mid-yawn when Tarron finished his sentence and started to laugh.

"I would have come in more. It's not like you had to get stabbed and show up at my place of work!"

At certain times, when silence between people seems pregnant with the unsaid, Tarron liked to stay quiet just a moment longer than necessary to hear out whoever was speaking. It was a trick his father had told him and one he practiced over his time working at the bar. People loved to talk when you gave them the floor. It had worked well enough with Darian at the graveyard. He figured he'd try again. Dr. Ulrich's clock ticked on.

"You're wondering about my dad, aren't you? Why I lied," Darian said.

There it is. Tarron thought, vaguely satisfied.

"Now, who said that you lied? I was just wondering what else you were choosing not to tell me. Listen, I'm not exactly a nosey guy. People tell me their personal shit unwarranted all the time, occupational hazard" Tarron held his hands up in a shrug, "But I'd appreciate a little more decency from my partner in crime for the foreseeable future."

"Ya got me there. T" Darian grinned. "Here's the thing: I'll tell you everything ya wanna know. Just ask me nicely."

"Alright then," Tarron responded. Slight suspicion crept up in his chest, and he felt a shake in his voice as he began to speak. "H-how," he coughed hard, "Mm. Sorry, what did you do with your father, then? If you weren't at the hospital."

Darian crossed his arms. "We had a chat. Threatened him. Asked where Jack was buried."

"So, you didn't go to the funeral?" Tarron beamed.

"I mean—I didn't know about it. I wanted to beat him to death for hurting my mom, but...." He trailed off.

"Are you even capable? I know you hit me pretty hard, but—murder?" Tarron asked, slightly taken aback.

Darian held up his hands in a shrug "Eh? I'm undecided."

"Why did you and your mom leave? If you don't mind my asking." Tarron changed the subject.

Darian's face darkened slightly, and he began to wring his hands; he stopped and finally exhaled. "Did you know that the average person's earliest memory they can recall is when they're two-and-a-half? It can be anything as simple as a nice memory of being held by a parent or pain from scraping a knee at a playground.

"I was probably three that night. It was just Ma and me'. Jack probably was at your house or something. But then James came home from work.

"I remember him screaming at mom. I was playing with a Tonka truck—Jack's Tonka truck. Actually, he never let me play with them when he was home. I remember looking into the kitchen and seeing James hit Ma. And hitting her. And hitting her. Kicking her over and over. And her screaming. I'll never forget that pure shriek of terror and pain. I remember just crying for what felt like forever until cops came and took James away. The neighbors had to have called. Ma was taken off in an ambulance, and this lady from CPS picked me up and took me away. But she let me keep the Tonka truck. They took care of me for a couple of days until Ma got out of the hospital."

"That's right... I remember Jack stayed with us for the rest of that week. My mom really tried to get you, too, but CPS wasn't allowing it. Something about parental consent or whatever."

Tarron broke in. "Sorry, I didn't mean to interrupt."

"You're fine, T. I haven't told this story in a long, long time. Anyway, though, about a week later, Ma and I moved to Tahoe with her sister, and Jack stayed here. I never knew why. But I never really knew about that night until she sat me down one day before I left for the Air Force."

"What's that?"

"Ma was pregnant when James beat her. Maybe four weeks or so. I'll never know if that was what they had been fighting over. But whatever it was, Ma came out of it changed forever. So did I, I'spose. It drew me back to Wyoming. I could be living out the rest of my short life at UCLA or some other fancy college. Air Force to pays regardless." Darian finished and sat back on the couch.

"Christ, Darian. I don't even know what to say. And I'm sorry to keep saying that, but—"

"Shut up. You're fine, T" Darian waved his hands.

"Listen, I'm... horrified and just sorry you had to live through that. No one should have to."

"Dude." Darian cut him off. "All this," He waved his other hand in the air, "is just a big dance before we get tossed in the soup."

Am I just that sleep-deprived, or did he just say soup? Tarron thought.

"Can you... elaborate on that?" He said aloud, bracing himself for another five-minute philosophy seminar.

"No. I'm gonna take a nap." He turned onto his side and stretched out his legs "Goodnight! Or good morning, rather."

He turned over once more to chirp, "I have a timer set for when we need to check the burner, so... yeah."

Tarron let his head hang back against the headrest of the chair and tried not to think about Tonka trucks.

***

Tarron didn't know how his body managed to wake up 5 minutes prior to the alarm going off. He sat there momentarily, unaware of where he was.

The alarm continued to blare and jolted him into fruition. The incessant ringing had no observable effect on Darian himself. The man did not stir. Tarron strode over to him and shook his shoulder. He heard him softly groan before silencing the alarm on his phone and rolling back over.

"Darian. Wake-up." Tarron began to shake him. No avail.

Darian would not wake. He had managed to take off his shirt and hoodie, and Tarron was tempted to slap back as hard as humanely possible to get the man to wake. Something he and Jack used to do.

He decided against it and stood up straight, stretching out his limbs, craning his neck side-to-side, and rubbing it heartily to eliminate the new knots that developed over the last few hours. He looked down and realized he had kicked off his boots in his sleep. He began to lace them up when a young woman in various brands of sports clothing walked into the clinic holding the leash to a comically large baby polar bear.

Tarron could see the women through the shudders on the office door. He rubbed his eyes.

It was a dog. A very large dog. With more fluffy, white fur than he could conceive on a canine. Tarron rushed to lace his boots up and cleared his throat loudly as he exited the office to catch her attention.

Time to bullshit. He put on his best customer-service voice.

"Hi ma'am, sorry we're closed today. The doc—uh, Doctor Ulrick is out today."

"*Ulrich?*" She corrected him. The dog beside her sat down and stared up wordlessly at Tarron.

"Uh... right. Yes him. Out sick. Sorry about that."

"But this is an emergency. Hap has terrible diarrhea. He is a Siberian Samoyed Ovcharka mix and should not be having issues like this. And this is an emergency veterinary clinic, isn't it?"

"Hap?" Tarron said aloud. The dog in question looked up to him at the mention of its name.

"Yes, he's obviously not his usual self. Can't you see?"

Tarron made eye contact with the oversized mutt again. He looked fine to him. Before he looked away, he could've sworn the dog narrowed his eyes at him.

"I'm not really qualified to help you, ma'am. But listen, if Hap is still having stomach problems, you can feed him chicken and rice. That's usually what my mom would do for our dog growing up."

"You don't work here, do you?"

Tarron began to feel a slight amount of panic rise up in his chest. His mind immediately went to Plan B: get rid of her as soon as possible. There was no plan C. Before he could even answer the woman, she furrowed her brow and stared intently at him before opening her mouth.

"You're Alina's father, aren't you?" She piped loudly.

"Yes, I am," Tarron answered immediately and instinctively. After the words left his mouth, he found himself wanting to ask the woman how, in the ever-loving-fuck, did she know that.

"Sorry, what's your name? Celestyna just always refers to you as 'Alina's Father.' A better title than 'baby daddy,' though."

"Uh—it's Tarron. But how do you know Cellie—"

"Hot Yoga!" she interrupted. Hap sat up suddenly at her outburst, and Tarron felt his heart drop for a moment, a feeling akin to how early humans must've felt. Recognizing that a predator was aware of his presence.

"Hap, sit!" The woman commanded. Hap sat, then exhaled loudly. Tarron thought it could've been a disappointed sigh.

"Anyways," she continued, "Celestyna and I go to hot yoga

every Friday night. We usually go out for drinks afterward, and she complains to me about you. She showed me a photo last week of you and Alina when you took her fishing—so cute!"

"Complains about me? Wow, I—"

"I'm not finished," She cut in. "She complains to me about how much she misses her baby daddy, how much she also hates him, and how much she wishes Alina wouldn't resent her for not being with him."

"Are those… recurring topics?" Tarron probed.

"Oh, almost exclusively. I thought once about cutting the girl off, but I figured a couple of rounds of drinks on her *always*—she insists, and some free advice from yours truly is a lot cheaper than therapy. That's all you sometimes need anyways, just someone to vent to."

"Well, in that case, I hope I don't disappoint you anymore than Celeste has led you to believe," Tarron managed to say, scrounging for any response that made him seem… not what she had already made him out to be.

"What's your name, by the way?" He asked.

"Juliet Florentine. Call me Jules." She immediately extended a hand. Tarron shook it apprehensively; Hap's eyes seemed to follow his every movement. The woman had a vice-grip handshake.

Tarron heard the metal clank of a door closing behind him and turned to see what had caused it. Darrian McConnell strode his way over to him, Juliet tund Hap, pulling on a white lab coat as he walked.

Juliet's demeanor changed immediately and noticeably. Tarron watched her tuck her already well-kept hair behind her ear.

"Hi there, ma'am. I see Tarron here, as I already greeted you and probably informed you that Dr. Ulrich, unfortunately, is not in the office today. If there's an emergency, I'm sure we can refer you to someone else. And if it's anything other than that, I'm sure I can help you." Darian announced. His customer service voice seemed considerably more practiced than Tarron's.

Nursing student with cancer — 1, depressed alcoholic bartender — 0.

Hap began to wag his tail furiously as Darian neared. He, noticing this immediately, bent down to rub the top of Hap's head.

"Is there something wrong with this beautiful pup right here?" He asked Juliet while holding eye contact with Hap and continuing to pet the dog.

"He had some stomach problems earlier—wow, he really likes you. Um, he seems better now, but—"

Hap suddenly rolled over. Offering his stomach for further rubs from his new best friend. Darian obliged. Juliet knelt down to scratch the canine's chest as well. She began small talk with Darian that Tarron couldn't quite make out.

"Hey, Dar, is the alarm set to go off soon?" He interjected while walking back to the door. Neither human nor dog acknowledged him.

Tarron was only hearing bits of the conversation between the two of them kneeling beside each other.

"So're you from here?"

"Mhm, born and raised."

"No way, you're far too pretty for Wyoming."

She blushed then laughed lightly, placing her hand invitingly atop Darian's.

Tarron cleared his throat "Darian."

This time it caught his attention, and he turned with a slight look of protest on his face. Tarron made hand signals and tried his hardest to mime that they needed to:

Get rid of her, pointing at Juliet and then the door.

Let's go, thumb hooking behind him towards the crematory.

Come on now, both hands gathering towards himself.

It started to click, and Darian stood up, excusing himself.

"I'm sure Donald can take a look at this sweetheart as soon as he's back, but until then, maybe my associate here can help you out." Darian nodded to Tarron, who tried to smile at her glance, then, with eyes widened, mouthed the word No to Darian.

"Uh… Donald?" She asked.

"Doctor Ulrich, my mistake. If you'd let me, I have something to attend to in the back. Tarron?" Darian looked back at his partner. Hap rolled upright and looked at Tarron as well.

Tarron accepted his fate. He had to distract the woman as much as he could without her raising any questions as to why the two of them were there in the first place, without a dog, the Veterinarian, or why the front door was left open.

If she had any more information about Celeste, though, Tarron wanted to learn all he could. All of his time serving drinks and bullshitting human interaction had led him to this point. Simple mission: extract as much information as he could about his failing (failed) relationship.

"So, you met Celeste through Yoga class?" He began.

Hap barked loudly, and Tarron flinched. The dog immediately rolled over and offered his stomach to Tarron this time. He obliged apprehensively. All he needed now was a bite wound from this fluffy, oversize dog.

***

The conversation was going exceedingly better than he could've hoped as long as he continued to pet Hap's head. It was soothing in a way. Petting the dog and listening to how your ex-lover may or may not still be in love with you. It was fairly hard to tell with the way Juliet told the story.

Tarron looked down at his phone and realized Darian had actually sent half a dozen texts with updates. He tried to read through them quickly.

Darian McConnell: Jack's done. We gotta figure out where to store him.

There's a LOT OF ASH

Juliet continued to orate. "And that's when I told her, you know, 'what are you doing with a man who doesn't believe in horoscope?' The lawyer guy, right? He gives me the creeps. I—"

Tarron needed to end the conversation: "Me too. Definitely. Sorry to cut you off, but Darian and I were actually working on some maintenance, so if you'll excuse me…."

"Oh, well, don't let me keep you any. Come on, Hap." She stood and started towards the door quickly. Hap followed closely. Before she reached the handle, she turned around.

"Here! Before I forget." She said as she handed him a piece of paper. Tarron looked and saw her phone number written on it.

"Oh… um, thanks, I'm flattered, but—"

"Not for you, silly. Give it to your friend for me. Ask him how he feels about polyamory," she said with a wink before exiting.

"Poly-what?" Tarron asked.

"See ya around." She exited through the door. Hap followed

at her heels, and Tarron breathed a sigh of relief and began to walk away. The door opened again.

"Oh hey!" Juliet shoved the door back open "Try to win her back this time. I think you actually have a chance; you know? Anyways, buh-bye now!" She exclaimed as she let the door close.

Hope fluttered within his heart again. This time with a little more foundation. He didn't know if he should trust it.

The moment passed, and he shook the feeling off. He made sure to lock the door of the clinic before making his way to the back of the building to rejoin his partner in crime.

Darian was waiting for him outside the crematory. He was fiddling with his tobacco can and spit as Tarron neared.

"Great! You show up when I'm all finished." Darian said.

Tarron scratched the back of his head. "Sorry man, that girl was friends with Celeste, believe it or not. Which isn't rare—for Cellie to have a friend, I mean, but it is rare for it to be a female friend," He stared at Darian's blank expression. "But that's neither here nor there. Anyway, I think she dug you. She wanted me to give you this." Tarron replied as he handed him the small piece of paper.

Darian looked at it for a second. Smiled, then crumbled up the piece of paper and tossed it into a trashcan next to the door. Tarron shot him a perplexed look.

"All's good. No time to chase tail now. We got a job to do. Besides, there'll be loads of Viking girls when we get to Iceland."

"I thought the point was to spread Jack's ashes there?"

"Hey, as far as I'm concerned—we're both bachelors. But also, before that, we gotta see Papa James again." He finished excitedly.

Tarron continued to look at him blankly with his jaw slightly ajar.

"I'll explain on the way. You're driving."

12

Bang!

"WE CAN'T just put his ashes in a coffee container."

"But it's the only thing here that'll fit it all. Besides, what's wrong with it?"

"It's just too… I don't know—derivative is the word, I think? Did you ever see that movie with Zach Galifianakis?"

"*The Hangover?*"

"No, it was with him and…fuck, I can't remember the other actor's name."

"Bradley Cooper?"

"No, dude. It's not the Hangover."

"*Between Two Ferns?*"

"What? No. That's not even a movie. Just forget it. Let's just find something else to put the ashes in."

"*Dinner for Schmucks?*"

"Dude!"

***

His childhood house had an air of mockery to it in the light of day. At night, he could've squinted, and it could be any other house in the suburb. But painted bright and true in the sunlight, it was undeniably the same house that was seared into his memory.

Welcome back. The toothy grin of the beaten-down wooden fence begged for Darian to tell it otherwise.

Tarron knocked on the truck window and startled him.

"C'mon, man, let's get this over with." the expression Tarron carried on his face implied: *this was your idea, after all.*

Darian swallowed hard, silently hoping that James wouldn't be there, that this would be a dead-end, and they could move on. He was conflicted, even suggesting they come here. But he had seen the way Tarron reacted when they unearthed Jack's body.

A look on his face that wouldn't settle for anything less than the truth or at least something close to it. It was a look Darian had recognized in his brother, as well. Maybe that's why he latched onto Tarron so quickly. In hopes of getting to know the man who was actually his blood. More than the short time he had.

Fate can be funny that way, he thought. He sighed and exited Tarron's truck.

He realized he was lagging behind as he walked.

Tarron was already at the door, about to knock. He wanted to shout out and tell him that they should just turn around. His voice caught in his throat. Before Tarron even brought his hand down on the door, James opened it up.

Darian watched them exchange a few words and a stiff handshake before James peered around Tarron to spot him. The expression on his face hardened; he ushered Tarron inside and then continued to wait outside the door, arms crossed and impassive.

The air felt heavy, as did Darian's chest. His heartbeat struck rigidly, and his legs stiff. He continued to walk forward and close the distance between himself and his father. *Hello, again.*

Neither spoke a word. It was a game of chicken. The consequences of losing felt lethal. He had no intentions of what he may do other than walk forward and say nothing. This was the purgatory that lay in between fight or flight—or the tendency to do neither and freeze.

Tarron broke the silence, calling to both of them from inside the house.

"Let's all head inside and have a chat, huh? We can decide if anybody needs to die or not afterward."

Darian pushed past his father and joined Tarron on the couch, feeling the tension in his chest ease up slightly. Enough for him to breathe. He heard the door shut behind him as James followed them in.

"Can I offer you boys anything to drink? Sorry, the place is a mess. I wasn't expectin' no one," He asked. Tarron answered for the both of them with a solitary 'no.'

Darian took a glance around the room. There was an abundance of boxes half unpacked with items that probably hadn't seen the light of day in several years. Sports trophies, a few yearbooks, and several photo albums. A framed picture sat atop the table next to the couch. He hadn't noticed it before. It was when Jack must have graduated high school based on the youth on his face. He was grinning ear to ear with Tarron's arm across his shoulder, who shared a similar expression. James' face was stern and unsmiling. Darian nudged Tarron to show him the picture.

Tarron leaned to pick it up and held it in his hands, faintly trembling.

"I was looking all over for this picture... I couldn't find it anywhere digitally, but I swore that you or my mom had a copy. Whadda, ya know, I should've just called you up for it."

James peered down at the photo and then sat in his armchair across from the two of them.

"That was the one we used at the funeral. Had to get it blown up and printed out all big n' nice-like. Cost like 50 bucks at Kinko's, but I couldn't find any other ones with him and me together."

"The funeral," Tarron began, lowering his tone, "right…."

"I meant to call your ma' up to send you the information, but it must've slipped my mind. Y'know, after you two moved out to go to college and shit was the last time I think we spoke."

"Well—I came back. Jack stayed," He paused. Darian saw him balling his fists. "You know, I live like five, ten minutes down the road." Tarron said, agitation building in his voice, "Yeah, I live ten fuckin minutes down the road, and I would've liked to know about my best friend's funeral and—"

"Actually, that's why we're here, pop." Darian interrupted. Wondering internally for a moment if he was trying to defuse the situation or shift some of the tension onto himself for Tarron's sake.

"Jack," Tarron said flatly.

"Wha—uh. What d'ya mean," James managed.

"Why was it that when you reported him dead to the world, it was suicide by shotgun? Imagine how surprised we were to dig up Jack's body and find his entire skull and face still there. How's that for confusing?"

James remained silent.

"You had to have known, right?" Tarron continued; voice raised, "You had to of…." He sprang to his feet. "So spit it out! Whatever you're hiding. I'm tired of everything being all kinds of fucked up!"

James shrank back in his chair with his mouth shut. He had stopped wringing his hands and hung his head. He mumbled, barely audible.

"It was that bitch…."

"I'm sorry?" Tarron replied.

"That Euro bitch who brought him here. His girlfriend, or fiancé, or whatever. I ain't never heard of her before, and suddenly she calls me up one day and says my boy is dead. I stopped asking questions after she said he killed himself. My heart already hurt too much."

Darian looked at Tarron's white-knuckled fists and patted his back, motioning him to sit down.

"Calm down there, cowboy. I got this one," he said quietly. He stood up and stretched out his legs before walking over to his father and backhanding him. The sound of his hand against the man's face was a crisp strike of bone against soft flesh. James held his cheek for a moment before he tried to rise out of the chair to retaliate. Darian grabbed the man by his throat and forced him back, pinning him to his seat. With Darian's hand around his neck, he managed to still speak.

"You son of a bitch, you fuckin' come here again and—" James managed.

Darian slapped him with his free hand, open palm this time, across the other cheek.

"Shut up, no, shut the fuck up. That's my mother you're talking about. But hey, this isn't about me. Answer T's question."

James desperately pawed at the hand Darian was choking him with. Darian relaxed his grip slightly.

"I'm gonna let you go, pops. But I will not hesitate to take that fire poker over there and put it through your eyes. Nothing would make me happier right now."

He watched James' eyes dart to the fireplace behind him and back before the man nodded in agreement. Darian released his grip and straightened up.

What are we doing right now? Good cop, bad cop? Tarron thought. He stood up and pocketed his hands into his jacket.

"I'm gonna ask slow and simply." He started, gathering the words he wanted to say. "How did Jack die?"

James opened his mouth before Tarron quickly added, "and don't say he shot himself. We're well past that."

"I—I don't know, then. I don't know what you want me to tell you." James said harshly.

"What about Diana, huh? What does she know? You meet her here?"

"Who?"

"The…" Tarron started, exasperated. "Diana! She's… "The 'Euro bitch'" Darian piped.

"Yes, The Euro bitch, her. The woman who called you. If Jack didn't kill himself, it had to be her."

"She showed up here, casket in tow. Already sayin' that Jack's body was prepared and ready to be buried. She and her weird posse."

"Okay. Now we're getting somewhere," Tarron resounded. He dug into his pocket and withdrew the black pendant they had found on Jack's body.

"Were they all wearing this?"

James recoiled slightly as he'd been hit again. He took one look at the pendant and began to wring his hands again, eyes not willing to meet the object once more.

"Yes." He muttered.

"Give me her number," Tarron demanded.

James wrote it down on a scratch piece of paper and handed it to him with shaky hands. Tarron was done here. He headed to the door and looked back to see if Darian was coming.

I'll be right out; the nod Darian gave indicated. Tarron nodded back and closed the door behind him.

"We still have some other business here, pop," Darian said, pulling out a Glock 19 from his waistband. He held it pointed towards the floor. The color in James' face drained.

"I'm sorry, Darian. I'm sorry. I'm so sorry—please just, don't kill me." He sobbed, rambling on, "I know I was hard on you and Jack, but it was to make you strong. I woulda never laid a hand on your mother if I'd've known. For chrissakes, I'm no murderer. No baby killer. Jesus, fuck. How—how did I ever…Why did she never tell me? Why?"

"Sheesh, I'm not actually threatening your life. Look—" Darian pulled the trigger of the pistol.

It squirted water on James, who jolted backward as if electrocuted. Darian laughed and tucked the pistol back in his pants, then continued to exit the house.

***

They drove in silence back to Tarron's. Several times Tarron tried to make conversation, but neither of the men really wanted to say anything.

Tarron was at the edge of the precipice. He could take the leap to Iceland and spread Jack's ashes or track down the man's fiancé and try to get a definitive answer as to why he killed himself.

Darian, however, was coming to terms that the quiet rage inside him that had been burning for so long was gone. There was nothing left, back to the matter at hand. Support his friend.

The fact that Iceland was several thousand miles (and dollars) away didn't help either's the situation, but neither did the suggestion of facing a mysterious cult alone. Tarron thought about this a lot as he drove.

He figured Darian would want to tag along on the journey, but the man was finishing nursing school as well as battling breast cancer—which, in and of itself, sounded like the setup to a bad joke. The punchline of which he didn't know yet.

He parked his truck in his driveway and looked at Darian before turning off the vehicle.

"How bad is it?" He asked, pausing "your cancer, I mean. How bad?" Darian breathed in deeply and shrugged.

"Why? Are you worried about me or what, T?"

"No, I just mean like… ah, forget I asked." He responded as he pulled the keys from the ignition and started to exit the truck.

"Wait, wait. Alright, yeah, it's bad but not bad, bad. You know what I mean?" He rambled, "It's not like 'hey, you got a week left to live' bad. It's just—I didn't want to keep it a total secret, but I know I wasn't gonna be able to hide it forever. It's my demon

to face and I'm gonna do it my way."

"By ignoring it?"

"You're funny. Anyway, here take Jack." Darian handed him Jack's ashes. Contained entirely in a large metal dog food tin they had emptied, cleaned, and ripped the label off of. Darian had taken a sharpie and written JACK W. FINNEGAN in big letters and 1992-2018 underneath.

"What're you gonna do for the rest of the day?" Tarron asked casually.

"Uh, go to the hospital. Email professors. Tell them all I'm taking the rest of the semester off."

"Uh. What? Why?"

"Dude, we have to go to Iceland. Duh. I can afford to miss all my finals for this. Just gotta say something like, 'Hey, sorry, teach, I can't take my exams because of the trauma of my brother's passing. Blah, blah, blah, or something like that. Then they gotta let me take my exams late, or they're assholes. And if they choose to be assholes, the Air Force pays my tuition, either way. I don't. So, fuck 'em', that's why."

Tarron glanced at Jack inside his metal tin for support.

You hearing this shit, Jack?

He looked at Darian's grinning face and stayed silent for a minute before realizing that the man had decided for him. As Robert Plant wrote: they were going to the land of ice and snow where the midnight sun and the hot springs glow.

***

'What to pack to visit Iceland.' A simple google search led Tarron down a rabbit hole of information. There was a regular assortment of information and travel blogs. But they were akin to recipe blogs that insisted on telling you a very long and detailed story before actually listing the items you came to the page for.

He sifted through dozens of these websites before landing on a very clear-cut guide called "RUCKING THE WORLD WITH GUNNY SIMMONS." The website was plain -looking and very poorly designed. That's what Tarron initially liked about it. The author was a 20-year Marine Corps veteran-turned backpacker who laid out the bare essentials of what you needed—wherever you were going. Gunny then offered a brief description of what was necessary for traveling and what was "pointless, backpack touristy bullshit."

The colorful prose in which Gunny wrote reminded Tarron warmly of his father. Men from the same generation.

Tarron was basing his packing list on Gunny's trip across Scandinavia. Entitled: *How I froze my twig and berries off, then fought a Swedish wendigo.*

```
1xLarge backpack/ruck -
  Invest in a reliable backpack. This is like
the foundation of a house. Places like REI might
charge you an arm and a leg for one. Avoid
places like that. I like Sportsman's or
Cabela's.
1xSleeping system (sleeping bag) -
  Unless you want to freeze your twig and
berries off, do not skimp out here. Try to visit
your local military surplus store and ask for a
USMC sleeping system.
1xPair of hiking boots -
  Iceland is an active volcano in disguise as
an island. One false step on your hike, and
your trip ends early.
1xHatchet -
  No matter where I ruck or camp, I always keep
a hatchet handy. It'll get you out of whole
lotta situations, like fighting a Norse demon.
```

Tarron read through the rest of the list and felt relieved when he realized he already owned a majority of the items listed out, save the hatchet. They were packed away in storage in his shed, and he could mentally picture the blue storage tub they were in.

He scoured every nook and cranny for the tub but to no avail. Frustrated, he sat on the cement ground of his back patio and thought about where else it could be packed. He pulled out his phone and dialed his mother's phone.

"What do you mean you gave all that stuff to Celeste… no, it's just one box… yeah, I'm uh, going on a trip with friends… yes, mom, I have friends… yes, I've looked there…that was in our old apartment ma'… yes, I looked there… ma' you know she lives with that lawyer guy, you know this… uh, huh. Yeah, bye ma'… Yes, I'll bring you back something. Okay. Okay. Love you too."

He sat at his desk and rubbed his temple. If his mother was correct, Celeste somehow ended up with his box of camping gear. He looked at everything else he had laid out on the floor.

Winter clothes, check, boots, check… Alright, no sleeping bag, no hatchet, and no ruck.

He unlocked his phone and navigated to his banking app. Then back to Gunny's travel blog, then back to his bank app. Finally, sighing, he opened up his contacts list and dialed.

"Hey, it's me… oh hi chicken, no, put mommy on the phone, please…Thanks, chicken. I love you… *hey* Cellie, I need to come by. My mom said you had a box of my camping stuff for some reason…yeah, a big blue storage tub…no, it's okay; I'll come to you… awesome…okay, love you, bye."

As soon as the words left his lips, he felt a flutter in his heart, realizing what his head had let the mouth say. It was something that was so routine for so many years while they had been together. He asked himself if he meant it or if it was simply a faux pas. With a resounding 'yes' in his heart, he knew he did.

Cellie was still on the line.

"I love you too, Tarron."

Click.

He felt trepidation creep up from somewhere in his stomach. The drive from his house to Celeste seemed to pass in an instant, and he found himself quickly approaching their driveway, watching the snowfall and waiting for the courage to walk into the house. This was a lull-in-between moment of action, and moving forward felt impossible.

He drove on. Anxiety told him it was gonna blow up in his face. He told anxiety to go fuck itself.

He parked and walked to the front of the house. Snowfall seemed to be coming to a halt, and the sun was beginning to peak out. Tarron looked at his watch. It read 12:23 PM.

He rang the doorbell.

Alina opened the door and immediately frowned when she recognized him.

"Hmph. Mommy said you're leaving us."

"Well, hello to you too, chicken. Not even a hug for your dad, and what'd mommy say? huh?" Tarron responded as he scooped her up and started tickling her sides. "Yeah, I'm leaving forever! You're never gonna see me again," He joked with her.

She giggled and played along. "Good! I hope I don't."

"Alina! I told you I'd get the door," Celeste called as she appeared from behind. Tarron put Alina down to greet Celeste. They locked eyes for a split second before she brushed her hair back and got down to business.

"Tarron, hello." She said awkwardly.

"Hello yourself," he responded.

She pursed her lips and turned around without indicating him to follow. She talked as she walked. Tarron shot Alina a look and gave her a very exaggerated eye roll. She mirrored him and did the same. Their secret.

"—So, I don't actually know where your box of camping stuff is, but I swear I've seen it in the garage, so you can help me look. Ian's in Cheyenne for a couple of days with his office, so…" Celeste stated.

"You're kidding me" He sighed, almost inaudible. She didn't seem to notice. "You can back your truck into the garage so we can load the stuff when we find it, though."

"Alrighty then," Tarron looked down at his daughter, "Do you wanna ride with daddy while I do that? I'll let you drive." Alina agreed gleefully.

Celeste was out of view, and he heard her call once more. "I'll open the garage but hurry up!"

Alina was happy to sit on his lap and pretend she was controlling the steering wheel as her father backed into the garage. She gave up quickly and started crawling around the front seat. She was humming an almost unidentifiable Christmas song. The tune ran laps in Tarron's head curiously before he reminded himself that it was mid-December.

"You like Mariah Carry?" He asked her

"Hm?" Alina responded, looking up at her dad's chin.

"The song, baby. The one you're humming."

"Oh yeah." She began, *I don wanna lot for Chrissmas…*" and continued the rest in a hum.

"What'd mom say about me leaving?" He asked. He saw the garage door open up and shifted the truck into reverse. Alina stopped humming.

"She said you have to go somewhere with your friend, Jack."

Tarron's eyes darted to the glovebox in which he had put the dog food tin, then back to watching Celeste in his rearview mirror wave him back into position.

"Something like that, hun…." He agreed.

"Are you gonna miss my birthday again?"

The question took him by surprise. Celeste and Tarron had

always made a point to celebrate Christmas on Christmas eve. That way, Alina had her own day.

"I'll be there, chicken. I promise." He spoke.

"What're these?" Alina asked, holding up a baggie full of black and white seeds.

"Uhhh…" Tarron said quickly, snatching the bag and tossing it onto the dashboard. "Just something a friend gave me."

Alina crossed her arms and pouted as her dad pulled the truck in, eyes not leaving the baggie.

With the combined efforts of two able-bodied adults and one partially distracted, 4-nearly-5-year-old, they successfully unloaded, combed through, and scoured just about every compartment of Ian's garage with zero lead on the storage tub. One innocuous box remained. Perched on the very top shelf.

Celeste left to retrieve a step ladder. Alina had grown bored with the search, so Tarron committed the cardinal sin of 21st-century parents and gave her his smartphone.

He let his mind wander as he waited. Darting back and forth from Iceland to the path of actually getting there. The excitement of being on the cusp of something he fantasized about for over a decade. He tried to remember when he last genuinely felt excited about something. It was the same giddy feeling of anticipation the night preceding an elementary school field trip.

He realized he'd been pacing beside his truck. Alina had opened the door to the house and disappeared inside. He could hear the footsteps of Celeste rounding the corner. She entered and placed the step ladder down. Climbed up and reached her hands assiduously towards the top shelf.

"Cel, let me get it. You're not tall enough," Tarron said. She ignored him, reaching still, fingertips barely away from the edge of the box.

"Celeste…" He insisted.

"I got it, okay, I got—" Celeste's hands grasped the outside of the box as she lost her balance, pulling the box free from the shelf with her as she fell. Tarron rushed to catch her and flung his hands around her waist. As he braced her from falling, Celeste released her grip on the box. It landed with a curious sound of glass crunching.

"Thanks…Celeste gasped as she stood upright.

"Did you hear that? When the box fell?" He asked as he bent down to move the box from where it landed. As he did, his eyes confirmed what his ears had suggested. The shattered, blinking screen of his smartphone lay underneath. "Goddammit, Alina…" He whispered.

"Hey, you said your stuff was in a blue storage tub, right?" Celeste began, pointing towards the spot where the box had been withdrawn. Lo and behold, Tarron recognized his own handwriting scrawled out in a black sharpie: Camping Shit.

"Yeah, that'd be the one," he sighed, scrapping up the leftover remains of his overpriced talk box from the ground. He tapped the screen a couple of times with his palm and tried the home button on the device.

No response. Time of death… he checked his watch.

"Oh shit, did the box fall on your phone?" Celeste asked before covering her face and stifling back laughter.

"I'm sorry—" she began. "I know this isn't funny," she continued, trying to reclaim her composure before clearing her throat loudly. "Mm, yeah, okay. Fuck, sorry, Tarron. I should've just let you get the box and—"

"It's fine. I mean, it's not really fine, but I'll manage… it is pretty funny, though. 'Lina is gonna be mad she can't play any more games on it tonight."

"Oh, if that's why it was on the ground, then I take it back. That's all your fault there, buckaroo."

Tarron nodded, *yeah yeah, I know*, and exhaled. He climbed the step ladder to grab the blue camping tub, brought it down, and placed it in the bed of his truck.

He walked back around and stood in front, searching for something to say but not finding any words to suffice. He figured he'd get out before he said something stupid.

"Well… I guess I should head ou—"

"Your hand!" Celeste gasped suddenly.

Tarron looked down; the crease of his left hand was slick with blood. He hadn't noticed the shattered screen of the broken smartphone had worked tiny incisions into his palm.

"We have a first aid kit inside, c'mon" Celeste grabbed his right hand and led him inside before he could raise a protest. She dressed his wound with the same care as he'd seen her treat their daughter. The daughter, who, after making sure dad was fine, made her way to the designated corner of the living room to graffiti her Disney princess coloring book. Quietly entertained by her own design.

"That should do it," Celeste said as she wrapped Tarron's hand in gauze.

"Thanks, doc. Do I get a jolly rancher?"

"No, sorry, those are reserved for special patients." Celeste laughed, "So, when do you and Darren leave?"

"Darian." He corrected, "And tonight. He's picking me up in his jeep, and we're gonna drive from my place to Cheyenne and then fly out from there to New York City. Then onto Iceland…"

"Ohhh. Ok, cool."

"Did you wanna… talk about what you said on the phone?"

Celeste crossed her arms. "I stand by what I said. There's no double-depth there."

"So, what about Ian?"

Celeste laughed sheepishly *"Zrobili mnie w konia…* why did I know you were gonna say that? I don't know why I was hoping you wouldn't. Listen, Tarron—" She sat down next to him. "I'll tell you a secret. Ian, the guy that you must hate and must think, is the villain in your own road to redemption story, is just a man. A very nice man. But I don't love him, and he knows that. He opened up his home to your daughter and me as a favor to a friend in need because I couldn't be around you last year.

"You let your father's death be an excuse for you then, and now Jack's death and you in the hospital. But you are not allowed to give up on the responsibilities you have to me. But more importantly to her" She pointed at Alina. "I'll tell you another secret about Ian," she continued, grabbing his hand and leaning in close to his ear, and whispered, "We've never even slept together."

As she pulled away, their eyes locked. Tarron felt his heart palpitate. He was looking at her lips. The curve of her cupid's bow. The cleavage of her breasts barely peeked out from her blouse.

He kissed her. And she kissed back. Hands moved quickly as they rose from their seats. Alina hardly looked up from her coloring book as her parents hurriedly exited the room.

13

Everyone Remain Calm

"SO, WHAT changed your mind, son?" Officer Graft asked as Tarron handed him the keys to his truck.

Well, to be honest, I'm not sure if my mind is made up entirely.

"I'm taking a big trip overseas. Need someone to look after her while I'm gone." He said sarcastically. The joke must've gone right over Graft's head, given the deadpan look on his face.

"I'm not gonna—uh, foster your truck, son. We actually only drove over here 'cause' my partner and I were on our way back to the station," he said, digging out his wallet from a back pocket. "So, three large is what we agreed?" Graft asked.

"Yessir. Uh, do you just—have three thousand dollars in cash on you at all times?"

"Listen, buddy. You called me. Now, do you want to sell the truck or not?"

"Yeah, screw it. Need the money." Tarron whispered under his breath.

"What was that?"

"Sold. To the man who saved my life!" He extended his hand,

and Graft shook it heartily.

"Do ya need to clean it out or anything like that?" Graft asked.

"No, sir. When y'all impounded it, originally, it got pretty scrubbed—minus the blood, of course. But that came out with some peroxide and patience."

"Well, in that case… Merry Christmas, sir." Graft said as he began to count out $100 bills.

As officer Graft and his partner drove away, Tarron felt a sudden weight drop in his heart. Saying goodbye to that truck felt rough but necessary.

There was a lot of history within its four' doors and the miles laid down on the road. Old memories, new inflections.

So long, and thanks for all the fishing trips!

He returned to the house to retrieve his pack. As he did, his landline rang.

***

Celeste's pace quickened as she heard the pre-recorded voicemail greeting of Tarron's landline. The call had been diverted immediately, and as she waited to leave a message, she felt callous for laughing at his broken cell phone earlier.

She paced across the floor, around the house, into her room, the garage, and back. Searching again all areas she had already poured through looking for her daughter. There was no greater fear that could grip her heart since she had become a mother.

Any resentment left for Tarron she had left was now replaced by guilt of her own. She asked how she could've been so careless to lose their daughter.

Celeste tried to recall the last time she had seen her. It had only been an hour but felt like an era apart. She retraced that last hour carefully.

Tarron and her had been in bed for at least thirty minutes. The last twenty-five of which they spent embracing and talking about the future before she went to shower and he departed. She had heard him say goodbye to Alina before he left, and she had made a mental note to heat up leftovers for the two of them to eat for lunch. But when she exited the bathroom, Alina vanished. Apparated into thin air.

Celeste wanted to scream until her lungs burst. Instead, she took a deep breath, sat down on the living room couch, and prepared to leave Tarron a message.

"Tarron, call me immediately. Alina is gone, and I can't find her anywhere. I'm leaving now to drive around the neighborhood and look. Please call me. Please."

As she pulled the phone away, she heard an automated voice informing her that *the person's number she had dialed had a mailbox that was full. If she would like to leave a call-back number, press 5. For other services, please—*

"MOTHERFUCKER!" She yelled, slamming the phone into the couch cushion.

***

"Okay, got it. See you in a bit. Cedar Street, Darian. Just—no, just honk when you get here. I'm already packed. I gotta let you go. I think there's someone else calling me. Yeah, gotcha. Later."

Tarron hung up the phone and tried to redial the number that was trying to reach him. Darian was going to be here in about 30 minutes and needed to be reminded how to get to his house. Tarron walked around his living room with the phone pinned between his shoulder and ear, hauling his blue Osprey backpack. It was heavy with clothing, cold weather gear, and miscellaneous hiking supplies.

The line continued to ring. No response. If it was important, then whoever it was would call back or leave him a message. That's what his parents always said. He shrugged and continued to take a mental inventory. He had the tickets in his back pocket, printed out last night. He was amazed that the vouchers were redeemable with such short notice and that flights to Reykjavik were even available.

He pulled them out and turned the envelope around curiously. There was a black, smudged handwritten note tucked inside he hadn't noticed before. He peered intently at the lines and tried to discern them. Only a couple of sentences, but the smudging turned it into nonsense:

"I couldn't stop?" Tarron wondered.

Hidden clues and cryptic endings are back on the table. He rushed back to his bedroom and pulled out Jack's letter to re-read it. Line by line.

Nothing. He sighed loudly to an empty room in frustration. He walked back into the living room, collapsed on the couch, and closed his eyes. He let his mind wander, and fantastic ideas take over.

C-h-r, 2013. 2013... What happened in 2013? That was college. That was sophomore year... the year Jack broke up with Cellie. The same year I started dating her. And also, around the same time, I knocked her up. Or was that 2014?

Alina was born in December of 2014, so that means... um... subtract nine months, never mind.

Christmas 2013? There was the Christmas party. The party that Jack wanted to go to since it was a Pi Kappa winter rush event. And he dragged me too. Cellie came later, and...that wasn't a good night.

But I can't even fully remember it either... Too drunk, too drunk. Everyone was too drunk that night. And we only found out later it was because...?

His acute lack of sleep the night before was dragging on him. The cryptic message was just another thing for another day. He knew he had about 20 or so minutes before he had to leave. He tried to relax and rest his eyes. He was asleep in a minute.

Twenty minutes passed in an instant. Tarron sat up quickly, hearing a car horn loudly announce Darian's arrival. The blue jeep was impatiently waiting for him outside. He picked up his pack and rushed out the door. Adventure calls.

***

As soon as it occurred that Mr. Faust had not given him the title to the truck he had just purchased, Robert Graft hopped back in the driver's seat and started it up. The truck sputtered to life, and he reminded himself to take a look at the alternator with his multimeter at home.

He sorely wanted to make it home before late tonight. Today had already dragged on with its share of arrests and other petty crime enforcement. Glenrock was supposed to be the quiet, harmless city he spent his twilight years as a cop in after transferring from Cheyenne, but that didn't seem to be in the cards tonight.

He stomped on the gas pedal of the Hilux and darted out

195

of the police station parking lot. He was still in uniform and figured if any of his coworkers gave him trouble, he'd get on his radio and ask them to piss off.

What he hadn't counted on, however, was the abrupt appearance of a small child who popped up from the backseat of the truck. Demanding to know who he was and where her daddy was. She also rattled off some words. Graft didn't understand that it sounded very foreign. Russian or something, maybe. The surprise caused Graft to swerve the truck off the road, which drew a small scream from the little girl. He gained control of the vehicle, pulled over to the road shoulder, and turned around.

"Alright, talk!" He growled. The child only yelped and shrunk back in her seat.

"Oh right… cop voice off. Sorry." He said in a quieter tone, "Long day at work. Wait, I remember you. You're Mr. Faust's daughter, ain't cha's?" She cocked her head slightly.

"Mr. Faust is your dad. I mean, Tarron?" Graft repeated.

"Mhm," the girl confirmed.

"Ah, jeez. Well, glad I found ya now instead of you getting locked in here. I mean, what were you thinkin'?"

The girl didn't respond. She held up a small baggie.

***

Celeste dialed Tarron's home phone number again and put the phone on speaker while she drove. She had driven a lap around the immediate neighborhood and was letting her mind come to the worst conclusions. Conclusions led to figuring out steps of filing a missing child report, going on a search for her daughter, and accepting the worse possibility of all—that she may not see her again.

The anxiety in her chest had been coming in waves. She

had been trying to get her breathing under control since she jumped in the car. When the automated voice told her that Tarron's voicemail box was full again, she sighed loudly and pulled the car over. She rested her head on the steering wheel and held her breath. Six seconds in, six seconds hold, exhale it all.

Repeat.

They tell you to have plans for things like this. When your child goes missing or when you can't reach the other parent. A way to cope when you have so much worry and anxiety you feel like you're drowning. All of the plans you're told about seem fine and logical. Until the day it happens to you, and that little voice in the back of your head tells you everything is not okay, you're a horrible parent, and you'll never see your child again.

A phrase her father often used popped into her head as she sat there:

Tonący brzytwy się chwyta. The drowning man clutches at a cut-throat razor.

Celeste didn't have time for any bloodied palms. She sat upright and wiped her eyes dry. Steering the car back onto the road, she hit the gas pedal.

***

Darian arrived with bravado. He was wearing a bright green winter jacket and a similarly colored pom beanie to match. Mötley Crüe's Kickstart my Heart blasted from the jeep's speakers, and brakes squealed as the vehicle came to a halt. Tarron loaded up his ruck in the backseat and hopped in. He hadn't even clicked his seatbelt into place before Darian sped away.

"You ready, T?!" Darian asked excitedly. "I am *beyond* hyped!

I haven't been out of the country in a minute!"

"Yessir!" Tarron replied, unsure. He was excited, but at the same time, he was desperately clutching the jeep's overhead handle to stabilize himself from Darian's driving. They made it around the block before Tarron realized he had majorly fucked up.

"Sorry! Turn around! I forgot something."

"Turning around!" Darian echoed loudly. The brakes screeched again, and Darian wheeled the jeep around in a wild U-turn. Tarron felt the vehicle very nearly tip.

"I'll be just a second!"

Tarron raced to his front door, into the kitchen, and grabbed Jack Finnegan. Secured tightly in a semi-airtight dog-food container.

Before rushing back out to leave, he stopped himself and looked at one of the few pictures hung up by a magnet on his fridge. The sunlight coming in from the kitchen window was evaporating quickly, but it held for a moment in the photo. Cellie and he, holding baby Alina—barely four months old. They were standing in front of the house he was standing in now—when it had been their place. He took the picture from the magnet and put it in his back pocket. He couldn't exactly say why he wanted to take it with him, only that he should.

Back out the front door. Locking it behind him. Hop in the jeep. Gas pedal to the floor again. Less than 5 hours until their flight to New York, then the following morning out to Reykjavik. Darian's plan was to get to save money and stay overnight at the airport. Tarron didn't know how those logistics would work out, but he was past asking questions about specifics.

Tomorrow!

***

Once the little girl warmed up to him and remembered who he was, she was a chatterbox. Filling Graft's ear with all sorts of nonsensical, halfway-connected stories that preschoolers love to tell anyone who'll listen.

"…and that's when I caught a fish, but daddy said sometimes, they get away and we got ice cream after! *Lody* means Ice cream!"

"Is that so? In what language?"

"Polski!" Alina replied.

Graft smiled warmly. Little Alina reminded him much of his own daughter when she was that age, now on her way to high school. Minus the bilingual skills. Alina continued to tell him all the facets of her life.

"But we aren't supposed to tell mom cause weekends are with daddy, and we get ice cream."

"Weekends are with dad?" Graft asked, curious.

"Yeah… the rest of the week, mom and I live with Ian."

"Who's this Ian, hm?"

"He's mom's friend. I don't like him."

Mom's friend. Graft thought *poor thing must have to split time between parents.* He was also doing his best to navigate to Alina's father's house. His partner had been driving when they originally came to pick up the truck. Relating his brief knowledge of Glenrock with the wonderfully puerile memory of his assistant navigator was a puzzle. He knew which streets connected to which, but the landmarks that stuck out to the child were wildly different.

"Turn here… there's the big tree. No, next to the gas station! That's where we always get drumsticks. I love drumsticks. They're my favorite." Alina shouted.

"And where to now?"

"Ummm. I dunno…it's dark out now," she responded, staring blankly out the window.

"Well, darlin', do you know which street your daddy lives on?"

"Cedar! Like the tree."

"Cedar. Okay, there's a start. East or West Cedar?"

The distinction was almost negligible as the streets were one and the same.

The separating factor was a small ditch that marked the end of West Cedar Street and the beginning of East. A distinction, all the same, one that'd help Graft return the girl to her father and for him to rush home to his wife in time for dinner. There was a storm set to make its way through town he'd rather avoid, as well.

"East!" The girl said firmly. "Wait. No. West!" She added.

"West it is." Graft replied. He turned left off Glenrock's main road, Birch, then left again onto West Cedar. He slowed the truck to 20 miles an hour and turned the high beams on to compensate for the lack of streetlights in the neighborhood.

Graft marveled at how quickly the sun had descended this evening. A full moon was supposed to make its appearance tonight.

"Any of these homes look familiar?"

"Hmmm." Alina put both hands up to the window to peer out. "Nope. Nope. Uh uh, not that one."

They reached the end of the street. Graft slowed the car to a halt and shifted the truck in reverse to try and turn around. "That one! That's daddy's house." Alina exclaimed, pointing forward.

Graft hit the brakes and followed the girl's index finger to the indicated house across the ditch. On East Cedar. There was a blue jeep with its lights on in front of it. It quickly peeled out down the street. Though Graft's first instinct was to turn on his lights and follow to chew out and issue the driver a ticket, he reminded himself he had a duty to return Miss Alina. He watched it speed off to be another cop's problem.

Graft drove back down West Cedar, turned left, then left again to East Cedar. They parked in front of Mr. Faust's home, and he led Alina by the hand to the front door. He knocked several times loudly and waited. Peered through the windows and knocked more.

"Alright, Miss Alina. Do you know how to get to your mother's house from here?"

"Mom doesn't have a house!"

"Right. My mistake. Your mom's friend?"

"Nope!" Alina exclaimed. "I'm hungry!"

"Me too, kid." Graft said from under his breath. "C'mon now. We're gonna go to the station and figure this out."

They walked back to the truck. Graft helped the girl up and buckled her into the back seat. When he hopped into the driver's seat and turned the key, the truck once again sputtered, but this time, the engine failed to turn over.

He tried the key again.

Click, click, click.

"Miss Alina, know any bad words in Polski?"

"*Spierdalaj!*" She replied cheerfully.

"Spear—da—lie." Graft repeated phonetically. "And what does that mean?" Alina had no reply. She offered only a small shrug.

***

Celeste had been told she had a habit of "jumping to

conclusions" too quickly. Mostly told by Tarron. Almost entirely. It was a bad habit she found herself guilty of once or twice. Albeit, She'd only ever admit it to herself. It went along with things men tell women when they think they're wrong about something. But looking forward to what might go wrong had helped her out of bad decisions.

Watching a police car with its lights on speed away from Tarron's house, seeing Tarron's truck still in the driveway, and Tarron not home after she let herself in with her spare key all did not bode well for conclusion-making. She sat down on the couch and tried to think.

He said they were leaving tonight. Then why is his truck still here? No, wait.

Tarron said that his friend was driving! Do I chase after them or...?

That "or" was what scared her. She didn't have an answer to "or." She also didn't want to tell Ian what had happened and let him make his own conclusions on how the hell she had managed to lose Alina. But she had run out of resources. She needed to call on someone who could help.

Maybe Alina was with Tarron this whole time, and he was taking her back. Or what if he was taking her with him to Iceland? But that made even less sense. Would he want to take their daughter from her? After sleeping together and giving her a shred of hope that things between them were changing for the better?

Spierdalaj!

She pulled out her phone and dialed 911. When the operator connected and asked her what the emergency was—all her words and thoughts seemed to pour out at once. She told them firstly about her daughter missing and her boyfriend—well, not exactly boyfriend, but Alina's father also missing but not exactly. That he and his friend were probably headed to Cheyenne in a jeep, and Alina probably wasn't with them, but she just wanted some assurance that she'd be found.

The operator took her statement and asked her to slow down. Then to return home just in case her daughter came back. They'd send a unit out to find her *boyfriend*.

***

Alina loved that Graft turned on the lights of the patrol cruiser again. Much to the annoyance of his partner, who picked them up. Graft didn't care, rather let the kid have fun before she started to freak out about being away from her parents. It had been about 30 minutes since they left her father's house. Graft was late for dinner, too, so the lights gave them the excuse to drive at fuck-you-I'm-a-cop-speed through town.

What came over the radio as they drove was enough to distract him from keeping Alina occupied in the backseat with *I-spy*. He turned around and keyed the mike.

"Hey, central, can you repeat that? Over."

"Missing person's report: tall, white male, late 20's, Tarron Faust. In the company of another unknown white male. Reported to be headed to Cheyenne in a jeep. And a missing child report, Alina Fau—" *That damn jeep!*

"Thanks, Central! I got Alina right here. Responding to the white male—that's her daddy" He cut them off and keyed the mike again. "All available units: be on the lookout. Blue jeep Wrangler. Early 2000's model. Most likely headed south on I-25. Standing by on 1-4, out."

***

"Copy on that missing pers, 1-4. This is unit 2-3 responding.

Hey, gents, I gotta get out of here. Thanks for the drinks," Sergeant Frank Hollands said. He had been taking a dinner break from his graveyard shift at his favorite dive bar, right outside Cheyenne.

A very nice divorce lawyer had given him his card and offered to buy him a round. *Must be how these guys find clients,* Frank thought, sit around at cop bars and find whoever is most miserable. The bar was damn near deserted, save for the lawyer and his friends, and Frank knew he had a long night ahead of him, so he took the offer happily.

"What were the details on that missing person? If you don't mind my asking. The name sounded familiar," the lawyer asked.

"Uhhh. Faust or something? White male, late twenties, headed this way. Listen, man, I'm one of the few I-25 guys on duty tonight, so I gotta go. Thanks for the drink." Frank rose from the bar, threw a $20, and began to leave. He turned around before he opened the door and added, "I'll call ya, though. Ian, right?"

"That's right. You take care now." The lawyer replied. He watched the cop exit the bar, start his car and pull off. He exited the bar himself and hopped in his own car. Once on the freeway, he pulled out his phone and dialed. "Hi, Celeste. No, I'm just checking on you. Everything alright?"

***

"Yes, everything is fine. I'm just having wine with Jules." Celeste lied. The phone call took her by surprise, as did Ian's inquisitive tone. When he was hinting at something, he was very obvious. She did her best to hide any panic that may have been left over from the 911 call.

"You know," she continued, "Jules from hot yoga... yes,

you've met her at least twice. Anyway, I'll text you… Okay… Hope you have a good business trip. Bye."

It wasn't a total lie. Juliet Florentine was over, standing behind her counter, currently popping the cork on a bottle of Barefoot Moscato. She was not fine, however. But the presence of her friend accompanied by alcohol made her nerves take pause.

"I bet she's with her dad. You said his phone was broken, right?" Juliet said, pouring Celeste a tall glass before pouring herself one too, slightly less full.

"Yes. It just shattered when a box fell on it. And then Tarron cut his hand up from the screen, and I put a bandage on it. That… that was probably the last time I remember seeing her."

"How'd she just disappear on you?"

"Well…" Celeste bit her tongue. She knew that Juliet would happily escalate any drama she could get. But this wasn't the time to lie to everyone. "Tarron and I slept with each other. I don't know how it happened, but…."

"Oh my god. You whore!" Juliet laughed. Celeste sniffled a laugh and wiped her eyes. They were still slightly reddened.

Juliet continued, "I'm actually pro-Tarron and you now. His friend was cute too. And Alina needs a father."

"Yes, she does," Celeste said quietly before taking a long sip of her Moscato.

"And we need each other. Maybe in a toxic, sort of way."

"And that's okay!" Juliet bayed, "Gaia and I were married for two years before we found out we hated each other. She knew I was bi before we were even together but didn't fully accept it yet. What I learned after the fact is that relationships work because they work every day. It's you and your partner coming together over any personal bullshit, any disagreement or difference of opinion because you love one another—you do love him still, right?"

"I do." She admitted.

"Then dump Ian's ass and move back in with Mr. Bearded dadbod."

"It's just not that simple. We can't just jump back into where we left off like we're still in college. We have to get better at being partners as well as parents. Honest and open. But all of that doesn't even matter if the cops can't find my daughter!"

"Hey now," Juliet put a hand on her back, "Just trust. As I said, I bet Alina is with her dad right now."

***

Darian boldly proclaimed that the speed limit was more of a speed *suggestion* when *Freebird* was playing. Tarron only heard half of what his friend was saying as they barreled down I-25. The engine of the Jeep was drowned out by the music as the speedometer needle inched towards 90.

Tarron thought how fortunate it was that the freeway was empty on this Friday evening.

"This is Skynyrd, right!?" Tarron shouted. He knew the answer to his question, but he needed to say anything to Darian in hopes of keeping his own sanity.

"Fuck yeah, it is! Hey, we gotta stop!"

"What?" Tarron shouted back.

"Gotta get gas! I forgot to fill up before we left!"

Darian took the next exit and coasted the jeep back down to a reasonable 60. They pulled into a solitary gas station with an attached coffee shop. Tarron's stomach grumbled.

"Hey, I'm gonna get something to drink from the coffee shop. Want anything?" Tarron asked.

Darian shook his head. "I'm gonna grab a 4-pack of

something else caffeinated. And some road snacks! Don't wait up."

Tarron actually needed to flush out whatever was left in his stomach from this morning's breakfast as soon as humanly possible. He didn't typically get car sick. But with Darian's driving….

The coffee shop was about to close and denied his bathroom request. The barista did, however, offer him the key to the outside bathroom. The key was conveniently attached to a broken half of a broom handle. The bathroom was attached to the outside of the gas station, and Tarron was grateful for the seclusion. Less chance someone would come in and hear him puke his brains out.

He unlocked the door and was struck with how clean the commode was, even for the standard set by the hundreds of highway gas station bathrooms he'd had the misfortune to use in his life. Tarron squatted down to eye level with the toilet and took a deep breath. Waiting for whatever would come up from his stomach.

It grumbled and churned. But nothing. Tarron debated pulling the trigger and forcing himself to throw up. But decided that he'd be fine. As he rose up, he heard the murmurs of shouting from the opposite side of the wall facing the toilet. One of the voices sounded close enough to be Darian's. He quickly exited the bathroom and ran around to the front of the gas station entrance.

Darian seemed to be arguing with the nervous-looking teenage cashier.

"It's a fake gun! I'm sorry. It's a toy, I swear!" Darian protested. Tarron ran up to him quickly, apologizing to the cashier. He wrapped an arm around Darian and began to walk him out. Whispering under his breath.

"Dude, what the fuck? Why do you have a gun?"

"Well, first of all, it's not real. Second of all, I still need to pay for these snacks, man." Darian replied. He had a canned energy drink and bag of beef jerky in his hand. They were almost to the door.

"Just give me em'. I'll go pay, and you can go in the car. You scared the kid shitless, man."

"I did?" Darian turned around and glanced at the cashier. "I'll go say sorry. Here hold these." Darian shoved the can and bag of jerky in Tarron's free hand and began to turn around. "Oh, and this too!" Darian moved to pull out the black pistol from his waistband. Tarron immediately gripped his hand to halt him.

"Dude. Do. Not. That kid is a second away from calling the cops on us."

"No way. He's not even there."

"What?"

They both looked over in unison to the cashier. Or lack thereof.

***

After the phone call with Celeste, Ian decided he was going to cut his work trip short and head back home to see what was up with her. He knew she was a bad liar, and there was an inevitable fight coming. He'd try to mitigate any damage with surprise flowers and chocolate. But first, he needed to get there, which required gasoline. The drive itself was about an hour and a half, and his Benz was on less than a quarter tank. He pulled off I-25 to a Conoco. The yellowish, pearlescent lighting made the gas station stick out amongst the miles of moon-soaked freeway. Upon parking and inserting his credit card into the machine, he peered at a large cardboard sign that said: "CARD MACHINE DOWN, PAY INSIDE." He swore and withdrew his metal credit card.

Despite almost a dozen other pumps available, the gas station was close to vacant—only one other vehicle, a blue jeep which was parked opposite him. Whoever drove it appeared to be inside. There were two of them in what looked to be an argument. Ian walked to the entrance of the station and opened the glass door. It chimed loudly, and the two men froze. One was holding a pistol, and the other...

"Tarron?" Ian asked, dumbfounded. His hand shot down to his own concealed carry pistol, which he had holstered in front of his appendix. A practiced maneuver he had done probably a hundred times in practice at the range. He had his pistol, a Smith & Wesson M&P 9, per recommendations from friends in law enforcement, unholstered and trained on Darrian McConnell in an instant.

"Hey, Woah! Woah! Let's take it down a few notches!" Tarron yelled, putting both hands up defensively, his voice almost breaking.

"Tarron, I never pegged you for petty theft, but...Who's your friend?" Ian asked in a flat tone.

"He's not a problem. We were just leaving—"

"Either of you takes another step, and I'll put you both down. Now you, jolly green giant, drop the pistol."

"What, this?" Darrian started to explain, waving the pistol in the air. Ian clicked the safety off his own. Tarron saw him do this and felt his entire body stiffen.

"It's not even real. Look—!" Darian chimed

Before he could finish his sentence, Tarron wrapped his arms around his friend and tackled him to the ground. He felt as if they fell in slow motion. The sound of a gunshot was ringing in his ears, drowning out whatever Ian was shouting at him. Tarron felt a searing pain on the right side of his face and warm blood trickling across his face as he and Darian crashed into a shelf full of beef jerky.

His ears continued to ring. Actually, he was only sure one of his ears was ringing. He sat up and raised a hand to his right ear. His fingertips connected with bloody tissue and struck waves of pain.

"You shot my ear!" He screamed. Ian's mouth was moving as he stared back at him, but he couldn't make out his words.

"What?!" Tarron yelled. He was able to hear his own voice this time. The ringing was dying down in his good ear.

"I said you're a brave fucking idiot, Tarron." Ian re-holstered his pistol and walked over to Darian's unmoving body. He picked up the toy pistol, studied it for a moment, and tossed it away. He then knelt down and placed two fingers on Darian's neck, searching for the carotid artery.

"You knocked your buddy out with that tackle. Lemme take a look at you" Tarron stood up, holding his bloodied ear.

"Fuck off. No, you're gonna buy me a new ear, you bastard. Why the fuck did you shoot? Darian said the gun was fake."

Ian crossed his arms. "Can never be too sure."

"You're sadistic...FUCK, this hurts."

"We sell first aid kits!" A voice suddenly said from behind the counter. Belonging to the previously absent, pubescent cashier. The kid pointed towards shelving which held a collection of meager-looking, travel-sized first aid kits for a conveniently priced $9.95.

Tarron continued to hold his damaged ear and thought it might be ringing again. The flashing red and blue lights which painted the gas station, however, determined that the ringing belonged to a very real police siren. Darian sat up and rubbed his head before making eye contact with Tarron.

"Tarron! Gun!" He slurred.

14

Another Happy Landing

THE ATTEMPT to get to Iceland and spread Jack's ashes was going phenomenally as the two conquering adventurers sat arrested at a gas station between Glenrock and Cheyenne. And the fact that the arresting cop knew Ian when he arrived did not surprise Tarron. As he sat on the curbside of the gas station, handcuffed and head bandaged, he desperately wished he had a cigarette. His ear was still ringing.

Pain from the injury crawled down from the side of his face to his jawbone. He wasn't sure if the cop had tried to lighten the situation when he told him that the bullet had only "taken a little off the top." As if Ian was a barber with a pistol and Tarron's ear was a haircut. Absurd, but he did appreciate the phrasing.

"I'm sorry, T, I—" Darian started to apologize.

"Don't." Tarron cut him off.

The two had been waiting in silence. Officer Hollands informed them they were awaiting another unit. He didn't tell them why.

Darian shuffled his way closer to sit next to him. He had a

comically large bruise on the crown of his head. The two were the Three Scrooges missing a member. Comedy in tragedy, laugh at my pain.

Officer Hollands is bald; maybe he's our Curly. Tarron thought. The officer was about a dozen yards away, talking into his radio in an unintelligible cop-speak-ese language. Ian stood abreast of him, trying his hardest to look intimidating.

"Well, now I feel like I have to explain," Darian said.

"Yes, please, explain, Darian. Why did you have a toy pistol tucked into your pants, and why were you brandishing it?"

"Oh, that's simple. Remember how I told you I threatened James?"

"Your *father*?"

"Yeah him. Anyway—"

"For what reason?" Tarron asked, tension rising in his voice.

"Put the fear of God into him? I dunno. Originally was gonna use it to find out which gravesite Jack was in. But I called him one time, and he was drunk and blurted it out. Guess I forgot it was in my pants. Listen, buddy, I'm truly sorry if this is coming as a surprise to you."

"A surprise?"

"Yeah! We were talking about it in the car, ya know? Facin' our demons."

"So, what about just now?"

"Oh, that. I was simply showing him that it was a toy so he would calm down?" He responded as if the question itself didn't make sense.

"How the fuck does that make sense, Darian!?"

"Quiet!" The police officer yelled from afar before lowering his radio to start chatting with Ian.

Darian inched his way closer to Tarron awkwardly and

leaned in close to whisper.

"I guess I can see now how that may have been a bad idea."

"Oh, you think?" Tarron hissed back.

When the cop had initially shown up, Tarron's mind immediately started searching for outs and plans to escape the situation. Speedbumps like this seemed indicative of the specific flavor of luck he'd experienced throughout his life. Wanted a brother, got a best friend, wanted a girlfriend, got a baby girl, wanted a change of scenery. Here he was curbside waiting to be read his rights.

Tarron tried to eavesdrop on the conversation between the cop and Ian. He was able to make out sparse whispers.

"…awaiting additional unit… Glenrock PD…something about a BOLO for the jeep… kinda figures."

"I'd like my phone call!" Darian loudly announced.

Both Hollands and Ian turned sharply at the outburst with looks of surprise. Darian continued.

"You can't arrest me for a crime I did not commit! Is this how America treats its veterans? I have rights!"

"You'll get a damn phone call when we get back to the station. Now shut the hell up." the cop responded.

"I have the right to remain silent…and I choose to waive that right," Darian hit back. He then opened his mouth, inhaled deeply, and began to wail at a high pitch.

"EEEEEEEEEEEEEEE—hey!"

The cop walked over and kicked Darian softly in a less-than polite gesture to reinforce *shut the hell up*. Darian took this as an opportunity to fall deftly off the curb and roll over to continue to scream at medium volume.

"PO-leese bru-tal-ee-TEEEEEE!"

The cop rushed forward to deliver another gentle nudge

when an additional police squad car roared into the parking lot. Lights flashing and tires squealing. It came to a stop at the parking spot barely 6 feet away. The backseat door opened first.

"Woohoo!" A courageous 4-nearly-5-year-old half-Polish little girl yelled.

"Hey, Woah, now, Miss Alina. Wait until the car is turned off." the officer chided as he exited from the passenger's seat. The driver stayed inside.

The sight of his daughter coming out of the back of a cop car with a giant grin on her face gave Tarron whiplash. This was God's sick joke, and Jack was at his side cackling along with him —probably making suggestions like the two were orchestrating an afterlife version of Impractical Jokers.

"Daddy!" Alina exclaimed as soon as she saw him.

He stood up as Alina ran to him and hugged his legs. Childhood innocence was bliss. He attempted to hug back with his handcuffed arms.

There it was, pure shame where happiness should've been. What an exemplary moment of childhood trauma this would turn out to be when Alina grew up.

"It all started when I saw my father arrested in front of a Conoco gas station when I was four, almost five years old. My mother thought I was missing, and my father's ear had been shot off."

Well, not shot entirely "off." Tarron's adrenaline had all but run out, and he could feel the lower two-thirds of his ear that remained screaming out in pain.

"Well, how about that? Found your father. What's going on here, Frank?" Officer Graft asked.

"64-golf. I'm told it was a toy gun. Got a call from the kid at the register inside. Unconfirmed at the time," Frank replied,

"And then a good Samaritan here, Mr. Ian Friezmont, was able to stop the robbery before it even began. Minor GSW on this perp." He added, nodding towards Tarron. "Who's the little girl?"

Alina was holding onto her daddy's hand. She looked up and around with thralls of confusion. The wheels in her young brain had begun to turn. Her excitement from riding around in a police car had expired, and realization set in that her superhero appeared to be wounded and in trouble.

"Believe it or not—that's Mr. Faust's daughter. He and his friend here are the BOLO I've been trying to track down." Graft said, turning to Tarron, "How'd we end up here, Mr. Faust? And you don't happen to have that title for the Hilux on you, do ya?"

"It's at my house, sorry, Bob. Knew I forgot something when ya left." Tarron said.

"Looks like it was a couple of things," Bob responded.

Tarron looked down at his daughter, unsure how she had ended up here. His primal plan to escape the situation was gone and forgotten. Shift gears. He needed to call Cellie.

"Ya, so about that phone call—" Tarron started out.

"I'll take her home, bud. Don't you worry?" Ian cut in, turning to Graft and then Hollands. "Miss Alina's mother and I live together, actually, officers. Unbelievably fortunate how this turned out."

"Fortunate, you get to shoot me *and* make me the bad guy. You're not taking my daughter," Turron attested.

Alina shrank back behind her father's legs. Graft placed his hands atop his hips picturing how he was going to recount this tale to his wife later. Mrs.Graft loved a drama-filled story about how her husband's day went. *And guess who was at the end of this 64-G call?*

"Tarron. She needs to go home. She needs to be with a responsible adult. C'mon, doll, let's go," Ian said, extending his hand toward Alina.

"The fuck you will!" Tarron shot back angrily.

He felt the energy in the air change as both policemen shifted defensively. Officer Hollands' right hand rested atop his service weapon, and so did Graft's. Tarron thought this must've been a picturesque situation of death by a cop. Begrudged father gunned down in his prime over disputes and love triangles.

Alina's grip around his hand trembled lightly.

He knew the right decision at this moment was not the easy one. And it pissed him off, mostly because it was Ian.

"You're right." He said to Ian in a smaller voice.

"What's that Tarr-bear?"

Tarron clenched his jaw tightly and said, through gritted teeth, "Take my daughter home to her mother. You can manage that much in your lawyer-mobile, can't you?"

"Can do, champ. C'mere Alina." Ian responded, gesturing with open arms to the girl. She turned her face away and hid it against Tarron's hand. Ian locked eyes with him, a smug nod on his face. *You gonna tell her?*

Goddamn it, he was.

"Hey, Lina—chicken?" He said softly. Her head popped up.

"You're gonna go home to mommy with Ian. Okay?"

"But you and mommy were gonna have another sleepover!" She protested.

Tarron's face grew red, and he made failed attempts to laugh it off. "Maybe next time, chicken. Now go with Ian. Daddy has a boo-boo on his ear."

"Mommy can fix that too! Like your hand! Before you guys went to mommy's room." Alina started to ramble. Her speech was a darling mix of child-babble and determined storytelling "…but then I wanted to ask you, um. About those seeds in your truck! But then I uh—there's a part in Ice Age where Peaches surprises her parents and um—"

"Well, now we know not to hide in daddy's truck, ok!" Tarron cut her off quickly. "Now go with Ian, and I'll call you and mommy to tell you I'm okay." Alina slowly lessened her grip on her father's hand. She turned towards Ian and began to trot before turning around suddenly.

"Here's the seeds, dad!" She held out the small baggie proudly. He awkwardly looked around to the surrounding men who were simply watching it all go down, then attempted to grab the baggie.

"Yeah, I'll take that," Hollands interjected, grabbing the bag from him and shoving it into a pocket.

"Let's go, boys—" Hollands added, grabbing Darian and Tarron's shoulders and starting towards his squad car. "Thanks for the backup, Bob. I'm booking them at the station in Cheyenne."

"Hey, wait, we committed zero crimes here, none!" Tarron protested.

"Zip it, bud!" Hollands shot back. He began moving the two arrestees dead to rights.

"' Lina, I love you. Tell your mom I love her too." Tarron added, "The fuck?" Ian asked flatly.

"No English bad words! Only Polski. *Spierdalaj*!" Alina piped.

"That's right, chicken. Spear-da-lie! Oh, and Ian, I liked the satin sheets! Real absorbent!" Tarron jeered.

"It was nice to meet you. Miss Alina," Darian shouted as they were led away. Hollands shoved the two and quickened the pace. Throwing open the backseat door to the police car and ushering them in.

Graft, Ian, and Alina watched the trio load up into the squad car and disappear into the darkness. Ian attempted to grab the girl's hand and lead her to his sedan. She pulled her hand back sharply and announced, "I can walk!"

Ian looked to Officer Graft for any sort of countenance. Graft simply returned the look, pursed his lips, and shrugged. *What d'ya want me to say? The girl said she could walk herself.* He thought.

"Y'all have a good, safe night," he said aloud. He opened the door of the cruiser; his partner had fallen asleep and was startled when it opened.

"Bye, Bob!" Alina said cheerily before waving goodbye.

15

"This is a Less Than Ideal Time to Take Psychedelic Drugs, Darian..."

...IS WHAT Tarron had wanted to tell him initially. But the immaculately logical way in which Darian phrased their conundrum made sense to him. He talked rapidly.

"They're gonna search us and find it. So, you're gonna have to swallow it. Us getting arrested for the gas station thing is weak, but if they find schedule 1 drugs on me, we're done!" Darian said once the police cruiser came to a stop at the station and Officer Hollands stepped out.

"What is it?" Tarron asked quickly. There was no indication of how much time they had alone.

"Doesn't matter. Look!" Darian turned his torso around to fish out a plastic baggie full of an ambiguous dark substance from his back pocket.

"Quickly!" Darian added.

"Chrissake!" Tarron said.

There was no good way to do it. The handcuffs already posed a challenge, but Darian had managed to free the substance from his pocket. He barely held onto the bag with his fingertips.

Tarron came to terms that the only way the drugs were disappearing was via him gutting them. He bent over and desperately bit at the baggie with his front teeth, caught it, and withdrew his head to tilt back and open his mouth.

Gulp, down the hatch. All hands-free like a manic barn animal.

...And *this* little piggie was going on a trip.

For a moment, he thought that the drugs might have no effect. They were all wrapped up in a plastic baggie, after all. *You have stomach acid; dumbass,* Tarron reminded himself. The drugs definitely didn't look like the mushrooms Darian had given him, either. They were a dark green, not exactly powder but small clumps. Not fuzzy like the marijuana buds he had seen once upon a time.

Hollands opened the backdoor, startling the two.

"Woah now. Touchy ain't ya's? Out we, go now." He said while grabbing Darian by the shoulder, then Tarron behind him.

"I thought we were going to the hospital?" Tarron announced. His eyes met the emblazoned sign that read out CHEYENNE POLICE DEPARTMENT.

"Mr. Ian didn't shoot your entire ear off, did he?" Hollands jested.

"Fu-wha? Yeah, he may've," Tarron babbled. *Oh god, this is how I die. In the waiting room of a police station, tripping on whateverthefuck Darian made me eat.* Panic was setting in as well as the perceived effects of whatever the fuck he just took.

He looked to Darian. His friend mouthed slowly: Stay calm! Just breath! Before imitating over-exaggerated breaths.

In through the nose and—

Breathe in, count to four, hold it, count to four, and let it all out.

Oh god. Just keep breathing. Oh, now we're moving. Here we go. Wow, It's super bright in here. Okay, sit down and wait. What's my blood type? How the damn hell should I know?

Cheyenne PD had two RNs that worked at the station. One, Franny D'addario, could very obviously tell Tarron was inebriated when he was brought out. But she assumed that Officer Hollands knew, so she didn't mention it and simply added it to her in-processing notes. She disliked all the late shift cops, anyway—always rude and always tried to make a pass at her like they didn't have someone waiting at home.

Also distracting her was the other hand-cuffed man brought in with Mr. Faust, who appeared to be winking at her from the waiting area. Tarron followed her gaze towards Darian, who waved happily at him.

Despite the hugely effective and heavy-duty plastic barrier that the peyote was contained in, Darian knew his friend was on his way to the top of a very high roller coaster. Tarron was headway towards falling helplessly into the sweet and caring arms of Mother Mescaline.

High-grade shit. Given to him by a dear friend from the Nambé pueblo Darian had made in Taos, New Mexico, during his post-cancer-news period of soul searching. Jesus spent 40 days in the desert, and he figured he'd try the same. He had heard of how beautiful northern New Mexico was from an Air Force buddy who grew up in Albuquerque.

Darian had originally planned to share the hallowed peyote plant with Tarron when they landed in Iceland and were able to see Aurora Borealis.

Damned shame.

He needed to act fast and put out the fire he had lit. He watched a muscular male nurse lead Officer Hollands Tarron away. Once they were gone, he stood up and walked towards the beautiful redheaded Miss D'addario at the desk and put on his best James Dean voice. She reminded him very much of his late wife.

"Good evening, miss. Don't mind the handcuffs. My name's Darian McConnel, and I'm actually a nurse myself. Have you ever seen the film *Pulp Fiction*?"

***

Nurse Sampson didn't read the notes that Nurse D'addario left him. He was 5 minutes away from freedom before Tarron came in. A quick stitch job, and he was home free to his husband and corgi. Every day he regretted moving to Wyoming a little more, but it was his partner's home state, and he was agreeable. Even if it meant harsh winters and dealing with the most ridiculous injuries working at a police station could offer.

A GSW that barely took off half the ear? Sure thing, sutures, and morphine are coming right up. He cleaned up the ear handily, re-wrapped it, and calmly talked Mr. Faust through what he was going to do next; he was trying to practice bedside manner.

Things were moving very quickly. The overhead lights in the exam room were reflecting bright spots into Tarron's eyes. They seemed to radiate heat and vibrate intensely. His entire body felt as though it were vibrating, actually. He had an overwhelming sensation of numbness spreading throughout his fingertips. Everything that made contact with his skin seemed to tingle. He looked down and saw he was unconsciously running his fingers over the sanitary paper on the exam table. He stopped and tried to process what the nice nurse had just said.

223

The pain? What pain?

"Oh, my ear!" Tarron said. It had almost slipped his mind.

"Actually, Mr. Faust, I don't need to give you any sutures, so if you're okay with it—and if it's okay with Officer Hollands here. I can just administer the morphine."

Hollands nodded in agreement. It was in the doc's hands now. A little shot of morphine for the kid was easy. Lucky bastard.

He needed a smoke. "Hey, Doc, I'mma step out real quick. Holler if he tries to bolt." Hollands said.

The door clicked shut, and Tarron turned sharply to Nurse Sampson. His eyes felt like they were bulging. Words swam around his mouth before he opened it.

"D-d-drugs."

"Yes, Mr. Faust. Morphine is a drug. You're in shock, okay? It should help with the pain in your ear and mellow you out." The nurse continued, but Tarron wasn't listening.

The idea of mixing whatever psychedelics Darian had fed him with morphine did not exactly strike Tarron as a good idea. It almost didn't strike him at all. He was fascinated with the personalized decoration on Nurse Sampson's name tag. Its illustration was bleeding the color into his irises.

"Rainbow," Tarron said. He pointed at the name tag.

"Yes, there's a rainbow on my name tag. I'm the only other RN here, though, so if you want someone else—"

"No! I love you."

"Oh. I'm flattered, Mr. Faust, but I have someone waiting for me at home. Now I'm going to just get a syringe and have you on your way."

"*No!*" Tarron tried to say. No sound came out. His mouth was agape. He was fighting hard to create multi-syllable words to convey to the man that if he gave him any more substance that he may effectively launch Tarron Faust into a completely different plane of existence.

It was too late. Sampson had the syringe and a clear vial of morphine. The needle was in Tarron's arm, and Miss Em made her way into his bloodstream.

Tarron's world shut down and rebooted. His brain started running a full diagnostic sequence and analysis to figure out what the fuck just happened. He tipped backward on the padded exam table. He sat right back up. The crinkle of the sterile paper covering was incredibly loud in his ears.

Ear?

"What's wrong?" Tarron heard Sampson ask.

Tarron pointed to his head and then began to make circles with his hands.

"Your ear?" Sampson guessed. Light panic in his voice.

Tarron shook his head, which was a mistake. As he did, everything fell out of focus. He squinted and tried to refocus his eyes. He then tapped his forehead.

"Your head?" Sampson guessed again. Tarron nodded slowly. He was finally able o regain feeling in his tongue. He didn't want to waste the opportunity and chose his word carefully.

"Drugged," Tarron said, stressing the tense of the word.

Sampson picked up the clipboard containing Tarron's chart notes and flipped through them. And through them again. What had he missed?

"Oh shit." He said aloud.

The door re-opened. Officer Hollands strode back in. He reeked of nicotine and tobacco. Tarron slumped over deftly onto the table. The smell had hit him like a wall. Immediate and effective sensory overload.

"Oh shit." Hollands snorted.

Quickly behind the uniformed officer of the law came Darian McConnell with Nurse D'addario in tow.

"STAND ASIDE!" Darian announced. His hands were still cuffed behind him as he stood in the doorway, and the nurse pushed past him.

"Sam, you didn't administer Mr. Faust anything, did you?"

"I did. Shit. I didn't read your notes, Fran. He needs—"

"He needs five migs of epinephrine!" Darian interrupted

"Who are? I mean, that's right, but who are you?" Sampson asked.

"This man's best friend. And miss D'addario will agree with me! Before he goes into cardiac arrest!"

Nurse D'addario walked to Tarron's hunched body, grabbed his wrist, and felt for a radial pulse. It was weak, but it was there.

"Quickly!" She said sternly.

Sampson flew out of the room. His voice could be heard bellowing in the halls, barking at others to stand clear. Nurse D'addario flipped Tarron over and began CPR.

"You two need to leave!" She shouted to Darian and Hollands.

Hollands grabbed Darian and quickly exited the exam room.

Tarron was in between worlds. He felt the pounding on his chest but failed to stir. The mix of morphine and mescaline felt like a weighted blanket meant for God himself. It was beyond anything he felt while in his coma just a month prior.

He felt his brain was responsive, but he wasn't exactly in the pilot's seat. He was beside himself. Metaphysically, as though he were watching from the high corner of the exam room.

Oh god, this is how I die.

One of his eyes lulled open, and he shot back into his own body. He spottedDarian peeking through the window of the door before his eye closed again.

He swore he saw him wink.

***

The ambulance flew out of the station parking lot and onto the street. Darian was genuinely surprised they let him ride with Tarron. They were basically brothers! He told them. Yes, but no. Nurse Sampson had been too busy stabbing Tarron with an epi-pen to ask.

"Ambulance" was also putting it glamorously. Cheyenne PD had converted one of the SUV units that had been barely, not deemed "totaled" into the "emergency medical transport vehicle." The stenciling that spelled this out on the side was just starting to peel, but the vehicle did have official PD plates on the back.

"You sure he's gonna be alright?" Franny D'addario said from the driver's seat.

"Yeah, he'll be 100% in no time," Darian lied. Tarron wasn't supposed to be unconscious and semi-responsive. But he also hadn't counted on the other RN at the station administering a high dose of morphine instead of just giving Tarron a couple of Motrin and a pat on the back.

Officer Hollands drove behind them, struggling to keep up with the wild turns Franny was taking.

"Where'd you learn to drive?!" Darian asked. Officer Hollands had briefly uncuffed Darian so he could help move Tarron into the SUV. Now his hands were cuffed to the handle above the car window. He didn't mind, though. It helped him hold on as Franny drove.

"Mmhm. I'm flying." Tarron mumbled.

"Tarron!" Darian shouted excitedly, "Can you hear me, buddy? I got us a way out of jail! With this happening at a police station and Ian shooting you over basically nothing, they have to let us go!"

"I know a pretty good paralegal too!" Franny added.

"Just stay with me, buddy! We're almost there!"

When Darian glanced over at his halfway comatose companion, he noticed a black string hanging around his neck. He was sure that Tarron hadn't been wearing a necklace during their last few encounters. Darian chose to ignore it for the time being.

Tarron Faust was very, very far from there. In later years, when he'd recount these drug escapades, he'd wonder how he managed to be some sort of unconscious in every iteration that Darian drugged him.

His skin was still tingling numbly. He was spinning. Hallucinating too. Wild images, demons in angelic guise, really.

Mescaline, 3,4,5-trimethoxyphenethylamine for any interested biochemists, naturally occurs in a wide array of South American cacti. The most widely used of which: peyote. (It's also found in certain beans, believe it or not!).

Peyote had survived thousands of years. Its history was long, colorful, and partially racially biased. While it was chiefly used in religious ceremonies of Native Americans, German chemist Arthur Heffter first isolated it in 1897, and it was then synthesized by Ernst Späth in 1918. An English politician, Humphry Osmond, volunteered to take the drug for a BBC special in 55'. He called it "the most interesting thing [he] ever did."

A typical dosage of mescaline hydrochloride is 175-350 milligrams. A high dosage is considered around 500 milligrams, which was around the amount Darian measured out—for him and Tarron to split.

Break. Next.

Morphine: a pain medication hailing from the family of opiates. Naturally found in a resinous form from the poppy plant. It can be used to make heroin. The drug has a pretty long and colorful history as well; in short, many an addict would agree that Morphine is fuckin' awesome.

The morphine was currently engaged in a mighty battle with the epinephrine for positive control of Tarron's heart rate. It was hard to see which was winning from an outsider's perspective. Mescaline sat in the background, watching.

Later in life, Tarron would also liken the experience to sitting in an open-top Cadillac, floating around in outer space and foot hard on the gas pedal. No burning rubber and going nowhere, but the engine sure was screamin'.

And you, the driver, look over to your left and see the USS Enterprise from Star Trek zooming by you. You wave. Captain Kirk waves back and wishes you the best of luck. Holler all you want, but he can't hear you.

But the shine and color of the stars? Well, brother, it was worth the price of admission.

Somewhere along the ride to Cheyenne General hospital, Tarron's body heard Darian mention to Miss Franny D'addario that it was a heroic dose of mescaline that Tarron had ingested. That would explain the buffalo.

It spoke to him. A giant, celestial buffalo floating out there with him in the middle of forever. He watched it float as he sat in the leather seats of the Caddy. Like a drive-in movie at the end of the universe.

"Are you my spirit guide?" He shouted to the buffalo.

"I can be," it replied. The voice boomed and flowed through him. It was awesome and terrible.

"Okay, good. That's a relief. My second guess was the state animal of Wyoming."

"That—I am as well. You may call me… Bill."

"Buffalo Bill?"

"William to my friends. But Bill…will suffice."

"Buffalo Bill. What is it—?"

"No. Just Bill." Bill corrected

"Oh, great and powerful Bill—"

"No, no, no. Do not grovel. I hate groveling. Start over."

"Bill, my spirit guide. What is it that I'm seeking?"

"Your heart desires closure from someone very dear to you. They have departed, and you seem to chase after them. You must not lose sight of those who surround you." The tone and inflection in Bill's voice changed drastically as the guidance continued.

"And also…figure out your shit with your baby momma, damn!" Tarron could've sworn Bill sounded like a bad Chris Tucker from Friday impression.

"This is my advice," Bill said again. Returning to a God-on-the-mountain-like tone.

"Wait. I knew all that already."

"THIS IS MY ADVICE. TAKE IT OR DO NOT. I AM BUT A BUFFALO."

"Uhhh—ahem! I will take your advice Smokey, uh—I mean Bill. Now um, how do I leave this place?"

"You must wake up soon. Before you forget how."

***

Tarron sat up. Looking around. He appeared to have traversed space and time to a different vehicle and one which seemed to be moving and dirty.

The light was blinding and translucent. It seemed to bleed from the source through the air like dye in a river. They were still in Wyoming, as far as he could tell. Snow and road salt illuminated by street lamps lined the street, and a passing billboard seemed to resemble the State of Wyoming tourism's ad campaign he saw everywhere along I-25.

It read out in bold letters "GATEWAY TO THE WEST, MEET THE WEST. *WyomingTourism.org*" on a green field with the trademark state animal to the right.

"Goddamn Buffalo bill…." Tarron muttered.

"Oh good, you're up. Tarron, this is Franny D'addario. A fellow practitioner of the medical field and a Casper College alum. She's sympathetic to our cause."

"Fuck yeah, I am," Franny said. "Turns out getting a nursing degree from community college doesn't get you much other than a shitty job at a police station."

"Looks like I have much to look forward to." Darian said before putting a hand on Tarron's shoulder, "Now sit back down and play dead. We have a plan."

Tarron laid back down in the converted backseat of the SUV. It was retrofitted to fit a collapsed stretcher, just barely, and had an interesting hodgepodge of medical supplies strewn against its walls. Tarron was fine asking all questions from a supine position. Easier to ride the wave. The stretcher made a fine surfboard.

"Why does time feel like I can taste it?" Tarron asked.

"Might have something to do with the double dose of *peyote* you were brave enough to take, the morphine the nurse at the station shot you up with, and the shot of adrenaline we gave you so you wouldn't flatline. All that should've evened it out, so you should just be feeling the peyote."

"We're here!" Franny announced.

Officer Hollands screeched to a halt behind them. He hopped out of the cruiser and then immediately back in to shut off his siren.

"Uncuff him so we can move him," Franny barked to Hollands, nodding her head towards Tarron lying in the back of the SUV.

"Excuse me? He was brought in on the attempted armed robbery and—"

"This patient was brought in injured on very flippant causes and received negligent care under your purview. Now I can record you as cooperative in the first-aid efforts, or I can report that you weren't. Either way, we can't move him until he's uncuffed. If he dies under your care, that's your ass, Hollands."

"Now, Franny… c'mon."

"None of that. It's Nurse D'addario or ma'am. I can't cover any more roughed-up people you bring in. Now uncuff him."

Hollands clenched his jaw and complied while mumbling swears under his breath. He removed the metal restraints from Tarron's wrists and placed them back in his belt pouch.

"Him too." She tilted her head towards Darian, who stuck his head against the window and grinned.

"When we get back to the station, women, I swear…."

"Chop, chop, let's goooo."

With Darian's help, Tarron was loaded up and rushed into the ER. The hardest part was over. Now they needed to shake the cop.

Franny took over in explaining what she needed to the Cheyenne General staff. She had friends here. Tarron was admitted as a run-of-the-mill emergency. The story was that

Tarron and Darian had come into the Police station to report Tarron taking a stray bullet to the ear, and then his poor heart had given out. The daring Officer Hollands had performed CPR and, with Nurse D'addario's expert help, got him to a hospital better equipped to deal with an unresponsive patient.

Hollands stayed in the waiting room and twiddled his thumbs. He was afraid Franny was right, more than right—legitimate about going over his head.

Let alone that he completely forgot to read the two criminal masterminds' Miranda rights before putting them in cuffs. The toy gun at the scene and the fella's ear shot off by the lawyer had been enough to sidetrack him. Not to mention Bob showing up with the fella's daughter! He might've been getting too old for this shit.

He waited for close to ninety minutes; moreover, he was growing impatient. It was nearing 11 PM. An anxious voice in his head had been running rounds suggesting that he didn't have enough to make any charges stick. That this could be a slam dunk case for any halfway decent state-provided lawyer.

Speaking of lawyers, he felt downright lousy for letting himself be fooled by that silver-tongued divorce lawyer! He knew it was too good to be true. A half-cocked, attempted armed robbery by two with zero priors and one of the perps having a love triangle with the good Samaritan? Shit, he didn't even talk to the cashier for a statement. Just trusted Ian's word on everything.

That anxious voice rang out in a mocking staccato like a playground bully.

You-didn't-do-your job right. You-didn't-do-your job right. You-didn't-do-your job right. His leg didn't stop bouncing once he sat down.

Finally, Franny, or nurse D'addario rather, emerged from the double doors which led further into the hospital. Darian McConnell, quick behind her,

pushing a semi-comatose Tarron Faust along in a wheelchair. An IV fed clear liquid to

Tarron's arm. Hollands stood up quickly with bewilderment on his face.

"You and I need to talk." Franny told Hollands sternly. The two walked towards the door out of earshot from Darian and Tarron. Darian drove Tarron over to a quiet corner of the waiting room near the water cooler.

"Is he buying it?" Tarron mumbled, attempting to peer out of one eye.

"Shhh. You'll blow the cover," Darian whispered while filling a disposable dixie cup up from the cooler.

"Here, drink up—no, don't grab it, just let me. You're supposed to be sedated. Yeah, it looks like he's buying it. Man, this woman is an angel." Darian said,

"She cute?" Tarron mumbled again, attempting to maintain the act.

"She looks like Scarlet," Darian said softly, almost inaudibly. "Who?"

"Never mind. Quick, they're coming. Play dead."

Tarron slumped back further into the wheelchair and did his best to appear drugged out of his mind. It wasn't much of a challenge. He had traded a stretcher/surfboard for a wheelchair to ride the chaotic peyote wave.

While in the exam room, all the doctor had done was check his vitals and give him a Snickers candy bar to keep his blood sugar levels high, then a Gatorade for the electrolytes.

He was lazily staring at the opaque floor pattern of the

hospital. The waiting room was carpeted in what resembled a bowling alley-esque space pattern that was brightly littered with colorful dots and ribbons on a black background. Where the carpet ended, subdued yellow vinyl began patterned almost akin to brickwork. The colors, lines, and patterns on the floor seemed to glow to him. Alive even, shimmering and expanding like as though it was breathing.

Chocolate, Gatorade, and an IV to sober me up. Then we watched Shrek 2 Tarron cackled, formulating his own corny customer review. Care received at Cheyenne General was suburb, but they should fire whoever did their interior design.

Officer Hollands and Nurse D'addario walked over. Hollands was holding his patrol cap with both hands and had a cheerless look on his face.

"So uh, got some good news for you boys."

Hollands began to explain how, in a very roundabout way, he wasn't going to arrest or book them. Not because Tarron could very potentially sue for negligent care while under federal custody or that Hollands had forgotten to perform one of the most basic necessities to policework, but because he believed that they had been through a "rough night" and it would save him some paperwork. Franny nudged him with her elbow after he finished.

"Oh, right. Ahem, uh, I'd also like to express my apologies for how you were treated, Mr. Faust."

Darian pretended to whisper into Tarron's ear. Tarron nodded slowly and gave a thumbs up. Greedier and more opportunistic men may have sought after a perfect opportunity like this to rip off the state government. They were just trying to catch a flight.

Franny politely speared Hollands again with her elbow.

"Christ woman… yeah, and we'll waive the impounding fee on your vehicle. It actually just got brought in about 10 minutes ago. And here's the little bag that little girl was trying to give you. It's funny—when I saw it, I almost thought it could've been pot."

"Hilarious!" Darian cut him off, rising to his feet, grabbing the bag from the officer and then the handles of Tarron's wheelchair. "We'll see our way out. Er—if the lovely and heroic miss D'addario would give us a ride back?"

"It would be my pleasure." She answered. The three followed the yellow vinyl bricks and headed towards the exit in stride (and roll). All they were missing was a cowardly lion and a little dog too.

Officer Hollands called out after them just before they passed through the automatic doors

"Y'all go right home after this, ya hear? Don't go leaving the state or anything like that. Still have to appear before a judge!"

Yeah, right.

16

Don't Forget to Write!

WHEN THE trio was loaded up in the car and back on the road, Darian let out a burst of laughter and excitement he'd been holding in.

"Oh, man! You were amazing, Fran! Can I call you Fran? We owe you big time! And how'd you know all that about negligent care and stuff? Your paralegal friend?"

"Um." She bit her lip as she drove. "I may have fibbed. It's me. I'm the paralegal. Graveyard at the station is slow, so I've been taking night classes so I can pass the bar. Been getting pretty burnt on nursing. Sometimes when it's quiet, and I'm doing my classwork, I sit there and pretend that the police station is some kind of study hall and I'm going to a big university like CU Boulder or Kansas." She laughed nervously.

"College is a scam," Tarron said deftly from the back. His head was leaning against the window. He was feeling the beginnings of a crash. When the drug clock had run out from the psilocybin, nights ago, it had felt like a breath of relief like when he'd cross the line at the end of track sprint. The comedown from tonight felt more like he'd gone ten bloody

237

rounds in a cage match against a grizzly bear.

"Yeah, it is!" Darian agreed before turning to Franny and saying in a quieter tone, "Don't listen to him. He dropped out."

"You like the nursing program at Casper?" She asked.

"I do, actually. But I think I have more of a desire to get into clinical psychology if I had more time on my hands."

"Oh, I remember those days. Studied until my eyes were dry and still only managed to get as high as a B in most of my classes."

"They say C's get degrees and D's spell diploma."

Franny liked that. She laughed hard enough to snort and quickly apologized.

"Don't be sorry! I think it's cute, actually," Darian said.

"Darian McConnell, you're gonna make me blush. And I'm four years your senior."

"Age ain't nothin' but a thang, Franny. I've been told I have an old soul. By Tarron, actually."

"You are an old soul. Pure of heart but dumb of ass." Tarron interjected.

"I'll take that as a compliment, good buddy." Darian replied.

They drove on in no particular rush. The police station wasn't too far away, but there wasn't any pressing desire to get there. The city of Cheyenne was quiet tonight. Tarron smiled as he continued to stare out the window and listen to Darian and Franny go back and forth in conversation.

The smile faded when he remembered Darian's confession at the cemetery and his spray tan story.

"Cancer, Tarron."

The SUV came to a stop. They had arrived at the impound lot at the police station. Tarron changed out of the hospital gown and waited by Darian's jeep while he and Franny disappeared inside. Tarron was in awe at how easy it was for his friend to pretend things were normal with this girl who obviously liked him. It was a great how-we-met-cute story. But the punch-line hadn't been rung out: cancer. Zing! Cymbal's crash. Thank you, everybody. I will not be here all week.

He heard ringing in his injured ear and raised a hand to softly touch the bandage they had applied at the hospital. Some of the numbness from the cocktail of drugs he had taken tonight was fading as well. He gingerly felt where the top of his ear should've been and grimaced at the shots of pain.

The ringing stopped. He had a change of heart; in spite of ear-related injuries, tinnitus would be better than losing the entire ear. He knew he'd quickly get tired of hearing Van Gogh jokes until he died or until some mad scientists grew him a new ear on the back of a mouse in a lab.

The wind had kicked up and cut a chill through him. He spotted a couple of cops smoking near the entrance to the station and walked towards them.

"Woah buddy, you alright?" one of the two cops said as Tarron neared.

"What, this?" Tarron said as he pointed at his bandaged ear, "Gettin' stabbed was worse, believe it or not. Can I bum a cig?"

One cigarette had turned into two and three as he waited and talked to the two policemen. After telling the story about how he got stabbed and partially lying about the gunshot to his ear, they told him he had a special type of luck any cop would kill for. Shot, stabbed, both non-fatal. All he was missing was: getting blown up and walking away with a migraine. He took a long drag of his cigarette at that suggestion and prayed silently.

***

Tarron was relieved when he saw the glint of Jack inside the metal dog food can in the backseat of the jeep. He had been thinking about it the entire time he waited. They were back on the highway, flying once again at a more reasonable speed.

"Why are we still going to the airport? The flight left already, dude." Tarron asked. They had just left the impound lot and were back on the road.

"We're making one stop first. And aren't you used to staying up late? Being a bartender and all."

"Maybe if I was SOBER."

"Oh, we're gonna change that very soon."

"So, 'd you get her number?" Tarron asked, changing the subject.

"Who? Franny? I actually tried to convince her to come with us. But she insisted that she couldn't take off work or school. Even though, after tonight, she may get fired. Lovely girl, though."

"You had said she reminded you of Scarlet. Was that your wife?"

"Yup," Darian said slowly in a monotone.

"Now, I'm not one to judge, but—"

"No, you're not. But go ahead."

"Well, now I feel guilty."

"Guilty or not, you have something in your head that you think is worth mentioning. Go ahead, dude. Remember who you're talking to here."

"Shit, okay," Tarron took in a sharp breath, "Girls seem attracted to you. The lady at the vet, this girl. Hell—my mother thinks you're charming."

"Your mom is a sweet lady."

"My point is—" Tarron didn't actually know what his point was. He was trying to talk through it "if you've got this thing.

Cancer, I mean. Maybe, I dunno, dude. If I was six years younger and, in your situation, I'd be at bars trying to find as many vices as I could to fill that void. Y'know what I mean?" Darian laughed. Hard.

"Maybe you don't remember who you're talking to. I don't need any of that, Tarron. I've had my slew of hook-ups using the cancer card and feeling ashamed about it afterward. I drove all over this country from Lake Tahoe and back and probably had enough coke and pussy to last a lifetime. But when I got back and looked at myself in the mirror, I knew it was all just a distraction. It was poisonous to live that way. I know I'm gonna die. We all are. And so what if I might be closer in line? I can't let this disease stop me from living right."

"And you wouldn't want to let yourself share that with anyone? A partner?"

"I'm not sure yet. I wanna do this thing with you and help put our brother to rest. Maybe after we come back, I'll look up Miss D'addario and see if she could handle my baggage."

"Is that an innuendo? Or do you mean, like, emotional baggage?"

"Why not both?"

The two shared a laugh. They were headed southbound on I-25 and out of the city as far as Tarron could tell. He watched the runway lights that surrounded the airport comes into view and disappear behind them.

"Dude, I think you missed the exit."

"I told you we're making a stop first, silly goose."

"Okay, yeah, but where exactly?"

"Taos," Darian said flatly.

"Taos as in Taos, New Mexico?"

"That'd be the one, yes, sir."

"You're joking."

"No, I'm Darian."

"Shut the fuck up." Tarron snorted.

"Shutting the fuck up." Darian smiled.

"New Mexico is like 400 miles away, isn't it? And what about our flight?"

"It's an easy drive. We can even stop in Denver or Springs. And as for our flight, we can still use your ticket vouchers to fly the same airline out of New York, if I'm not mistaken?"

"Yeah. That's right. Okay—Taos it is."

Tarron was surprised at how okay he was about the change of plans. He hadn't been on a road trip in years. The last time had been moving back from Tempe to Glenrock, a year after Alina had been born. He felt like he was ready for whatever came next.

"So, what's in Taos?"

"My good friend Frank Greensboro. Run's small greenery out of his Earthship."

"His what?"

About the Author

Collin Johnson would like to make it known that writing about one's self in the third person will never, not be weird. University of New Mexico 2021 Alum, sko' bo's. This is his first real novel. He likes using semi-colons and beginning sentences with and. He and his wife currently live wherever the Navy sends him but wants to make this writing thing a full-time gig one day. Be kind, be a cowboy.